My Heart

Also By Allie Everhart

The Haydon Falls Series:
1. *Keep My Heart*
2. *Break My Heart*
3. *Take My Heart*
4. *Protect My Heart*

Protect My Heart

ALLIE EVERHART

embla books

First published in the UK in 2025 by

embla books

An imprint of Bonnier Books UK
5th Floor, HYLO, 105 Bunhill Row,
London, EC1Y 8LZ

A CIP catalogue record for this book is available from the British Library.

ISBN: 9781471420856

Also available as an ebook and an audiobook

1

Typeset by IDSUK (Data Connection) Ltd
Printed and bound in Great Britain by Clays Ltd, Elcograf S.p.A.

FSC www.fsc.org MIX Paper | Supporting responsible forestry FSC® C018072

The authorised representative in the EEA is Bonnier Books UK (Ireland) Limited.
Registered office address: Floor 3, Block 3, Miesian Plaza, Dublin 2, D02 Y754, Ireland
compliance@bonnierbooks.ie
www.bonnierbooks.co.uk

Chapter 1

January

Jason

'Singles table?' a guy says as he sits across from me at the round table near the back of a large ballroom where the reception is being held.

'Looks like it,' I say, noticing the different last names listed on the place cards around where I'm seated.

'Trust me,' the guy says with a laugh. 'It's the singles table. I've been to enough of these things to know. They always throw us single people together and put us in the back of the room. So are you friends with Noah?'

'Yeah, we went to college together.'

'Were you on the team with him?'

'I was supposed to be, but I messed up my shoulder the summer before college and couldn't play.'

The guy nods. 'That sucks.'

It more than sucked. It was devastating. Growing up, I dreamed of being a professional baseball player. I knew it was a long shot, but that didn't stop me from trying. I'd be out every day, practicing my swing, trying to get better. By high school I was the best player the school ever had, good enough to get a college scholarship.

When I heard my shoulder snap during a workout, I knew it was over. Just one wrong move, a simple over-extension with just the right amount of force behind it, was all it took to tear my rotator cuff and end my dream of playing baseball.

'It turned out okay,' I tell the guy. 'I coach now. High school baseball, and I run a baseball camp in the summer.'

'Got any kids of your own?' he asks.

'No. Never been married.'

'I haven't either, but I've got two.' He picks up his phone and shows me a picture of two young kids, a boy and girl. 'Kenny and Sierra. They're five and three.'

The guy's probably around my age and already has two kids. I don't think I'm ready for that. I definitely want kids, but not until I've had time to save up some money and maybe get a house. And I need to find the right girl, which is a challenge in a small town.

'Looks like this is my seat,' someone says from beside me. I look over and see a gorgeous girl with long dark hair, fair skin, and the most beautiful smile I've ever seen.

My breath catches in my throat as I try to respond. The guy across from me beats me to it.

'Chuck Sanderson,' he says, standing up and reaching across the table to shake her hand.

'Mia Daniels,' she says, her smile fading slightly as Chuck keeps hold of her hand. He's being too aggressive, making her uncomfortable. I don't even know her, but I can see the tension on her face.

'I'm Jason.' I hurry to get up and offer Mia my hand so Chuck will let her go.

She frees herself from Chuck and shakes my hand, her smile back, sending my heart soaring, beating faster by the second. 'It's nice to meet you, Jason.'

'Nice to meet you too.' I move her chair out for her, wait for her to sit down, then gently push the chair in before sitting beside her.

'You friends with the bride?' Chuck asks Mia before chugging down his drink.

'Yes, we were sorority sisters back in college.' She laughs. 'That seems so long ago now.'

'It's only been what . . . four years?' I ask, knowing Lacey, the bride, is 26. I'm guessing Mia's the same age, or close to that.

'It feels longer than four years,' she says. 'When I work with students that age, they all look so young.'

'You work at a college?'

'I'm in grad school,' she says, turning to me. 'But I counsel students as part of my studies.'

'You're a psych major?' Chuck huffs, rolling his eyes. 'My ex was a psych major. She's fucking crazy. If anyone needs therapy, it's her.'

Mia glances at him, then turns back to me. 'So what do you do?'

'I'm a teacher. High school science.'

Her face lights up. 'Me too! I mean, I used to be a teacher. I taught high school English.'

'And you decided you didn't like it?' I ask, knowing it's not for everyone.

'I loved it! But when I saw how many of my students were struggling with issues outside the classroom, I decided to go into counseling instead.' She laughs a little. 'I had already kind of become the school's counselor by default. When anyone had an issue, they'd go to Miss Daniels.'

Miss. So she's single. I guess I should've already known that since she's at the singles table.

'I'm going to the bar,' Chuck says, getting up. He smiles at Mia. 'What can I get ya?'

'Nothing right now, but thank you.'

Chuck gives me a look like I better not try to take his girl while he's gone. I ignore him. She's not his girl. He just met her. And from the way Mia's looking at him, I don't think she's interested.

'Do you know him?' she asks when he's gone.

'No, I just met him.'

She sighs and sits back in her chair as she watches Chuck walk to the bar. 'I can already tell he's going to be bothering me all night. Pressuring me to dance with him. Trying to get me drunk.'

'I could help you out.'

'What do you mean?'

Maybe I shouldn't suggest this, but I really like this girl and don't want Chuck ruining her evening.

'Be my date for tonight. We'll talk. Maybe dance. We'll pretend to really hit it off so Chuck gets the message you're interested in someone else and stops bothering you.'

She smiles and extends her hand to me. 'Deal.'

As we shake on it and I look in her eyes, I feel something between us. A spark. Chemistry. A connection. Maybe all three.

'Oh, and . . .' She leans toward me, her hand still in mine. 'That part about us pretending to hit it off? I don't think we'll need to pretend.'

My heart skips a beat and my smile widens. 'I think you're right.'

I might've just met the girl of my dreams . . . at the last possible place I'd ever imagine meeting someone. I've spent the past five years going to wedding after wedding for all my friends and never once met a woman, at least not one who's single that I'd want to date. I assumed tonight wouldn't be any different.

'Do you live here in Chicago?' Mia asks, reaching for her glass of water.

'No, I live in Haydon Falls. It's a small town in Wisconsin.'

She nods. 'Yes, I've heard of it. My friend, Nora, goes there every fall for some kind of festival at an apple orchard. She said it's beautiful and that people come from all over to go there.'

'It's my family's orchard. And yes, it's beautiful in the fall.'

'Wait.' She sets her water down and puts her hand on my arm. 'Your family owns that orchard?'

'Yeah, my dad started it right after my parents got married. My oldest brother runs it now, but my parents are still involved with it.'

She squints her eyes like she's thinking hard, then pops them open. 'Kanfield! Kanfield Orchard! Am I right?'

I nod. 'You are. I'm Jason Kanfield.'

She sits back, that intoxicating smile still on her face. 'What a small world. Nora was just telling me about the orchard and here I am, talking to the owner. Well, not the owner but the owner's son.'

'You should come to Haydon Falls sometime,' I say, already wanting to see her again after tonight. 'The orchard isn't open in the winter, but you could check out the town.'

'I might just do that. Nora said it's adorable with all the cute little shops and restaurants. And she mentioned they have a new microbrewery.'

'Kanfield Brewery. My brother, Sawyer, owns it. And his girlfriend owns G's, the brewery just outside of town.'

Mia laughs. 'Does your family own the whole town?'

'No, just the brewery and the orchard. And Brody, my younger brother, has a snowplowing and lawn mowing business. He's also getting into renovating houses. I come from a family of entrepreneurs. I'm the only one who took a different path.'

'Why is that?'

I shrug. 'I just always wanted to teach. Well, actually I wanted to play baseball, but when that didn't work out, I went into teaching. I'm also the baseball coach.'

'Hope you weren't talking about me,' Chuck says with a laugh as he joins us back at the table, a drink in his hand.

'Jason was just telling me about his job,' Mia says.

'I'd tell you about mine, but you probably don't want to hear about pouring concrete,' Chuck says before taking a swig of his drink. 'So where are you staying tonight?'

'With a friend,' Mia answers. 'She's picking me up after the reception.'

'I got a room here at the hotel.' He winks at her. 'Just saying.'

'Jason, would you like something from the bar?' Mia asks as she hurries to get up.

'Yeah. Let's go.'

'I thought you didn't want anything,' Chuck says as we leave.

'I was hoping he'd get the hint by now that I'm not interested,' Mia says, holding onto my arm as we walk.

'We might have to step up our efforts,' I say.

'How?'

We stop as we reach the bar. There's a line with three couples ahead of us.

'What if I did this?' I take Mia's hand as we stand side-by-side, facing the line.

'I'd be okay with that.' She glances at me. 'And maybe you could put your arm around me when we're sitting at the table.'

'I could do that,' I say, trying to hold back my smile. I don't want to get my hopes up, but I think Mia and I might be seeing each other after tonight. We just met and we're already hitting it off.

'What would you like?' I ask, getting out my wallet as we reach the front of the line.

'Oh, I'll get it,' she says, opening her phone case where she has some money stashed.

'I'm your date. I think that means I get to buy you a drink.'

She smiles and closes her phone case. 'I'll have an old fashioned.'

'An old fashioned.' I eye her, feeling this immense amount of curiosity for a girl I just met. I want to know everything about her.

'Did you think I'd say wine?' she asks.

'I wasn't sure. I tend to date women who drink beer, but that's probably because we always end up going to my brother's brewery.'

'What can I get you?' the bartender asks as I step up to the bar.

'An old fashioned and a whiskey on the rocks.'

'That'll be 30 even,' he says as he makes the drinks.

Thirty dollars for two drinks? It'd be half that in Haydon Falls. I forgot how expensive things are in big cities. It's another reason I'd never want to live in one.

We take our drinks and head back through the ballroom to the table. The place is filling up as more people arrive. The cocktail hour goes on for another half hour and then dinner is served. After that, the music will start. Noah and Lacey hired a local band. I'm hoping Mia will agree to a dance or two, maybe more if the evening goes well.

'We got some company,' Chuck says as Mia and I get back to the table. There's a woman sitting next to Chuck and one heading toward the empty chair next to mine. Two guys are now on the other side of Mia.

'I'm Gary,' one of them says to her as she sits down.

Gary better back the hell off. Mia already has a date for tonight.

'Sorry,' the woman next to me says as she sits down. She bumped me when she moved her chair out.

'It's fine,' I say, smiling at her. She's hot, with wavy blonde hair and wearing a tight pink dress. But as hot as she is, my attention is drawn back to Mia. There's something about her, something I've never felt with anyone else.

'This is Jason,' Mia says, and when I turn to her, I feel her arm slip around mine as she looks at Gary.

'Nice to meet you,' I say, using my free arm to reach over and shake his hand.

Gary glances down at Mia's arm around mine. 'I thought this was the singles table.'

'It is,' I say.

'Them two have been giving each other the eye since she sat down,' Chuck says, motioning to Mia and me. 'They're both teachers so maybe that's got something to do with it.'

'I'm single,' the woman next to Chuck says. She's probably in her 40s, but the way Chuck's looking at her, I don't think he cares about their age difference.

'Why don't we get you a drink?' he says, giving her the same smile he gave Mia when she sat down, the kind that says he's hoping to sleep with her later.

The two of them get up and head to the bar.

'I feel like I know you,' the guy next to Gary says to me. 'Do you work downtown?'

'No, I'm a teacher and baseball coach in Haydon Falls, a town a couple hours north of here.'

He smiles. 'That's how I know you. My son wanted to go to your baseball camp. He showed me the website and I saw your photo. We live here in Chicago so I had to tell him no, but he really wanted to go. Do you run the camp yourself?'

'Yeah, I started it a couple years ago. It's getting to be really popular.'

'You must be a good coach,' Mia says, smiling at me.

The guy's phone rings and he answers it. 'Honey, you know I'm at that wedding tonight.' He nods, then gets up from the table. 'I'll be there soon.' He ends the call and says, 'That was my daughter. She's at a sleepover and got sick. I need to go get her. It was nice meeting you all.' He takes off.

'Glad I don't have kids,' Gary says, watching the guy leave. 'They ruin your life.'

'I can't wait to have kids,' Mia says to him. 'I want at least three, maybe more.'

'Good luck with that,' Gary says, getting up. 'I'm getting a drink.'

'Angela,' a guy says, coming up to the girl next to me. 'I didn't know you'd be here.'

'Larson!' She jumps up from her chair. 'Where are you sitting?'

'Over there.' He points to the table near the exit door. 'There's an open seat if you want to move.'

She takes off with the guy, leaving just Mia and me at the table.

'Thanks for saving me,' she says. 'As soon as I felt Gary's leg touching mine under the table I had to do something so he'd know I was with someone.'

'He was touching you under the table?' I ask, my anger rising as I think of that jerk touching her.

'He moved away when he saw me put my arm around yours.' She turns to me. 'I hope you don't mind.'

'Not at all.' I lean down to her and talk in her ear. 'Feel free to use me however you like tonight.'

She slowly backs away.

'Sorry,' I say. 'I didn't mean—'

'No, it's fine.' Her smile turns flirtatious, along with the tone of her voice. 'I was just surprised. You seem so . . . polite.'

'Polite doesn't mean I'm . . . well, I'll let you finish that thought.'

She takes a sip of her drink, then turns to me. 'Tell me more.'

'More what?'

'Tell me more about you. So far I've learned that you're an amazing coach and that your family owns a very famous orchard. I'm already impressed and I've known you for less than an hour.'

'I'd rather know more about you. I don't even know where you live.'

'Madison. I'm going to grad school at the university. I have one semester left.' She lets out a sigh. 'This is my last weekend to have some fun and relax before hitting the books again. Monday's the start of another semester, my busiest one yet.'

'Madison, huh? That's not that far from Haydon Falls. Well, it's over an hour but—' I shake my head. 'Never mind. I'm getting ahead of myself.'

'Are you seeing anyone?' Mia asks.

'I go on dates, but I don't have a girlfriend. How about you? Are you seeing anyone?'

'I was, but we broke up a few months ago.'

I'm staring into her eyes, knowing I should look away, but I can't. She's got beautiful eyes, a deep brown color with specks of caramel. There's kindness in her eyes, which I know sounds strange, but it's what I feel when I look at them. Like she's a kind person with a big open heart.

'Hey, everyone!' Noah says over the microphone. The noise in the room quiets down. 'I just want to thank you all for coming and hope you have a good time tonight. We're doing the toasts after dinner before cutting the cake, so be sure to stick around. Free booze for the toast if that makes a difference,' he says with a laugh. He takes his seat at the head table. I'm so far back in the room I can barely see him. There's so many people here, I probably won't even talk to him tonight.

'Want another drink?' I ask Mia, noticing hers is empty.

'I could have another,' she says as she watches a woman walk by. 'What a beautiful dress.'

'Yours is better,' I tell her, my eyes going to her dress. It's black and fitted to her body with tiny straps at the top and ending just above her knees.

'I've had this forever,' Mia says, looking down at her dress. 'I've probably worn it to at least three weddings.'

'It looks great on you.' I put my arm around her as Gary comes back.

'They're out of the vodka I wanted,' he says as he sits down. 'I hate these damn weddings. I don't know why I keep going to them.' He downs whatever drink he got, then stares at the waitress as she serves the table next to ours.

Mia moves closer to me, turning so her back is against my chest. I keep my arm around her and gently rub my hand over her bare shoulder. She looks up at me and smiles.

I wish I knew what was going on here. Are we just pretending to date or is this real? It feels real. I feel like we're a couple, not two strangers who just met. Why am I feeling this way with someone I barely know?

Chapter 2

Jason

During dinner, Mia and I get so wrapped up in our conversation it's as if nobody else is there. My mom would scold me for not being more social, but there's no way I'm giving up precious time with Mia to talk to Gary, who's done nothing but complain, or Chuck, who keeps touching the woman next to him. She's touching him too. And they're both drunk. They're definitely hooking up tonight.

'Have you heard of this band?' Mia asks as we listen to them warming up.

'I don't know. I didn't see their name.'

'I think it's Vandyl. It was on the sign when we walked in.'

'Vandyl? That's my cousin's band.' I stand up so I can see the front of the ballroom where they're setting up. Austin's there with his guitar. 'Yeah, that's them.' I sit back down. 'I didn't know he was playing tonight.'

'Your cousin's in the band?' She gets up. 'Which one is your cousin?'

'The guy with all the muscles. He's obsessed with working out. He also works construction so he basically works out all the time.'

'He's really hot.'

'Hey!' I take her hand and tug on her to sit down. 'We're on a date. And he has a girlfriend.'

She sits down, smiling at me. 'You're even hotter.' She kisses me, a quick kiss, but I wasn't expecting it. I wasn't sure how far we were taking this pretend date.

Seriously, what is going on here? Is this a real date? Because if it is, that's not going to be the only kiss of the night. I already want to kiss her again—a real kiss, not a quick one like she just gave me.

'I think I'm done,' she says, pushing her plate away. 'I'm saving room for cake.'

'Champagne?' the waiter says, stopping by with a tray of champagne. 'It's for the toast.'

Mia and I take one, but Gary waves the waiter away, telling him he hates champagne. He's a real downer. I wish he was sitting somewhere else.

Noah's brother gets on the microphone and makes a toast, followed by one from Lacey's sister.

Then Lacey gets up and speaks, with Noah by her side. 'We just want to thank all of you for celebrating with us tonight. We hope you're having a great time and will stick around for the band.'

Noah takes the microphone from her. 'I just want to make one last toast.' He holds up his glass of champagne. 'To love, and to finding the person who makes you feel as amazing as I feel right now.' He swigs his champagne, then kisses his bride.

'To love,' I say to Mia, holding up my glass.

'To love.' She smiles as we clink our glasses.

I don't know if it's because of all the drinks I've had or because I've been wanting to do this all night, but whatever the reason, I can't help myself. I lean over and kiss Mia.

I feel her set her glass on the table, but she doesn't pull away. I cup my hand around the side of her face, becoming completely immersed in the kiss, loving the feel of her soft lips and the way she keeps moving closer to me.

'Get a room,' Gary says.

Mia pulls back, just slightly, and smiles at me.

This girl is so damn perfect. She's everything I've been looking for. She's smart, sexy, easy to talk to, and we have so much in common. She's as passionate about teaching and helping kids as I am. She even likes baseball.

'What the hell?' Gary says, looking over at Chuck and his new lady friend as they make out at the table. 'You gonna eat her damn face?' Gary gets up. 'I've had enough of this shit. I'm leaving.'

He stumbles away from the table.

'I hope he's staying here,' Mia says. 'He's way too drunk to drive.' She looks back at me. 'What about you? You're not driving home tonight, are you?'

'No, I got a room. I'll drive back in the morning.'

'Me too. I didn't want to be driving back this late, and I knew I'd be having a drink or two.' She looks at her empty champagne glass. 'Or three.'

'I thought you were staying with a friend.'

She shakes her head. 'I just said that so Chuck would stop bothering me.'

We're both staying at the hotel, meaning our evening wouldn't have to end after the reception. I wonder if she's thinking the same thing.

'They're really good,' Mia says as the band plays.

'Yeah, they played for my mom's birthday last year. Everyone loved them. My brother Nick's thinking of having them play for his wedding. Well, the reception, not the wedding.'

'When's the wedding?'

'In May. Maybe you could come. This could be our thing. Being each other's wedding dates.'

'I'd be open to that.' She sways to the music. 'I love this song.'

'Let's dance.'

We get up and I take her hand as we walk to the dance floor. It's full of couples, some so drunk they're falling on each other. I feel kind of drunk myself, not falling-over drunk, but drunk enough to do stuff I typically wouldn't do. Like inviting Mia to Nick's wedding? That was a bold move, especially since I don't know how tonight's going to end or if we'll see each other again. Mia said she was open to the idea, but she's had a lot to drink. Her response could've been the alcohol talking.

'I'm having a really good time tonight,' she says, looking up at me as we dance. We're not really dancing, but more like swaying side-to-side. It's a slow song and there isn't much room to move with all the people around us.

'I am too,' I tell her. 'I kind of don't want tonight to end.'

'Maybe it doesn't have to.'

I wait for her to say more. I know what I want, but I'm not going to say it. I want her to tell me what she's thinking.

'Jason, would you maybe want to . . .' She looks away.

'Would I want to *what*?'

'I never do this.' She lays her head on my shoulder like she doesn't want me seeing her face when she says whatever she's about to say.

'Do what?'

'I can't believe I'm doing this. I told myself I never would. It always seemed like a bad idea, but for some reason with you, it doesn't.'

'Mia, what is it? Just tell me.'

She looks up at me. 'Would you spend the night with me? I'm not saying we have to—'

'Yes.' I smile at her. 'I'd love to. And I'm not expecting anything, if you're worried about that. I just want more time with you.'

'Excuse my interruption,' a waiter says, coming up to us with a tray of shot glasses. 'These are from the bride and groom.'

'No thanks,' I tell him.

'I'll have one,' Mia says, taking a shot glass.

'Then I guess I'll join you.' I take a shot and down it, then set the glass on the tray.

'Have all you want,' the waiter says. 'They're free.'

Mia and I take another one.

'Okay, maybe that was a bad idea,' Mia says as the waiter leaves. 'Those shots went straight to my head. The room's starting to spin.'

I don't feel the room spinning, but I definitely feel drunker than I did a few minutes ago.

'Let's go sit down,' I say, putting my arm around her as I lead her away from the dance floor. The music just ended. The band must be taking a break.

'Jason!' I hear someone yell.

Turning back, I see Austin coming up to me, a big grin on his face. 'I thought that was you. What are you doing here?'

'I'm friends with the groom.' I look at Mia. 'You okay, or you want to go sit down?'

'I'm okay.' She smiles at Austin. 'I like the band. You guys are really good.'

'Thanks! I'm Austin, Jason's cousin. You must be Kasey.'

'No, this is Mia,' I rush to say. Kasey was a girl I dated last month, but it didn't work out. 'I'm not seeing Kasey anymore.'

'Oh, shit, sorry,' Austin says.

'Jason and I just met,' Mia says, smiling at me.

'She was seated next to me at the table.'

'Austin!' one of the band guys yells.

'Yeah, I'm coming!' Austin yells back. 'I gotta go,' he says to us. 'But hey, hope it works out.' He takes off.

'Sorry about that,' I say to Mia. 'He didn't know about Kasey.'

'Let's go sit down.' She takes my hand. 'I need some water.'

We get to the table and see that Chuck and that woman are gone.

'Looks like we've got the table to ourselves,' I say, picking up the water pitcher and filling Mia's glass.

'Thanks,' she says, taking a sip of water. 'I probably should've passed on the shots.'

'Yeah, me too. I'm feeling pretty drunk right now.'

Mia turns to me. 'Was it serious? You and that girl?'

'Kasey?' I chuckle. 'No, not at all. We only went out a few times. She's a teacher at the middle school. We chaperoned some school dances and got to be friends.'

'So you're definitely single,' Mia says.

'Hopefully not for much longer.' I turn to Mia and look in her eyes. 'I really like this girl I just met.'

'I really like this guy I just met.'

I slide my hand though her silky hair and gently pull her toward me. I hear her let out a soft breath before I press my lips to hers. The moment I do, I no longer hear the band playing or people talking or dishes clanking. All my focus is on Mia and how good it feels to kiss her. I can only imagine how good it would feel to do more, but like I told her, I'm not expecting that. I'd be happy just holding her in my arms all night.

'Let's go,' I whisper over her lips.

She nods and slowly backs away.

As we leave the ballroom, we speed up our pace, like we can't wait a second longer to be alone together.

'Where's your room?' Mia asks as we go down the hallway.

'First floor, just past the lobby.'

'Let's go to yours. Mine's on the fifth floor and the elevator's painfully slow.'

'Are you in a hurry?' I ask, giving her a smile.

She just looks at me, but I know that look. I take her hand and walk faster.

'Wait.' We stop and she reaches down to take off her heels. 'Okay, let's go.' She takes off running.

I almost trip trying to keep up with her. We're both laughing, probably because we're drunk. I wish I'd skipped the shots. If I had, I'd be sobered up by now.

'Hold on,' I say, pulling on Mia's hand as I stop at my room. 'This is mine.'

'Oh!' She starts laughing again, which makes me laugh.

'You have the best laugh,' I say as we go into the room. 'And beautiful eyes.' I pull her into my arms. 'And an amazing smile.'

She looks up at me. 'I really like you, Jason.'

'I really like you too.'

'I never do this.'

'I don't either.'

'But I really want to. I just . . . I don't know.'

'How about this?' I slide the straps of her dress down as I kiss the side of her neck. 'We go slow, and if you decide you want to stop, just tell me.' I move her hair back and kiss just below her ear. 'How does that sound?'

'Perfect,' she whispers.

Reaching behind her, I lower the zipper on her dress, then gently tug on it until it falls to the floor. She steps out of it and drops the heels she was holding. She's left in a lacy black bra and matching panties.

'You look absolutely gorgeous,' I say, my gaze moving down her body.

'Thanks,' she says, glancing away.

I take her hand. 'If you don't want to do this, it's not too late to change your mind.'

Her eyes lift to mine and she smiles. 'I'm not changing my mind. Are you?'

I answer by wrapping my arms around her and pressing my lips to hers. Now that we're finally alone, I can kiss her the way I've wanted to all night, a deep passionate kiss that makes it clear how much I want her.

We make our way over to the bed but remain standing. She tugs at my tie, trying to undo it.

'I got it,' I say. I yank off my tie, then take off my suit jacket. I start to unbutton my shirt, but Mia stops me.

'Let me do it.' She slowly undoes each button as we kiss. When she reaches the last one, I take the shirt off and toss it aside. Mia runs her hands down my chest. 'You're in good shape for a teacher.'

I crack a smile. 'I think you just insulted teachers.'

She laughs. 'I didn't mean it that way. I just mean you're in really good shape.'

'I play baseball and spend time in the gym.' I turn her around and kiss her shoulder.

'What are you doing?' she whispers.

I unhook her bra and slide it off, then wrap my arm around her waist and pull her against me, her back against my chest. As I kiss the side of her neck, I hold her closer and feel her body relax into mine.

She starts circling her hips, pressing her ass against my cock, making it hard as steel, like it's about to burst through my dress pants. My hand slides up to her breast, caressing it, my thumb rubbing over her nipple.

She softly moans, then whispers my name as she arches back, lifting her face to mine.

I lean down and kiss her as I slide my hand down her stomach, then lower, my fingers slipping under her panties. She's soaking wet, making my cock throb and pulse, begging to be inside her.

My fingers move over her slick center, back and forth, before settling on her clit, circling over it, softly at first, then harder. I slide a finger inside her, then another, my thumb still working her clit.

'More,' she whispers.

My hand moves faster and I add more pressure, quickly learning what she likes. Her legs tremble and her breaths speed up. 'Oh God!' She grabs hold of my arm. 'Yes!' she yells, her whole body trembling as she comes.

Her head falls back against my chest as she takes a moment to breathe. If she wants to stop now, I'd understand, but I really hope she wants to keep going or I'm going to need a very cold shower, and fast.

She turns and sits down on the bed, smiling up at me as she undoes my belt. I guess that means we're continuing. She unzips my pants and rubs her hand over the front of my boxers, moving up and down my cock with just the right amount of pressure. It feels fucking amazing.

'You keep doing that,' I say, 'and this will be over before it's started.'

'But I'm not done yet.' She runs her tongue over her lips.

Fuck, that's hot. And although I'd love to have those lips of hers wrapped around my cock, I'd rather have it buried inside her.

'Why don't we save that for later?' I say, gently moving her hand off me as I lean down to kiss her.

I take a step back and quickly undress, keeping my eyes on Mia.

'You are so damn beautiful,' I say, watching as she slips off her panties.

She moves over on the bed, lying on her side and giving me a sexy smile. Fuck, she turns me on. I almost came while I was touching her, then again when she was touching me, but I held back, wanting more, wanting to be inside her.

I join her on the bed, my hand moving over her body as I kiss her. Her skin is soft as silk. If my cock wasn't so damn impatient, I'd keep this up, touching her, exploring every inch of her body.

She breaks from the kiss and turns so she's on her back. I lower my mouth to her breast, my tongue teasing her nipple as my hand moves over the soft curve of her hip, down her leg, then up between her thighs.

'Jason,' she moans, her hips rising. 'I can't wait anymore.'

Glancing up at her, I see the desperate look in her eyes. I feel the same way. I want her so fucking bad.

I move over her, my cock settling between her legs. She tilts her hips up so that the tip of me is touching her. I slide inside her, just barely, wanting to take this slow. But my cock takes over and I sink into her, all the way. I couldn't wait. I tried, but damn, I've held out long enough.

'Jason,' she moans, her hands raking down my back.

I love that sound, that sexy moan, and hearing my name come from her lips. I slowly pull out of her, then sink back in. She so tight. So wet. I just want to stay here, buried deep inside her.

I lean down to kiss her, gently rocking my hips. I'm going slow, or as slow as I can. But the feel of her lips, her soft skin, the way her body moves with mine, I can't hold back. I start going faster, thrusting harder.

Mia wraps her legs around me, changing the angle and letting me go deeper.

'Fuck,' I mutter. 'You feel so damn good.'

My hips move faster. I've lost control. There's no turning back now. I feel it building, my muscles tensing, my cock ready to burst.

'Yes!' Mia's fingers dig into my back as I thrust deep inside her. 'Don't stop!'

I feel her body tense up. Mine is too. I'm past the point I can hold back.

'Oh God!' Mia cries out. I'm right there with her, the feeling rocketing through me with an intensity I've never felt before.

That was fucking amazing. Every second of it, from the moment I touched her until now. There's another reason this girl is perfect for me. That was the best sex of my life. Mia and I are compatible in so many ways it almost doesn't seem real. I feel like I'm dreaming this, like I've dreamed up the perfect girl and tomorrow I'll wake up and realize I imagined it all. But it sure as hell feels real.

She opens her eyes and softly smiles when she notices me looking at her. I lower down to kiss her, then gently pull out of her and collapse back on the bed.

Mia lets out a sigh. 'I don't think I've ever felt this relaxed.'

I look at her. 'Stay with me tonight.'

She turns on her side, smiling at me. 'I was planning to. I didn't think you'd just kick me out.'

'What about tomorrow? It's Sunday. We could spend the day together.'

'I can't. I need to get back. I have a lot to get done before classes start.'

'What about next weekend? I could drive to Madison. You could show me around, give me a tour of campus.'

'I work at the student counseling center on the weekends.'

'So when can I see you?'

'I don't know,' she says, sounding disappointed and maybe a little sad.

'Mia, I want to see you again. I don't want tonight to be it.'

'Can we talk about this tomorrow?' She moves closer and wraps her arm around me, resting her head on my chest. 'I don't want anything to take away how I'm feeling right now.'

'Yeah.' I kiss her forehead. 'We'll talk tomorrow.'

But I'm worried I won't like what she's going to tell me. I thought she'd want to continue this, but maybe she doesn't. Maybe tonight is it.

* * *

'When can I see you again?' I ask Mia the next morning as she's getting dressed.

We're heading home soon and I'm not ready to say goodbye. We had such a great night, and a great morning. We were up at five—talking, kissing, making love. Then I held her in my arms, not wanting to let her go.

'Jason, we talked about this,' Mia says, slipping on her shoes. 'I have school. You have work. We live in different places.' She turns her back to me. 'Would you zip me up, please?'

I come up behind her and zip her dress, then wrap her in my arms and lean down to kiss her neck, then her cheek. 'I know what we said, but I'm changing my mind. I want to keep seeing you.'

'How?' She turns to me. 'My job at the counseling center takes up whatever time I have left after studying and going to class. And soon you'll be coaching baseball in addition to your teaching job. When would we have time to see each other?'

I sigh. 'I don't know. I just don't want this to be goodbye.'

'I don't either. But I'm moving back to Boston after I graduate. Why would we start something that's going to end in a few months?'

'You don't have to go back to Boston. You could stay here. You already live here. Why go back?'

She pauses a moment. 'My parents. They're in their seventies. My dad's almost 80. I don't know how much time I have left with them. If I lived here, I'd only see them a few times a year. That's not enough. I'm their only child and I need to be close to them, in case anything happens. In case they get sick.'

She didn't tell me that last night. I didn't know her parents were that old. They're even older than mine. And she's an only child. Now it makes sense why she wants to move back. Her family's important to her and she wants to take care of them. It's another thing we have in common.

'Is there any chance you'd consider moving?' she asks. 'Assuming we got to that point.'

I shake my head. 'My parents are getting up in age too. They're still in their sixties, but my dad had a heart attack last summer, which made me realize he may not be around much longer. And my whole life's in Haydon Falls. My parents, my brothers, my job, the baseball camp I started. I don't want to leave all that, especially my family.'

She softly smiles. 'I understand.' She gazes into my eyes. 'So I guess this is it.'

'I guess so.' I cup my hands around her face and lean down to kiss her. 'I'll never forget this night. Or you.'

She slowly backs away. 'I'll never forget you either.'

She gathers up her things from the nightstand, then walks quickly to the door.

'Mia, wait!' I race up to her. 'You didn't say goodbye.'

She looks at me, then reaches up to kiss my cheek. 'Goodbye, Jason.'

She turns and opens the door, then races off. I go out to the hall and see her running toward the elevator. I watch as she gets on, thinking she'll look back at me, but she doesn't.

She's gone. Last night and this morning will soon just be a memory, a memory of a girl I'll never forget.

Chapter 3

End of April

Mia

'You still haven't heard from him?' Nora asks as she comes into my office. She caught me staring at my phone again, which I'm embarrassed to admit I've been doing ever since I asked Jason if we could have dinner.

'Who?' I ask, as if I have no idea who she's talking about.

She sits on the small blue couch next to my desk, the one a student just left after crying her heart out over a guy who just dumped her. I remember when my problems were as simple as a guy breaking up with me. It felt horrible at the time, but now, having a much bigger, more serious issue to deal with, getting dumped seems like no big deal.

'You know who,' Nora says. 'Why don't you just call him again?'

'And say what? I already asked him to dinner. I'm not going to ask him again.'

'Tell him you need an answer so you can make plans about coming there. Friday is only a few days away. Tell him you need to make a hotel reservation or there won't be any rooms left.'

I shake my head. 'It's only been a day. I'll give him another day. Then maybe I'll text him, make sure he didn't forget.'

'He didn't forget.' She puts her arm up along the back of the couch. 'He's probably stalling because he's trying to figure out what this is about. You haven't talked to the guy in months and then you call him out of the blue and ask to have dinner with him? He's going to wonder why.' She pauses. 'Maybe you should just tell him.'

'Over the phone?' I say, like she's crazy for even suggesting it. 'No. This is not something you tell someone over the phone.'

'It is if you can't talk to him in person.'

I get up from the desk and pace the floor. 'Maybe I should just go there. I don't know where he lives, but I'm sure I could find out. It's a small town. And his family owns that orchard. He's practically a celebrity there. I'm sure if I asked, someone could tell me where he lives.'

'And you're going to what? Show up at his door without any notice? I think that's a bad idea.'

'Then what am I going to do?' I walk up to her, feeling more and more anxious as I think about this. 'What if he doesn't call me back? Or what if I call him again and he tells me he doesn't want to see me? What if he says he has a girlfriend and he wouldn't feel right having dinner with me because of her? What if he met the love of his life and he's about to propose to her and then I show up and—'

'Okay, calm down.' Nora gets up and grabs hold of my arm. 'Even if he's with someone else, you have to tell him this. You know that, right?'

'Of course. I wouldn't keep this from him.'

'So let's think about this rationally. Your goal here is to tell him what happened and figure out a plan for what to do next.'

Nora's a professor in the physics department. She approaches problems like a scientist would, with logic and reason. I'm the opposite. I'm very emotional, which is good when I'm counseling and need to feel empathy for my clients, but not so good when I'm trying to make decisions.

'I know what the goal is, but that doesn't solve the issue of him not calling me back.'

'I'm just saying, there's no reason to get your emotions involved here. If the guy's with someone else, who cares? It's not like you had feelings for him. It was one night. And you can tell him that. Say that you're not looking to have any kind of relationship with him. You just need to figure out a plan going forward, given what happened.'

'It's not that simple,' I say, sitting down on the couch.

'Okay, yes, you two have a lot to discuss, but at least it's not complicated by you having feelings for him.'

I look down, not wanting to admit that I actually do have feelings for Jason. Nora will tell me it's not true, that there's no way it could be, but she wasn't there that night. She didn't feel what I felt when Jason and I were together. She hasn't spent the past four months thinking about him, wondering what could've been.

Nora sits beside me. 'You don't, right?'

'Don't what?' I look at her.

'Have feelings for him.'

'No,' I say, laughing 'How could I have feelings for him? I only spent a few hours with him.'

'Yeah, I don't know why I asked. It's just that for a minute there I got this feeling that maybe you felt something for him, but that doesn't make sense. You barely know the guy.'

'I wouldn't say that. I mean, we talked for hours that night. It wasn't just . . . you know . . . sex. We actually have a lot in common.'

'Just teaching. That's it, right?'

'There were other things.'

'Like what?'

My mind drifts back to that night. When I got to the ballroom at the hotel, I couldn't find my table. A woman noticed me searching for it and directed me where to go. When I saw Jason, my heart skipped a beat. He was so incredibly handsome, sitting there in his suit and tie. He was talking to someone and when he smiled, I found myself smiling too. He has one of those smiles that's contagious. I smiled a lot that night. He did too.

'Mia?' Nora waves her hand in front of me. 'You still with me?'

'Yeah, sorry. What were you saying?'

'Forget it. I have to go.' She gets up. 'Want to grab a drink later? Oh, wait, you can't. I keep forgetting that.'

She motions to me. 'Probably because you still look like that. Shouldn't you be showing by now?'

'The articles I've read said everyone's different.' I look down at my boobs. 'These are definitely bigger. I had to get a new bra.'

'I guess that's one perk of being pregnant.' She walks to the door. 'Maybe we can meet up later for dinner.'

'Probably not. I'm counseling until nine.'

'Why so late?'

'It's that time of year. Finals week increases anxiety, depression, drinking. I've got one student convinced her parents will disown her if she doesn't get all A's this semester. She's studying so much she's not sleeping.'

'Are you sure you should be working this much? I thought you were going to slow down.'

'I will. I just need to get through this week.'

'Maybe it's good Jason didn't get back to you. You should stay here this weekend and get some rest. You don't have to tell him this week.' Her phone alarm goes off. 'That's my reminder to get to class. I'll talk to you later.'

When she's gone I consider what she said about waiting to tell Jason the news. I could, but then I'll just keep worrying about telling him. I'd rather just do it. He needs to know. This is his child too and I don't feel right waiting to tell him. If he tells me he doesn't want to be involved in the baby's life, I'll understand. But I don't think he'll want that. He loves children as much as I do.

On my way back to my desk, I stop next to the wall of pamphlets, the ones we give out to students. I take out the one that says 'Could you be pregnant?'. There's an image of a teenage girl on it, looking confused as she holds her stomach.

I've given this pamphlet to several girls I've counseled. I've talked to them about it, gone over the symptoms. So how did I go all those months without knowing I was pregnant?

I thought I had the flu. I was tired. I kept throwing up. I didn't even consider I might be pregnant. All the signs were there—the same signs that are in the pamphlet—and yet I didn't put it together.

Putting the pamphlet back, I notice the one next to it about birth control. Jason and I didn't use protection that night. How could we be that careless? I'm always reminding students to be careful, and yet that night, I didn't follow my own advice. I'd been drinking, so that's part of the reason, but it's not a good one. I should've known better.

'Ms. Daniels?'

I turn and see Kirk standing at the door, his hair a mess and wearing wrinkled clothes that look like they came from the dirty clothes pile.

'You're early,' I say, giving him a smile.

'Actually, I'm here to cancel my appointment.'

I walk up to him. 'Do you want to reschedule?'

'No.' He rubs his hand over his face, then through his messy hair.

'Kirk, is something wrong?'

He shrugs. 'I just failed a test. My alarm didn't go off and I got there late and couldn't finish. The test was half our grade and I was already failing that class.'

'Which class? I could talk to your professor and see if you could take a make-up exam.'

He shakes his head. 'I'm done. I don't want to do this anymore.'

'Do what?'

'School. I hate it. I'm dropping out.'

'Did you talk to your parents about this?'

'I talked to my mom. She's going to talk to my dad.'

His dad is verbally abusive, which is why Kirk has been seeing me. His father is always putting him down and telling him he's lazy and not good at anything.

'Anyway, I just wanted to say you've been a big help. I'm not afraid to go home anymore.' He smiles a little. 'And I know what my dad says about me isn't true. So, thanks for that.'

'You're welcome.' I smile back, but I'm tearing up. I'm going to miss Kirk. He's one of those guys who tries to act all tough but deep down he's caring and sensitive and really sweet.

'I'll be okay,' he says, noticing me tearing up.

'I know you will.' I pull him in for a hug. 'You keep in touch, okay?'

'Yeah, okay.' He pulls away. 'Oh, and congrats on the baby. You'll make a great mom.'

'Wait—how did you know?' I ask, because I haven't told anyone except Nora.

'I heard you talking to your friend when I was waiting in the hall. I didn't even know you were married.'

'I'm not.' I clear my throat. 'I mean, not right now. But we're planning on it.' I put my hand on my stomach. 'This was somewhat of a surprise.'

'That happened to my aunt. She had twins.' Kirk glances behind him. 'I gotta go. I just wanted to say goodbye.' He takes off, meeting up with a girl who was waiting for him in the hall.

I shut the door, trying to figure out why I told Kirk I was planning to marry the baby's father when I'm not even talking to him. It's like I was ashamed to admit I'm doing this alone. But I'm not ashamed. Things like this happen all the time. So why did I say that?

My phone rings. My pulse races, assuming it's Jason. But when I look at the screen, I see it's my mom.

'Hi, Mom,' I answer.

'Hi, honey, are you working?'

'Yes, but my next appointment just cancelled.' I walk over to my desk and sit down.

'I was calling about your graduation. Your father and I decided to fly out there early and make a little trip out of it. Deloris was telling me there are some darling little towns in that area.'

'How early?' I ask, wishing she'd asked me about this before booking her flight. I need more time before I tell them my news. I need to talk to Jason first, and then I need to figure out how to tell my parents. They'll be excited about having a grandchild, but upset that I'm not married. They firmly believe you should be married before having a child. They're from a time when that's what everyone did.

My parents are in their seventies. My mom had me when she was 45 and my dad was 53. My parents didn't think they could have kids until I came along and surprised them. I guess surprise babies run in the family.

'Mom, I don't think you and Dad will like it out here. The towns are mostly farm towns. They aren't touristy like out there.'

My parents live in a suburb just north of Boston. Now that they're retired, they're always looking for things to do.

'We've already looked online and found some wonderful places we'd like to visit. We found a town to stay in at night and then during the day we'll take little side trips. We'll head to Madison on Friday. We didn't want to get there early and be in your way. We know you're busy.'

'So when are you getting in?'

'The 16th, and we're staying in Haydon Falls. It's supposed to be a beautiful little town. Have you heard of it?'

'Haydon Falls? Um, yeah. I've heard of it.'

It's where the father of my baby lives. The father of your grandchild.

Out of all the towns in Wisconsin, they just had to pick Haydon Falls?

'If you're able to, would you like to meet us there for a day or two?'

'Where? Haydon Falls?'

'Yes. Your father and I would love to spend some time with you since we won't be seeing you this summer.'

'I don't know, Mom. I'll have to check my work schedule.'

My summer job doesn't start for a few weeks, but I don't want to tell her that or she'll guilt me into spending time with them in Haydon Falls, just like she tried to guilt me into coming home this summer. I'm done with school, so I could've gone back to Boston, but I decided to stay here a few more months. I'd like to say it had nothing to do with Jason, but that's a lie. I took a job here this summer because I wasn't ready to leave.

Even before finding out I was pregnant, I wanted to call up Jason and ask if we could meet for dinner. I wanted to see if the way we felt that night was real or just a side effect of the alcohol. But I never got up the nerve to call him. I kept coming up with reasons why I couldn't. I was too busy with work. Too busy with school. I had to finish a paper first, or a project, or clean my apartment. There was always something holding me back, but I can't put it off anymore, not after finding out about the baby.

'Mom, I need to go,' I say, suddenly feeling sick.

'Let me give you our flight times.'

'Just text it to me. I really need to go. I'll talk to you later.' I end the call and race to the bathroom. I've gone a couple weeks without morning sickness, which makes me wonder if this is something else, like my nerves acting up because I'm afraid to tell my parents about the baby. I hate disappointing them, and finding this out will definitely disappoint them.

Back in my office, I find my boss standing at my desk.

'There you are,' he says, smiling. He's head of the student counseling center and also teaches some classes in my graduate program.

'I just stepped out for a moment. Did you need something?'

'I wanted to ask if you'd like to continue doing some counseling this summer.'

'I'd love to, but I already have a job. I'm assisting Professor Abrams with some research.'

'Yes, I heard, but he said it's only part-time. I thought maybe you could fit in a few hours a week of counseling, unless you have other plans.'

I do have other plans. I want to use the time I'm not working to get ready for the baby and figure out my life as a single mom. The research job is easy and I can do it online, which is why I took it.

'Could I think about it? I'd love to help out, but I don't want to commit to it just yet.'

'Of course. Think it over and let me know.' He walks to the door, then turns back. 'You've done a wonderful job here. The students rave about you. I'd be happy to give you a recommendation when you start applying for full-time positions.'

'Thank you. I'll take you up on that.'

He leaves and I'm reminded of the job I was going to apply for in Boston. The job is for director of a teen crisis center that works with homeless teens. I'd planned to work at a high school, but this job would give me more responsibly and better pay. I was going to apply for it the day I found out I was pregnant. I decided to wait, but if I wait much longer, the job will be taken by someone else.

There's so much to think about. So much to decide.

I need to talk to Jason. I really wish he'd call me back.

Chapter 4

Jason

'Mr. Kanfield?' Joel, one of my students, comes into the classroom, waking me from my thoughts.

'Hey, Joel.' I get up from my desk. 'Did you need something?'

'Yeah, I um,' he checks behind him, 'wanted to ask you something.'

'Go ahead.' I move to the front of my desk as he walks up to me. Joel's a freshman, but he's taking my junior level chemistry class and getting an A. He's really smart but tries to hide it because he doesn't want to be labeled a nerd.

'You know Abigail, right?' he asks, keeping his voice down.

'Yes, I know Abigail,' I say, trying not to laugh. I know everyone in the school, and their families. That's how it is in a small town and a small high school like Haydon Falls High. 'What about her?'

'I really like her and want to ask her out, but I don't know what to say. I always see you around town with a different girl.' He shrugs. 'I'm guessing that means you know something about girls or what to say to make them go out with you.'

I clear my throat. 'I think you're getting the wrong impression. I don't go out with that many women.'

'I saw you last Tuesday having dinner with some blonde lady and last weekend you went out with that girl who works at the dentist's office. And Zach saw you out with Ms. Ennis.'

Ms. Ennis is Mary Ennis, the librarian at the middle school. We went out for coffee. It wasn't a date. The two other women Joel mentioned I went out with in the past but it didn't go anywhere. Now we're just friends. In fact, Lydia, the blonde I had dinner with, is going out with a guy in my apartment building this weekend. I set them up after he saw her in our building and asked about her.

Getting dates isn't my problem. It's getting those dates to turn into something more that I struggle with. If I don't feel something for the girl—a connection, a spark—I don't see a reason to keep dating her. My brothers keep telling me I need to give it more time, that a few dates isn't enough to know if she's the right girl, but I've dated girls for months and still didn't feel anything.

The only time I felt a true connection with someone was that night I spent with Mia. From the moment she sat down next to me, I could feel something between us. An immediate connection, almost like we'd known each other for years. And there was definitely a spark. More than a spark. It was a flame, burning so hot we barely made it back to my room.

I've thought about Mia, and about that night, every day since, wanting to call her but not letting myself. We agreed not to see each other after we said goodbye. So why did she call me? Why does she want to see me?

'Mr. Kanfield?' Joel says. 'Did you hear me?'

'Um, sorry, no.' I focus back on Joel, who keeps looking behind him. He does that when he's nervous. Either that or he shoves his hands in his pockets and shrugs his shoulders. 'You were asking about Abigail. About asking her out?'

'Yeah.' He nods really fast. 'My friends say I'm a fucking—I mean freaking—idiot to even think she'd go out with me.' He looks down. 'Maybe they're right. Maybe I shouldn't do this.'

'Hey.' I put my hand on his shoulder. 'Don't listen to your friends. If you really like this girl, ask her out. The worst that could happen is she says no.'

'And tells everyone at school that she turned me down.' He sighs. 'It's not worth it. I'm just going to forget it.'

'Then you'll never know what might've been. What if she said yes and you two really hit it off and dated all through high school and then college. Maybe you'd even end up getting married.'

I don't see that happening, but I'm trying to make a point here.

He laughs a little. 'She'd never marry me.'

'Maybe not, but I think there's a good chance she'd go out with you.'

'Really?' he asks, sounding hopeful.

'You'll never know if you don't ask.'

'So how do I do this? What do I say to her?'

'Say something nice. Compliment her. Tell her what you like about her.'

He smiles. 'I like her tits.'

'Okay, not that,' I say with a sigh. 'Think of something else you like about her, not related to her body.'

'I like her voice. And I like her laugh. And her eyes are pretty. Oh, eyes are part of her body. Forget that.'

'Eyes are fine. So is complimenting her smile. Just avoid mentioning her chest, or anything below the neck.'

'Okay, so I say I like her eyes and the way she laughs, and then what?'

'Is this the first time you've asked a girl out?' I ask, wondering why he has so many questions.

'I asked Tamara out a few months ago. My friends told me what to say and she turned me down. After that I figured out my friends don't know shit and I should ask someone who's old and knows what they're doing.'

Old? I'm not old. I'm 28. But I guess when you're 15, 28 is old.

'Well, after you compliment her, maybe ask what she's interested in, what she likes to do.'

'I already know all that. She takes dance classes and reads a lot and likes being in school plays.'

'Okay, yes, but asking her about that stuff shows you're interested in her, in more than her . . . chest.'

'Yeah, I could see that. Girls like talking about shit, so if you get them to talk there's a better chance they'll like you.' He smiles at me. 'You're really smart, Mr. Kanfield. I see why you get so many girls. So what do I do when she's done talking?'

'Ask her if she'd like to go do something. Make it something you know she likes, and if you're not sure, ask her. Like ask what her favorite ice cream is and then offer to take her for ice cream.'

'Ice cream?' He scrunches up his nose. 'That's kind of a lame date.'

'There's only so much you can do at your age and ice cream is cheap. That's another tip. Offer to pay. If she wants to pay for herself, that's fine, but at least offer. And remember to be nice, compliment her, and ask her questions.'

'I gotta write this down.' He reaches behind to his backpack.

'Here.' I hand him a notepad from my desk and a pen.

He scribbles down 'Nice. Compliment. Ask.' 'Thanks, Mr. Kanfield. You've got a lot better advice than my friends.' He hands me the notepad and pen. 'I'll see you around.' He walks to the door. 'Hope you win tomorrow!'

He's talking about the baseball game. It's one of the last games of the season. We have a weak team this year. My best players graduated last year and I was left with kids who aren't as skilled or as interested in the game. The past few years, football has become the sport everyone wants to play and baseball is suffering because of it. For awhile, football was losing players because the team sucked and nobody wants to be on a losing team. But then they started getting good, good enough to go to the playoffs, and now younger kids are wanting to play football over baseball. That's why I started the summer baseball camp, to get younger kids interested in the game so they'll want to play on the team when they get to high school.

It's almost four, which is when I'd usually be out on the field, practicing with the team. But it's raining and I saw some lightning, so I cancelled practice for today. It's Friday. I should be going home and getting ready for a date, but I don't have one. And I can't go out with my brothers because they'll be out with their girlfriends. I'm the only single one left, something my mom reminds me of on a regular basis. Just last week she was asking who I was taking to Nick's wedding, as if I couldn't possibly show up without a date.

My older brother Nick is getting married in a couple weeks at the orchard our family owns, the one he now runs. I still can't believe he's marrying Lyndsay, the girl he had a crush on all through high school. I was even more surprised when he proposed to her after only dating her a few months. Nick is always very cautious and overthinks every decision, so proposing to her that soon tells me he knew Lyndsay was the one after just a few dates. He had no doubts.

That's what I'm looking for. That feeling of knowing the girl I'm with is the one for me, without a doubt. Thinking about that brings my mind back to Mia. She's waiting for me to give her an answer about dinner. I don't know what to tell her. I really want to see her, but what if I have dinner with her and all those feelings come back?

All the feelings I had that night? Feelings that ended in disappointment and months of thinking about a girl I can't have. I've been trying to get her out of my head so I can move on with someone else. Seeing her again is only going to make that more difficult.

But I really want to see her.

Scrolling through my phone, I find Noah's number. I haven't talked to him since his wedding, but he's the only person I can ask about Mia.

'Hello?' he answers.

'Hey, Noah, it's Jason.'

'Hey, man, how's it going?' He sounds really happy. I guess married life has been good to him.

'I'm keeping busy. Baseball season's wrapping up soon.'

'How's the team this year?'

'We suck,' I say with a laugh. 'But next year should be better. I've lined up private coaching with some of the kids this summer. They're not bad players. They just need to work on their skills and practice more.'

'You still doing the camp?'

'Yeah, but I've changed it to be for younger kids. The older teens weren't signing up. They've got too much going on in the summer.'

'Yeah, I could see that.'

'How's married life?'

'Couldn't be better. We're looking at houses, got some trips planned for the summer. Next fall we plan to start trying for a kid.'

'That's great! I'm happy for you.'

'How about you? You seeing anyone?'

'Not right now. You know how it is around here. There's only so many single women and I've dated most of them, at least the ones close to my age. My brothers have been giving me a hard time for dating girls in their early twenties but that's all I've got left unless I want to go older. And the older ones are married. Hey, speaking of women, I wanted to ask you about Mia.'

'Mia *who*?'

'Mia Daniels. Lacey's friend. She was at your wedding.'

'Oh *that* Mia. Yeah, I know who you mean. What about her?'

'Has Lacey talked to her since the wedding?'

'No. I don't think so.'

'But they're still friends, right?'

'Yeah, they just got busy and haven't talked. Why are you asking about Mia?'

'I guess I'm just looking for some advice. That night of the wedding we um . . . got to know each other. I didn't think I'd hear from her again, but the other night she called me, saying she wanted to come here and have dinner.'

'What do you mean when you say you got to know each other? Like you guys talked or did something happen?'

'Something happened.'

'What? You guys kissed?'

'We did more than that. We spent the night together.'

'No shit? And you're just telling me this now?'

'I didn't tell anyone. Well, I told Brody, my younger brother, but that was an accident. I was drunk.'

It was Sunday night, the night after the wedding, and I was drinking to try to forget about Mia. By the time Brody came over, I was drunk. He asked me about the wedding and I told him about Mia but made it sound like it wasn't a big deal, like she was just some girl I met and we ended up back in my room. The next day I asked Brody to keep quiet about what I told him, but of course he'd already told Nick and Sawyer. When they asked me about her, I did the same thing I did with Brody. I pretended Mia was just some girl, not the girl I fell for in a way I've never fallen for anyone else.

'So what happened?' Noah asks. 'Did you guys go out after that?'

'No, we decided not to. She's graduating in a few weeks and going back to Boston. We didn't want to start something knowing she'd be leaving in a few months. We decided not to see each other after that night. That's why I'm trying to figure out why she called and why she wants to have dinner.'

'Maybe she just wants to say goodbye before she moves back.'

'But why? Why say goodbye to someone you haven't seen in months? It's not like we've been talking this whole time.'

'I could ask Lacey, but I don't think she'd have an answer. This sounds like something between you and Mia. She obviously still likes you if she wants to see you.

Maybe she wants another night with you,' he says, a smile in his voice.

'That's not it. If she just wanted sex, she could get it from someone else. She's gorgeous. She could have any guy she wants.'

'But she wants you, which tells me that night you guys shared was more than just sex.'

'It was,' I say with a sigh. 'Honestly, it was the best night of my life. We talked. We laughed. We—well, I don't need to go into details. The point is, I never forgot her. Even now, all these months later, I wake up thinking about her and go to bed thinking about her. I can't get her out of my head.'

'Damn, man, you got it bad.'

'I know, right? And the worst part is, we can never have anything more than that night. I finally find this amazing girl who's everything I could ever want and she's moving away in a few weeks.'

'Maybe she's not. Maybe she changed her mind. Maybe that's why she wants to talk to you.'

'I don't think so. She was adamant about going back. She told me about her parents and how she wants to be close to them since she's their only child.'

'Yeah, and her parents are old. She probably thinks she doesn't have much time left with them.'

'And I totally get that. I'm the same way with my parents. It's one of the reasons I want to stay in Haydon Falls. That's why Mia and I decided to end things that night. We both knew we wouldn't be able to make this work.'

'So what'd you tell her?'

'I didn't give her an answer yet. But I can't keep waiting. I need to call her back.'

'I think you should have dinner with her. She probably just wants to see you again before she leaves. As a friend.'

'Yeah, maybe that's all it is.'

'Hey, I need to go. I'm going to be late for a meeting.'

'Oh, yeah, sorry, I forgot you're still at work. I'll talk to you later.'

'If you decide to see Mia, let me know how it goes.'

'I will. Bye.' I end the call, still not sure if I should agree to have dinner with her. Maybe Mia only sees us as friends, but I still see her as more than that, which means having dinner with her could be a bad idea.

Looking at my phone, I find her number. My finger hovers over the screen. I need to do this. I can't keep waiting. I need to give her an answer.

Chapter 5

Jason

My heart thumps faster as Mia's phone rings. I'm nervous, but I don't know why. We're just talking. It's not a big deal, or it shouldn't be, so why am I nervous? I wasn't this way last time we talked, but I think that's because I was too shocked that she'd called to be nervous.

'Jason,' she answers, sounding out of breath. 'Hi.'

'Hey, are you busy? I should've texted first. Asked for a good time to call.'

'Now is fine. I had a counseling appointment, but he cancelled. So how was your week?'

'Good. Hey, sorry it took me so long to get back to you. I had a lot going on this week with work and baseball and getting ready for graduation.'

'I understand. When I was teaching, it was always crazy this time of year, but I loved it, sending the seniors off to whatever adventures awaited them. There was so much hope and excitement in the air. Or maybe that was just me feeling that way.' She laughs a little, and I feel myself smiling. I love her laugh. I've missed it.

'It's not just you. I feel that way too. It's exciting to see kids I've watched grow up go on to graduate and start a new phase of their lives.'

I'd love to keep talking to her about teaching and all the other stuff we have in common, but that's not why I called. I need to get an answer to the question that's been on my mind all week. Just as I'm about to ask, Mia starts talking again.

'So how's the baseball team this year?'

'Not great. We have a game tomorrow that I'm sure we'll lose.'

'Tomorrow? What time?'

'In the afternoon, but we're supposed to have rain so I'm guessing it'll get delayed until later.'

'Oh,' she says, sounding disappointed.

'Is something wrong?'

'No, it's just that we talked about having dinner and I thought maybe we could do it tomorrow, assuming you want to go. Did you make a decision?'

'I wanted to talk to you about it first. I'm a little confused.'

'About what?'

'When we said goodbye in Chicago, we agreed we wouldn't see each other again. I'm just wondering what changed your mind.'

'Could we talk about this in person? It's not something I want to do over the phone.'

'So there's a reason you want to meet. It isn't just to catch up or say goodbye before you move?'

'Actually, I'm not moving. Not yet. I'm staying here for the summer and helping one of the professors with his research.'

'But you're still moving, right? To Boston?'

'Um, yes, at the end of the summer.'

The phone is silent as I think about what to do. Why would I see her again if she's just going to leave? It's taken months for me to get to a point where I'm not spending all day thinking about her. If I see her again, I'll be back where I was in January, with her consuming my thoughts.

'Mia, I don't think—'

'Jason, please. It's just dinner, and I really need to talk to you.'

'Talk to me now. What do you want to say?'

'Can we please just meet for dinner? I could be there tomorrow night.'

'Tomorrow won't work. There's a good chance the game will be moved back a few hours if it rains, and after the game I'm meeting up with my brothers to figure out a wedding gift to give Nick.'

'That's right. He's getting married soon.'

'May 15th. So anyway, tomorrow isn't good. I could do Sunday.'

'That won't work. I have counseling appointments in the afternoon. How about next Friday?'

I quickly check my calendar. 'I could do Friday. What time are you thinking?'

'Six? I work that afternoon, but I could be there by six.'

'Let's plan on that and if it doesn't work, just let me know.'

'Great! Just text me where to meet you. Any place you want to go is fine with me. My next appointment just got here. She's early, but I should probably go.'

'Yeah, I'll see you next Friday.'

'Okay. Bye, Jason.' She ends the call.

I stare at my phone, wondering what the hell just happened. I agreed to see her again, having no idea what this is about. Why wouldn't she tell me? Is she just wanting an excuse to see me again? Why would she want that when she's leaving in a few months? None of this makes sense, and now I have to wait another week to get answers.

I go home and change clothes, then head over to Sawyer's to meet up with my brothers. We're going to have a beer before they go out with their girlfriends for the night. Nick invited me to go to dinner with him and Lyndsay, but I told him no. I'm not going to be a third wheel on their date. My family thinks I'm a lonely bachelor in need of company, but the truth is, I'm totally fine on my own. It'd be nice to have a girlfriend, but it has to be the right girl and I haven't found her yet. Or I did, but she's moving away.

* * *

'What are you drinking?' Sawyer asks as I go into the brewery. He's standing by the long high-top table where Brody and Nick are sitting.

'Give me the stout,' I tell him.

He takes off for the bar. It's awesome having a brother who owns a microbrewery and even better that he has a girlfriend who owns the one outside of town. I get all the free beer I want. Personally, I think Gina's beer is better, but I'd never tell Sawyer that. His beer isn't bad. He just needs more time to work on it.

'You get a date for tonight?' Nick asks as I sit across from him.

'Yeah, a date with my TV,' I kid. 'There's some good games on tonight.'

Brody laughs. 'Couldn't get a date, huh?'

'I could get a date. I just didn't want one. I need a break from dating. It's exhausting.'

'What about Brianna?' Sawyer asks, setting my beer on the table. 'Are you guys done?'

'I hope so,' Nick mutters before taking a drink of his beer.

I look at him. 'Why are you so against Brianna? There's nothing wrong with her.'

'I didn't say there was. I just think she's too young for you. And too immature. Matt said she showed up drunk to work yesterday.'

'And how would he know?'

'Tessa took one of the kids to the dentist and there was nobody there to check them in. Apparently, Brianna showed up drunk and was sent home so they didn't have anyone to run the front desk.'

'Are you guys still going out or not?' Brody asks me.

'We're not going out. She wants to see me again, but I told her we're better off as friends.'

'Did she get pissed?' Brody asks.

'No. It's not like we were serious.'

'I know someone you could go out with,' Sawyer says, returning with my beer. 'Liam's sister is coming to town next weekend and she'll need something to do when he's working. She's 25 and she's hot. He showed me her picture.'

Liam is Sawyer's new bar manager. He replaced Wade, the guy Sawyer fired last fall. Liam moved here from Milwaukee, so I'm guessing that's where his sister lives.

'Sawyer, you know I don't do the long-distance thing.'

'I didn't say you had to marry her. Just take her out. She's coming next Friday. You could meet her here for a drink, then take her to dinner.'

'I'm busy next Friday.'

'Doing what?' Nick asks.

I don't want to tell them. If I do, they'll ask me a million questions.

Brody shoves my shoulder. 'Hey, wake up. We're waiting for an answer here.'

'And I'm not giving you one. You guys don't need to know everything. I'm allowed to have some privacy.'

Sawyer smiles at Nick. 'Must be serious if he's hiding her from us.'

'Maybe it's that librarian he went out with last week.'

'It's not her,' I say, rolling my eyes.

'Then who is it?' Brody asks. 'You know we'll find out. You might as well tell us.'

I sigh in annoyance. 'Okay, fine. It's Mia. We're having dinner next Friday. It's not a big deal, but I know you idiots will make it one, which is why I didn't tell you.'

'Mia,' Nick says, rubbing his jaw. 'Do we know her?'

'The girl from the wedding,' Brody says. 'She called him earlier this week saying she wants to see him. We haven't met her.'

'This is the girl you slept with?' Sawyer asks.

I sigh again. 'Do we really have to talk about this?'

'Hell yeah.' Sawyer sits down next to Nick. 'Tell us about her. She's going to school, right?'

'Yes, in Madison. She graduates in a few weeks and then she's moving back to Boston.'

'So why does she want to see you?' Nick asks.

'I don't know. She didn't say. I'm guessing she just wants to tell me goodbye before she leaves, although she's not actually moving until after the summer.'

'Must've been a good night if she's coming all this way to see you,' Sawyer says, in a way that implies she's only coming here to have sex. 'Is she staying all weekend?'

'No, and it's just dinner. Nothing else.'

'Did she get a hotel?' Nick asks. 'She's not going to drive back that late. It's too far and it'll be dark and if she's been drinking—'

'Yeah, I'm sure she'll get a hotel,' I say, although she didn't mention it. I didn't even think about that until Nick brought it up, but he's right. It'll be too late for her to drive back to Madison. Should I offer to let her stay with me? No, that'd be bad. Really bad. We'd end up repeating the night of the wedding and I'd fall even harder for her.

'Kate thinks this girl wants to get back together with you,' Brody says. Kate is his girlfriend. They're living together. Kate's opening a store downtown and when I was there the other day, I mentioned Mia calling me, which prompted Brody to ask his girlfriend what it meant.

'Mia and I never dated, so there is no getting back together.'

Brody turns to me. 'I'm saying she wants to continue wherever you left off the night of the wedding. Like actually go out and see if it turns into something.'

'I thought the night of the wedding was just sex,' Sawyer says.

'It was more than sex,' I tell him, 'but it doesn't matter. She's moving at the end of the summer.'

'So date her for the summer,' Nick says.

'From an hour away?' I roll my eyes. 'Yeah, that'll work. Can we stop talking about this? Nothing's going to happen with Mia. We'll go to dinner, and after that, I'll probably never see her again. I don't have a reason to.' I look over at Sawyer. 'Let's talk about Nick's bachelor party.'

'I don't want another bachelor party,' Nick says. 'One was enough.'

Nick's bachelor party was in Chicago a few weeks ago, but Sawyer thinks we should have another one here, for people in town who couldn't make it to Chicago.

'How many strippers should we get?' Brody asks.

'No strippers,' Nick says, looking at Brody, Sawyer, and me. 'And there's not going to be another party. I'm serious.'

'We're just joking,' Sawyer says. 'Lighten up, man.'

'Hey, it took me a long damn time to get Lyndsay. I'm not letting you guys do something stupid to screw it up.'

'She's going to marry you no matter what,' Brody says.

'You're still not getting me strippers. And I don't want another party.'

'Then we'll save the strippers for *my* bachelor party,' Sawyer says. 'Jason, you're in charge of getting them.'

'Why him?' Brody asks.

'Because he's single. If you or Nick do it, your girlfriends will get pissed.'

'And Gina won't get pissed?' Brody asks. 'She's okay with you having strippers at your bachelor party?'

'She hasn't said she isn't.'

'You might want to run that past her,' Nick says. 'Why are you even talking about this? Are you guys getting engaged?'

'Not right now, but we will eventually.'

'What are you waiting for? You're not getting any younger.'

'Yeah, if you don't hurry up, you'll be old like Nick before you have kids,' Brody jokes.

'I'm not old,' Nick says to Brody. 'People have kids later now. It's not like when Mom and Dad were our age.'

'I always thought Jason would be the first to have kids,' Brody says. 'And now he's the single one and we all have girlfriends.'

'I thought you'd be first too,' Sawyer says to me. 'Ten years ago I would've guessed you'd be married with two or three kids by now.'

'Yeah, well, I'm not,' I say, getting annoyed. They say this shit all the time and I'm getting tired of it. If I'd found the right girl, they're right, I'd be married by now and have a couple kids, but that's not how it worked out. I don't need to be reminded of that by my stupid brothers.

'Kate's all baby crazy now,' Brody says. 'It's Nash's fault. Bringing his baby here all the time.'

'She is pretty damn cute,' Sawyer says. 'Even I think about having a kid when I'm around her. Then I come to my senses and realize it's not the right time.'

'It's never the right time,' Nick says. 'Kids change your life. You're never fully prepared for it, even if you think you are.'

'Are you and Lyndsay still going to have them right away?'

Nick smiles. 'We're already trying. The wedding's only a few weeks away. There's really no need to wait.'

Sawyer looks at Brody and me. 'We could be uncles by this time next year.'

Nick's phone dings and he checks it. 'That's Lyndsay. I need to get home.'

'To make a baby?' Sawyer jokes.

Nick laughs. 'That's later. I'm taking her to dinner first.'

'I need to go too,' Brody says, getting up.

We say our goodbyes and they take off. Sawyer goes back behind the bar to fill orders as the place fills up. I remain at the table and finish my beer, my mind going back to Mia, wondering what she wants to talk about and why she couldn't tell me over the phone.

I won't see her until next Friday, which means I'll be thinking about this all week. I wish she'd just told me.

Chapter 6

Mia

It's Friday night and I'm almost at Haydon Falls. I feel like I'm going to throw up, and not because of the pregnancy, but because I'm worried about seeing Jason. I'm worried about how he'll react to my news. I'm worried about seeing him again. I'm worried I'll fall for him even more, which will make leaving him even harder than when we said goodbye at the hotel.

I cried on my way home that day. I'd met this great guy, a guy I could see myself having a relationship with, maybe even marrying someday, and I had to leave him. I thought I'd never see him again. And now, here I am, about to have dinner with him. About to tell him that our night together created a baby, and that he'll soon be a dad.

What if he gets mad? What if he blames me for this? I was on birth control, but I'd just changed pills and was supposed to use a backup method for a month. What if Jason gets angry at me for not telling him that? We should've used a condom, but we didn't. That's both of our faults. He can't blame me for that.

My phone rings. It's Nora calling. I hit the button to put it on speaker.

'Hey, Nora.'

'Hey, are you there yet?'

'Not yet. I have about five minutes to go.'

'How are you feeling?'

'Like I'm going to be sick. Nora, what if he freaks out?'

'Then let him. You did when you found out. Then after you had some time to let it sink in, you were fine. I'm sure it'll be the same for him.'

'What if he gets angry?'

'Then slap the jerk and tell him he's being an ass. You didn't make this baby on your own.'

'I know, and I honestly don't think he'd react that way. I'm not sure how he'll react.'

'I think the biggest thing you have to worry about is how he'll react to you leaving. If he wants to be in the baby's life, he's not going to be okay with you living a thousand miles away.'

'That's what I'm worried about. How are we going to make this work?'

'Just focus on telling him for now and go from there. You're getting a hotel room, right? You can't be driving back tonight. It's too dangerous. It'll be dark and you'll be tired.'

'I'd be okay driving back, but yes, I'll get a hotel room just to be safe.'

'Or you could stay with Jason.'

'I'm not staying with Jason.'

'Why? Because you think something might happen?'

'No, of course not,' I say, but the truth is, it's entirely possible something could happen. I never planned on spending the night with him at the wedding, but then I ended up in his bed. 'I just think it'd be better if I stayed at a hotel.' I turn off on the road that leads to downtown Haydon Falls. 'I'm almost there. I should go.'

'Okay. Let me know how it goes.'

'I will. Bye.'

The small downtown is like a movie set with its historic buildings and all the storefronts decorated for spring. Large planters overflowing with flowers line the street along with black iron benches. Even the trash cans are pretty, made of black metal with a scrolling design on the sides. Nora was right when she said this town was adorable. I see why she likes coming here. I'm sure I'd love it too if I wasn't so nervous about seeing Jason.

Pulling up in front of the restaurant, my heart takes off when I see Jason waiting outside. He's just as handsome as I remember; tall with broad shoulders and thick dark hair. He's wearing jeans and a white dress shirt with the sleeves rolled up.

He hasn't seen me yet. His head is down as he looks at his phone.

I get out of the car and walk up to him. 'Jason.'

He startles and his head jerks up. 'Mia.'

He smiles and I get that feeling again, like I've known him forever. I had that feeling the night we met. It's why I felt so close to him, so safe, so connected.

'It's good to see you,' I tell him.

'It's good seeing you too.' He pulls me in for a hug. I wasn't expecting that, but being in his arms again, I don't want him to let me go.

This is already harder than I thought it'd be. I imagined myself coming here, telling him about the baby, and us discussing next steps as though we were business partners. I was going to keep my emotions out of it. That was the plan.

But seeing him again, feeling his arms around me, that plan is already shattered. The feelings I keep trying to shove away are there and stronger than ever.

He lets me go and motions to the restaurant. 'I got us a table. I just came out here to wait for you.' He smiles. 'And welcome you to Haydon Falls. You haven't been here before, right?'

'No, but I like what I've seen so far. The downtown is beautiful.'

'The falls are even better. If we had more time, I'd take you there.'

I'd love to go there with him, but I don't think he'll want to spend time with me after he finds out the news. He'll need time to himself to process the fact that he's going to be a dad. I've known for weeks and I'm still trying to process it.

'You look great, Mia,' Jason says, gazing at me.

'Thanks.' I glance down at my stomach. I'm not showing yet, but I feel like I am. 'We should probably go inside.'

'Right this way.' He opens the door for me and we go into the restaurant. It's not what I was expecting.

I thought it'd have a small town diner feel, but it's got more of a big city vibe with its black-and-white color scheme and modern decor.

'This is nice,' I say as we sit down at the table.

'It's new. Well, it's been here about a year, which is new for us.' Jason laughs a little. He seems nervous, or maybe I'm imagining it because I'm feeling nervous. But my nerves have calmed down a little being with Jason. He has such kind eyes and a gentle way about him. I can't imagine him getting angry. I'm sure he does, but I can't see him exploding with anger the way I imagined him doing in my head when I told him the news. Why did I think of him that way when I know he's not like that? Was I trying to imagine him being a jerk with a bad temper so it'd be easier to get over him?

I'm not over him, not even a little. If anything, I like him even more, seeing him in his hometown, wearing casual clothes instead of that suit and tie he had on at the wedding. He looked amazing in the suit, but it didn't seem right for him. He seems like a jeans and t-shirt type of guy.

'How was the trip?' he asks.

'Good. It was an easy drive. I'm just tired after the drive and a long day of counseling sessions.'

'Are you still going to class?'

'No, classes are over. I just have some assignments to finish.'

'It must feel good to be done. Congratulations on the degree.'

'Thanks.' I pick up my water glass and take a drink. Part of me wants to just tell him the news and not wait, but the other part of me wants to enjoy a nice dinner with him and pretend we're on a date.

If things were different, if our situation wasn't so complicated, I could see us dating. I could see us having a relationship. But it didn't work out that way.

'Hey, Jason,' the waitress says, stopping at our table. She's tall and thin with long blonde hair and light blue eyes.

'Hey, how's it going?'

'Great! Haven't seen you for awhile.' She smiles at him in a way that makes me think she's flirting with him. Does she not see that we're on a date? I guess it's not a date, but she shouldn't assume it's not.

'I've been busy with baseball,' Jason tells her. 'But the season's wrapping up soon. We had a rough year. We won't be going to any playoff games.'

'So you'll have more time soon.' She hasn't even glanced at me. It's like I'm not even here. 'Maybe we could go out again.'

Again? Jason went out with this woman? When? How long ago?

Wait—why do I sound like a jealous girlfriend? I'm not dating Jason. I never did. We just shared a night.

'Andrea, this is Mia,' Jason says, not answering her question about going out.

She finally looks at me. 'Hi.'

'Mia's going to school in Madison,' Jason says. 'This is her first time to Haydon Falls.'

'Welcome,' she says, but her tone isn't very welcoming. 'Do you want to start with a drink?'

'Just water is fine,' I say.

'You sure?' Jason asks. 'They have a good wine list here.'

'I'll stick with water.'

'I'll have the same,' he says to Andrea.

'Do you want to just order?' she asks, sounding annoyed that we didn't get drinks.

'I think we need a minute,' Jason says.

She leaves and I pick up my menu. There isn't much on it and everything is expensive, or expensive for here. It'd be cheap if I were back in Boston. How am I going to live there with a baby? My rent alone will be four times what I pay now.

'You sure you don't want some wine?' Jason asks. 'If you're worried about the cost, don't. Tonight's on me.'

'Jason, I don't expect you to buy me dinner. I invited you. If anything, I should be the one paying.'

'You're my guest. I'm not letting you come to Haydon Falls and pay for dinner. I'd be a really shitty host if I did. Now are you sure you don't want wine?' He smiles. 'Or how about an old fashioned?'

I smile back. 'That's probably not a good idea, given what happened last time I had one.'

'The wedding was the last time?'

'Yes. I swore off drinking after that, at least for awhile.'

'Why?' His expression turns serious. 'Do you regret what happened that night?'

'No,' I say, and I honestly don't. Even knowing what that night resulted in, I still don't regret it. It was the best night of my life. I doubt I'll ever experience something like that again. 'I just decided to take a break from drinking after that.'

Andrea returns. 'Did you decide what you want?'

'I'll have the chicken,' I tell her, setting the menu down.

'I'll have the steak,' Jason says.

She takes the menus and turns to Jason. 'Are you taking anyone to your brother's wedding?'

'Probably not.'

'If you change your mind, I have that night off.' She gives him that flirty smile again.

'I'll keep that in mind.'

Her face lights up, like she thinks he'll actually take her to the wedding. Maybe he will. There I go again, feeling jealous. I have no right to be jealous. I need to stop this.

'Are you two dating?' I casually ask once Andrea's gone.

'Not anymore. We went out a few times, but there wasn't anything there.'

'I think she disagrees.'

'Yeah, she wants to go out again. She saw my mom at the store last weekend and asked her if I was seeing anyone.'

'Are you?'

'No. Well, I was, but it didn't work out. We only went out a few times.'

'Sounds like you go on a lot of dates.'

'But they never turn into anything. I know right away if there's potential there and if there's not, I end it. I don't keep seeing someone just to avoid being alone.'

'I'm the same way. Or I am now. When I was younger I didn't like being single so I'd date a guy even if I wasn't that into him.'

'Are you seeing anyone now?'

'No,' I say with a laugh, imagining myself dating with a big pregnant belly.

'Why is that funny?'

I'm not ready to tell him the real reason so I say, 'Because I have no time to date. Between work and my classes, I barely have time to sleep.'

'You'll have time now that your classes are over. Do you think you'll start dating?'

'No.' I look down at the table, suddenly realizing I may be alone for a very long time. How many guys want to date a woman with a baby that's not theirs? And when would I have time to date? I'll have a job and a baby to care for.

'Because you're leaving?'

I look up at Jason. 'What?'

'The reason you don't want to date. Is it because you're leaving? Going back to Boston?'

It's because I'm pregnant. With your child. And because I still have feelings for you, which makes no sense since I only spent a night with you.

That's what I want to say, but instead I say, 'I'm just not interested in dating right now. I have to focus on finding a job for after the summer.'

'A job in Boston,' he says. 'So you're definitely moving back.'

'I have to. My father had a bad fall back in March and then hip surgery. He walks much slower now and has difficulty doing the things he used to. He's going to physical therapy and my mom is helping him, but if he gets worse, she'll need me there to help out.'

Jason nods. 'Yeah, I understand.'

He sounds disappointed. Did he think I'd changed my mind? Is that why he thinks I'm here? To tell him I'm staying? If so, I didn't mean to get his hopes up. I didn't think he wanted to see me anymore. I assumed he'd moved on by now. But maybe he thought my coming here meant I wanted us to have a second chance.

I need to tell him the truth and end any confusion about why I'm here.

'Jason, I need to tell you something.'

'Go ahead.'

Chapter 7

Mia

Just as I'm about to tell Jason my news, Andrea returns with our meals.

'The chicken,' she says, setting the plate down in front of me. 'And the steak.' She sets Jason's plate down and smiles at him. 'Can I get you anything else?'

Jason looks at me to answer.

'I think we're good,' I say to Andrea.

I wait until she leaves, then try again to tell Jason my news, but before I can, Jason starts talking.

'Do you work tomorrow?' he asks.

'No, but I need to finish a paper that's due next week. Why?'

'I was just thinking maybe you could stick around.'

'You mean stay in Haydon Falls?'

He shrugs. 'Just for the day. I could show you around. Maybe take you to the orchard.'

'I'd love that. But I don't know if—' I stop, deciding not to finish that thought. I was going to say he may not want to take me around town once he finds out my news.

What if I didn't tell him? What if I waited until tomorrow? Would it really be that bad to wait?

I want more time with Jason. I want to see what he's like when he's here, living his regular life. I want to see where he lives and what his family is like. If Jason decides to be in our child's life, I should know more about him. Spending a night with him in a hotel room isn't enough to tell me who this man is and what he's really like.

'I'll stay,' I tell him. 'I'd love to see more of the town.'

'But you hesitated. Why?'

'I was just rearranging my schedule in my head. I can get back Sunday and still have time to get everything done.'

'Great!' He cuts into his steak, but then stops. 'Oh, shit. I have a game tomorrow.'

'Could I go?'

'You want to go to a high school baseball game?'

'Sure! It sounds fun!' I'm not really into sports, but I'd like to see Jason coaching the game. I want to see how he is with the kids.

'We're probably going to lose, but if you really want to go, you can. I promise we'll do something fun when it's over. My parents might come. If they do, you could sit with them. Actually, that's a bad idea.'

'Why?'

'They might tell you things I don't want you knowing. Stupid shit from when I was a kid. Or they'll spend the whole time asking about us, trying to figure out if we're dating.'

'Do they know about me?'

'They know we met at Noah's wedding.'

'But they don't know we . . .'

'No, and I'd never tell them. But anytime I'm with a girl, even a friend, they assume I'm dating her or might in the future, and then my mom goes into matchmaker mode, trying to sell me to the girl in the hopes we'll get married.'

'She's pressuring you to get married?'

'She has for years, and now that my brothers all have girlfriends, it's even worse. She's determined to find me someone.'

'Is that what you want? Or do you like being single?'

'I don't mind being single. I'm not going to just pick someone to avoid being alone.'

'But you still want to get married someday, right?'

'Definitely. Like I told you the night of the wedding, I always thought I'd be first to get married out of all my brothers. I never had the desire to go out and party and meet girls. I ended up doing that, but only because I was single. Even my family thought I'd be married by now with a kid or two. But now Nick will be the first to get married and first to have a kid.'

'His fiancé is pregnant?'

'Not yet, but she will be. They're already trying.'

Nick won't be the first to have a child. Jason will. He just doesn't know it yet. I wonder what his family will think of that. Will his parents be upset that he's having a child without being married? My parents will. They'll be devastated. They'll be thrilled about being grandparents, but their excitement will be overshadowed by the disappointment of me not being married.

'Where are you staying tonight?' Jason asks.

'I don't know yet. I thought I'd stop at one of the hotels in town. Is there one you'd recommend?'

'There's a fancy historic one a few miles from here but it's kind of expensive and they're doing renovations so it could be loud. The other one has a tour group staying there so I'm not sure they have any rooms.' He pauses. 'You could stay with me.'

'That's probably not a good idea,' I say with a nervous laugh.

'Why? I'll take the couch. You can take the bed. It's a big apartment. Only one bedroom but there's plenty of room.'

'I don't want to make you sleep on the couch.' I glance at the table next to us where a couple is being seated with their baby. They look happy, the three of them together as a family.

'Mia.' Jason waits for me to look at him. 'Nothing's going to happen.'

'We said that the night of the wedding,' I say, lowering my voice.

'We never said that. In fact, I think we both knew exactly what was going to happen that night. This is different. We haven't been drinking and we've already decided there isn't a future for us.' He sounds sad when he says it. I feel sad hearing it.

I want us to have a future. We just can't. I need to take care of my parents and Jason's life is here.

'C'mon, it's just one night,' he says. 'You can even lock the door to my room if you're that worried about it.'

I smile. 'I'm not worried. I know you're a gentleman.'

'Not always,' he says with a smile, 'but I try.'

'Okay, then yes, I'll stay with you.'

The baby at the table next to ours giggles as her dad picks her up and holds her.

'She's adorable,' I say, staring at the baby.

'She is,' I hear Jason say. I look back and see him gazing at the baby, smiling at her. 'She reminds me of Nash's baby.'

'Who's Nash?'

'My cousin,' Jason says, looking back at me. 'He lives in Chicago. He's Austin's brother. Remember the guy playing in the band that night? The one with all the muscles?'

'Yes, I remember him. His brother has a baby?'

'She was born last February. Nash and his wife, Callie, come up here all the time. My mom insists on it. She can't go more than a few weeks without seeing the baby. Nash and Callie lived up here last fall while Nash fixed up a house on my parents' property.'

'Who lives in the house?'

'Nobody. My dad offered it to me and my brothers, but none of us want to live that close to our parents. My dad might end up renting it out. I can show it to you if we go over there tomorrow. Nash did a really nice job on it. It's got that modern farmhouse look people are into right now.'

'I'd love to see it.'

'I should also take you to Kate's shop. She's Brody's girlfriend. She's opening a home store just down the street from here. It's almost done. I think you'd like it. You could be one of her first customers.'

'It's nice she's opening a place in her hometown. Supporting the local economy.'

'She's not from Haydon Falls. She's from Chicago. She moved here to be with Brody and open her shop. Same with Gina, Sawyer's girlfriend. She's from Green Bay. She moved here to open her brewery. Nick's the only one who ended up with a local. He went to high school with Lyndsay.'

We finish our meals and Jason pays the check.

'Ready to go?' he asks, pushing his chair back.

'Yes. I'll just need your address to put in the nav system.'

'You can just follow me.'

We go outside and he walks me to my car, then I wait as he walks to his truck. I didn't know what he drove. I imagined him driving a small car, not a huge pickup. He looks really sexy in it, all rugged and manly.

I need to stop this. I can't be getting turned on by Jason. We're not dating. We're not even friends. I haven't talked to him in months. But it feels like we're continuing where we left off. After some initial awkwardness, we both relaxed and talked like we did that night, like we'd known each other forever. But we can't repeat the part of that night that resulted in my current situation, which is why my hormones need to get in line and stop making me want Jason.

'Welcome home,' he says as we go into this apartment. 'Or home for the night.' He laughs as he picks a shirt off the floor. 'I don't normally throw clothes on the floor. I was just in a hurry to change after the gym so I wouldn't be late for dinner.'

As soon as he mentioned the gym, my thoughts went back to that night, in his room, when he took his shirt off and I saw his chest. I couldn't believe how ripped he was. I still remember how his body felt, the weight of him when he was on top of me, how it felt when his—

'Mia?'

I wake from the memory and see Jason by the couch. I'm still standing at the door.

'You can come in,' he says, laughing a little.

'Yeah, sorry. I'm kind of out of it. I'm just tired from the drive.'

'You want to go to bed? I know it's early, but if you're tired you should sleep.'

'I'm fine.' I walk up to him. 'Want to give me a tour?'

'Sure.' He motions to the room. 'The expansive living area is perfect for lounging around watching sports, making a late-night snack, and hosting friends.' He walks over to the wall by the couch. 'Take note of the artful decor.' He points to a painting on the wall, then the wooden bowl on the coffee table that holds his remotes. 'The comfortable furnishings.' He points to the gray leather couch. 'And of course, the entertainment options.' He points to the huge TV on the wall.

I laugh at his performance. 'Very impressive.'

'The tour isn't over.' He comes over to me and takes my hand, leading me down a short hallway to the one and only bedroom. It has a dresser, two nightstands, and a king-sized bed covered in a dark blue comforter. 'I think you'll find the bed very comfortable and spacious.' He points to a walk-in closet. 'Feel free to use the closet if you need to hang anything up. Any questions?'

'I think I've got it,' I say, laughing at his formal tone. It's not at all him, which is why it's so funny.

Still holding my hand, Jason leads me out of the room. It feels natural to hold his hand, like it's what we always do. It's another one of those things that feels familiar about him, even though it shouldn't.

'And this is the bathroom.' He stands at the door to it, turning the light on so I can see. It's a large bathroom with two sinks, a shower-tub combo, and built-in shelves for towels.

'It's really clean,' I tell him. 'Your whole apartment is.'

'I might've cleaned last night,' he confesses. 'In case you came over. But it's usually not a mess. I don't like tripping over stuff so I keep it picked up. Anyway, that's the tour.'

'It's nice, and bigger than my place. I have a one-bedroom but it's really tiny.'

We walk back down the hall to the kitchen. He lets go of my hand and I find myself missing it. It has to be hormones making me this way. I'm feeling clingy, emotional, and extremely aroused, not a good combo when you're staying with a guy who's off limits.

'You want a drink?' he asks, opening the fridge.

'What do you have?'

'Pop. Sport drinks. Beer.'

'I'm fine for now.'

He shuts the fridge. 'We could run to the store. Get something you like.'

'Really, I don't need anything.' I walk over to the window. The apartment's on the third floor and looks out at a small neighborhood lined with trees. 'You have some nice houses here,' I say, noticing a craftsman-style house with a large porch.

'Yeah, I need to start looking again.'

I turn back to him. 'You're buying a house?'

'I would've already had one by now, but I used all of my savings to help out Brody last year. He paid me back so now I need to start looking again.'

'You don't want to wait? Until you get married, or engaged?'

'I don't see that happening anytime soon, maybe not ever if I'm limited to girls in town. I've dated almost every girl my age and the ones I haven't dated I'm not interested in. I'm not going to put my life on hold waiting for the right girl to come along.'

'Maybe she's close and you just haven't found her yet.'

'Yeah, maybe,' he says, his voice trailing off.

I turn back to the window. 'It's really beautiful here.'

'It's even better at the orchard. It's up on a hill. You can see for miles.'

I feel him beside me, his arm brushing against mine.

'Are we going there in the morning?' I ask, trying to ignore how close he is to me.

'We can. My mom makes these really great pastries every morning. If we go there, you've gotta try one.'

'She sounds like a great mom.' I turn to Jason, my heart beating faster.

'She is.' He faces me, gently moving my hair behind my shoulder. 'I like having you here, Mia.' His hand lowers to my arm as his eyes go to mine. 'I know I shouldn't say this, but I haven't stopped thinking about you since that night.'

'Why do you think you shouldn't say that?'

'Because we were supposed to move on. Not think about each other. Find someone else.'

'Sometimes our minds do things we don't want.'

'It's not just my mind. It's my heart. You really got to me Mia, like no one else has. I know we can't be together, but seeing you again, having you here, I just wanted to tell you how much that night meant to me, and how I haven't stopped thinking about you.'

I look down. 'Jason, I—'

'You don't have to say anything. I know you're leaving. I just didn't want you to go without me telling you how I felt. I didn't want you thinking that night was just sex.'

'I know it wasn't,' I whisper, my eyes tearing up. Damn pregnancy hormones. Then again, I'd probably tear up even if I wasn't pregnant. Hearing Jason say he hasn't stopped thinking about me confirms I wasn't the only one who felt something that night. I was telling myself I made it out to be more than it was, hoping it'd make me get over Jason. But we both felt a connection that night, something that doesn't come along every day.

I wish I could convince him to move to Boston with me. Maybe when he finds out about the baby he'd be open to at least talking about it. But he's so happy here—happy with his job, his family. I don't want to take that away from him.

'Mia, are you okay?' Jason asks, noticing the tears in my eyes.

'Yeah.' I laugh and wipe my eyes. 'It's allergies. I get them in the spring.'

'But we're inside.'

'I know. It's probably just something in the air.'

'You sure that's all it is?' he asks with concern.

I nod, smiling. 'Yes. It happens all the time.'

'You want to get out of here? There's not really anything to do other than watch TV.'

'Where do you want to go?'

'We could go to Sawyer's place. You like beer, right?'

'I do, but—'

'You're not drinking. I forgot. But we could go there anyway. You could meet Sawyer, see his brewery.'

I agree to go because being here alone with Jason is way too risky. My hormones are on overdrive and if we don't get out of here I'm afraid something will happen.

What was I thinking? I shouldn't be staying with Jason. But it's just one night. We can get through one night without anything happening.

Chapter 8

Jason

'Hey!' Sawyer yells from the bar, smiling at me.

'That's Sawyer, my brother,' I say to Mia. 'We can sit over here.' I lead her to a high-top table by the bar. It's the only open table. The placed is packed, like it always is on Friday night, so I texted Sawyer on our way here, asking him to save us a table if one opened up.

'You must be Mia,' Sawyer says, coming up to her.

'Yes. It's nice to meet you.'

'Welcome to Haydon Falls.'

'Thanks. I like what I've seen of it so far.'

'She's sticking around tomorrow,' I say. 'I'm going to take her to the orchard and the falls.'

'What about your game?' Sawyer asks me.

'She wants to go.' I smile at her. 'I don't know why. I already know we're going to lose.'

'I think it'll be fun!' Mia says, smiling back at me.

God, I love her smile. I love her eyes, her voice, her laugh. Seeing her again, I realize why I couldn't get her out of my head. There's something about her, something that makes me feel like we're meant for each other.

I don't usually believe in stuff like that, and I still wouldn't if I hadn't met Mia.

'What are you drinking?' Sawyer asks Mia.

'Oh, I'm not having anything.'

'You sure? It's on me.'

'She's taking a break from drinking,' I tell Sawyer. 'We just came so she could check the place out.'

'I hear you're getting engaged soon,' Mia says to Sawyer.

'I am?' He looks at me. 'Since when am I getting engaged?'

'You know you will. You and Gina are already looking at rings.'

'Doesn't mean we're getting engaged next week.'

'I didn't say next week. I'm guessing you'll wait until after Nick's wedding and then pop the question in June or July.'

'Maybe Brody will go first. He and Kate already have a house. They're the ones who should get married.'

'You guys have a lot of weddings coming up,' Mia says.

'You should come to Nick's.' Sawyer looks at me. 'You don't have a date yet, do you?'

Why can't my idiot brother keep his mouth shut? I can't take Mia to the wedding. We're not dating. We weren't even planning to see each other again after tomorrow.

'Mia can't make it,' I say to Sawyer. 'She's got graduation coming up.'

'That's actually the weekend after the wedding,' she says. 'My parents are flying in early to check out the area. They're actually coming here for a few days.'

'To Haydon Falls?' I ask.

'Yeah. One of their friends told them about it. They're planning to spend some days here before going to Madison.'

'You should come back for the wedding,' Sawyer says, 'then stay and hang out with your parents.'

'Sawyer, I think they need you at the bar,' I say, trying to get rid of him.

He looks back at it, then back at me. 'What are you drinking?'

'Surprise me.'

He finally leaves.

'Ignore him,' I say to Mia. 'He's always saying shit he shouldn't.'

'Sounds like he really wants you to have a date for the wedding.'

'He needs to stay out of it. I don't need a date. I went to Noah's wedding without a date.'

'And ended up meeting someone. Maybe you'll meet someone at your brother's wedding.'

'I already know everyone who will be there and none of them are single women my age.'

Sawyer returns with my beer. 'Try it. It's new.'

I take a sip of the light amber-colored beer. 'It's good. What is it?'

'A sour ale. They're getting really popular so Gina and I are each making one.' He looks at Mia. 'You sure you don't want to try it?'

'Here, have a taste,' I say, offering Mia the glass.

'I'd rather not.' She smiles at Sawyer. 'I'm sure it's good. I just don't like to drink during the school year. My brain works better without alcohol.'

'When are you done with school?' he asks.

'My classes are already done, but I have to turn in assignments next week. Then I have a week off before graduation.'

'Another reason for you to come to the wedding,' Sawyer says. 'You'll be done with school and can drink all the free beer you want.' He smiles. 'I'm supplying the beer. Nick's getting wine and my girlfriend Gina's bringing her hard cider.'

'It won the hard cider competition last fall,' I tell Mia. 'Sawyer entered too, but he didn't win.'

'You just love bringing that up, don't you?' Sawyer says to me.

I laugh. 'Just trying to keep your ego in check.'

'Gina does plenty of that. I don't need you doing it too.' He glances back at the bar. 'I need to go help out. We're getting slammed.' He looks back at Mia. 'Good meeting you. Hope to see you at the wedding.' He takes off.

'He doesn't give up, does he?' Mia says with a laugh.

'My whole family's that way. Always trying to set me up.' I take a drink of my beer. As I'm setting it down, I see my parents coming into the brewery, with Nick right behind them. 'Great,' I mutter.

'What's wrong?' Mia asks, following my gaze to the door. My mom sees me and waves. 'Do you know her?'

'Yeah,' I say with a sigh. 'That's my mom, with my dad and my brother Nick.'

'Is that a problem?'

'Kind of. I just wanted to come here and have a beer, not hang out with my family. How did they know I'd be here? Did Sawyer tell them?'

'Do you want to leave?'

'No. I mean, we can if this is going to make you uncomfortable.'

'Not at all. I'd love to meet them!'

'Can we join you?' Mom asks, stopping at our table. She's smiling as her eyes bounce between Mia and me.

'Go ahead,' I tell her.

Nick and my parents remain standing at the end of the table, all three of them looking at Mia.

'And who do we have here?' Dad says, smiling at her.

'I'm Mia,' she says, smiling back. 'I'm a friend of Jason's.'

'We met at Noah's wedding,' I say.

Nick extends his hand to her. 'Nice to meet you. I'm Nick, Jason's brother.'

'The one getting married.'

'Yeah, it's coming up fast. Lyndsay, my fiancé, is having her bachelorette party tonight so I tagged along with the parents and ruined their date night.'

Mom shakes her head. 'You didn't ruin anything. We love having you join us. And now we get to see Jason too.'

'Did you already have your bachelor party?' Mia asks Nick.

'Yeah, a few weeks ago. We went down to Chicago where our cousins live. We all went out. Had a great time.'

'Hopefully not too great,' Dad says, looking at Nick.

Nick glances at me. 'We were all on our best behavior, weren't we, Jason?'

'Of course. You know how we are, Dad. We never get into trouble.'

He shakes his head. 'I don't even want to know.'

Mia quietly laughs.

'You guys going to sit down?' I say, thinking Mia probably feels awkward having them all stand there, staring at her.

Mom takes the seat beside me. Dad sits across from her, next to Mia.

'Sawyer looks swamped,' Nick says, watching Sawyer race around behind the bar. 'I'll go grab our drinks. Mom, Dad, the usual?'

'That'll do,' Dad says, glancing at Mom who gives Nick a nod.

'What about you, Mia?' Nick asks.

'I'm not having anything, but thank you for asking.'

Nick leaves and I take a swig of my beer, preparing myself for whatever my parents are going to say. They knew Mia was coming to town and I made it clear she's just a friend. But that won't stop them from trying to set us up.

'So Jason said you're in graduate school?' Mom says to Mia.

'Yes.' She smiles at me. 'What else did you tell them about me?'

'I mentioned you were a teacher,' I say, 'and that you're going into school counseling.'

'Actually I haven't decided that yet.'

'I thought that's why you were getting the degree. To counsel teens.'

'I can do that without working at a school. I'm considering working at a community center for teens.'

'Are you already applying for jobs?' Dad asks.

She nods. 'I'm starting to, but I have all summer to look so I'm not in a rush.'

'She's staying in Madison this summer,' I tell my parents. 'Helping a professor with some research.'

'Madison isn't that far from here,' Mom says, giving me a smile.

She's so obvious. I'm sure Mia has already picked up on my mom's attempt at matchmaking. I hope it's not making her uncomfortable. I don't think it is. As my parents continue to fire questions at her, Mia's smiling and answering in a calm and relaxed manner.

I'm watching her, completely fascinated by her. She goes from being studious and sophisticated as she talks about her classes, to laughing and making jokes. I love that about her. I love that just when I think I've figured her out, she surprises me. Like that night of the wedding. I thought she was all prim and proper, then we got to my room and I saw a whole different side of her. A wild, sexy, seductive side.

Shit, now I'm thinking about that, about what we did, which is the absolute last thing I should be thinking about when we're sitting here with my parents.

Nick returns with the beers and takes a seat at the end of the table. 'So where are you staying tonight?' he asks Mia.

'With me,' I blurt out, saving Mia from having to explain. 'I offered her my room to save her some money.'

'She could've stayed in the Carson house,' Dad says before taking a drink of his beer.

'What's the Carson house?' Mia asks.

'Last year Mom and Dad bought the land next to theirs to expand the orchard,' Nick says. 'It came with an old farmhouse.'

'Oh, yes, Jason told me about that.'

'Our cousin Nash works construction and renovated the place,' Nick says. 'Dad's thinking of renting it out.'

'I'd rather have one of you boys take it,' Dad says. 'But if you don't want it, we'll figure something out.'

'I'd love to see it tomorrow if we have time,' Mia says to me.

'You're coming over?' Mom asks, sounding hopeful, like taking Mia there means we're dating.

'She wants to see the orchard,' I say. 'I was going to text you to let you know.'

'What time will you be over?' Mom asks.

'Jason's taking me there after the game,' Mia answers.

'Or we could go before,' I say, knowing the game will give us an excuse to get out of there.

'Yes, come over in the morning,' Mom says. 'I'll make breakfast! Nick and Lyndsay can join us. And maybe Brody and Kate could be there too.'

'Mom, Mia's met enough of the family. I'll just take her out for breakfast. I'll take her to Maury's.'

'Maury's doesn't have my homemade apple pastries,' Mom says, smiling at Mia.

She smiles back. 'Those sound delicious.'

'Well, then, it's settled. You'll join us for breakfast.'

'Wait—what?' I look between Mom and Mia. 'What just happened?'

'You're having breakfast with us.' Nick chuckles. 'Try to keep up.'

He thinks this is hilarious—Mom inviting Mia over, hoping to fix us up. The jerk should be helping me, not laughing at me. He's been there. So has Sawyer and Brody. Mom's tried to play matchmaker for all of us, but now I'm the only single one left and she's putting all her effort on finding me a wife.

I need to tell her Mia's not sticking around and that the only way I could date her is if I followed her to Boston. That'd instantly stop Mom's attempts to set us up. The last thing she'd want is for me to move away. She finally got Nick back to Haydon Falls after all the years he lived in New York. She doesn't want to see another one of her sons leaving town.

'He said they'll be there at eight,' Mom says, setting her phone down.

'Who?' I ask.

'Brody,' Mom says, as if I should know she just texted him. She turns her focus back to Mia. 'He's our youngest. His girlfriend Kate is opening a store downtown. You should have Jason take you there. She has some beautiful items for sale. She has such good taste!'

'Mom, isn't eight a little early for breakfast?' I ask. 'Mia probably wants to sleep in. She had a long day today.'

'I'm an early riser,' Mia says. 'Eight works for me.'

Sawyer comes up to the table. 'I didn't know the whole family was coming by tonight.'

'I didn't either,' I mutter.

'Can you and Gina come by for breakfast tomorrow?' Mom asks Sawyer.

'Sure,' he says. 'Any reason why, or is it just breakfast?'

'Jason's bringing Mia to the orchard,' Dad says. 'We can't let her come by without feeding her.'

'Get used to it,' Sawyer says to Mia. 'Every time you show up to Mom's house, she'll feed you.'

What's going on here? They're all acting like Mia and I are a couple when we clearly are not. I've told my brothers more than once that I'm not going to date someone who doesn't live in the area. They know Mia is moving away, so why is Sawyer talking like she's going to be spending time here and going to my parents' house? And why is Mom insisting on having Mia over for family breakfast? Are they really that desperate for me to have a girlfriend that they'll push me to date a girl who's leaving in a few months?

'It's getting late,' I say to Mia. 'You want to head out?'

'Um, okay.' She seems surprised that I want to leave, but she doesn't know my family. If we stay any longer, they'll have us engaged by the end of the night.

I go around the table and help her down from the barstool.

'It was really nice meeting all of you,' she says to my family.

Dad smiles at her. 'We'll see you bright and early in the morning. Be sure to bring your appetite. Martha really puts out a spread when we have company.'

'I'm looking forward to it.'

'See you guys tomorrow,' I say, taking Mia's arm and directing her away from the table.

We make our way outside and head to the truck.

'Sorry about that,' I say.

'About what?'

'My family. I love them, but they can be a little much.'

'I didn't think so. They seem like very nice people.'

'They are, but they're also meddling.'

She laughs. 'They just want you to be happy.'

'I *am* happy. I have a great job. Great apartment. Great friends.' I stop at the truck and open her door. 'The only thing missing is a wife and kids, but if it doesn't happen, I'm okay with that, and my family should be too.'

'You'd really be okay not having a family of your own?'

'It's not what I want, but I've accepted it may not happen. If I can't find the right girl, I may just end up single.'

'But the night of the wedding, you talked about how much you wanted kids.'

'Yeah, well, I kind of need a girl for that.'

'Jason, I—' She stops and grabs hold of the truck door.

'Are you okay?'

'Yes.' She takes a breath. 'I just got dizzy for a moment. I think I need to sit down.'

'Let me help.' I take her arm and help her into the truck.

As we're driving back to my apartment, she takes several deep breaths.

'Are you sure you're okay?' I ask.

She nods. 'I'm just tired. I'll be fine.'

We get to my building and I help her out of the truck, then take her hand as we walk to the door. Maybe I shouldn't hold her hand, but I don't want her getting dizzy again and falling down. And I like holding her hand. It's small and soft and fits perfectly in mine.

As we take the elevator up to my floor, I don't let go of her hand. She doesn't attempt to pull away so I keep hold of it as we walk down the hall to my apartment. I finally let her go as we go inside.

'Do you want something to drink?' I ask.

'No, I think I'll just go to bed.'

It's not even ten. I was hoping we could stay up and talk. We talked all through dinner but it wasn't enough. There's still so much I want to know about her, but it's probably better if I don't. It would just make me like her more.

'Do you need extra blankets?' I ask as I stand at the door to my room, watching Mia unzip her overnight bag.

'I think I'll be fine.'

'Let me know if you need anything. I'll keep the TV off so I don't wake you up.'

'Jason, I don't want you changing your routine because of me. Go ahead and watch TV.'

'I think I'll just go to bed, now that we have this early morning breakfast,' I say with a sigh.

She laughs. 'I'm looking forward to it. Your mom sounds like a great cook.' Mia walks up to me at the door. 'Thanks again for letting me stay.'

'I'm happy to.'

She pauses, her eyes on mine, then hugs me.

I'm so surprised by the hug that it takes me a moment to realize I should be hugging her back. I put my arms around her and instantly get that familiar feeling again, like she's been with me forever. Why does that keep happening? Why does being with her feel so right when I know in my head that it's wrong? I'm not getting involved with a girl who's moving away.

'It's really good seeing you again,' Mia says, resting her head on my shoulder. She almost sounds sad, but maybe that's just how she sounds when she's tired. 'Goodnight, Jason.'

'Goodnight.' I kiss her forehead before letting her go. I wasn't even thinking. I just did it, but I shouldn't have. She's just a friend, staying here for the night.

I close the door and grab a blanket from the hall closet. I take it to the living room and toss it on the couch.

'Shit,' I mutter, realizing I forgot to grab something to sleep in.

I don't want to go back to my room. Mia might already be in bed. I take off my jeans and shirt. I'll sleep in my boxers and put on my clothes before Mia wakes up. I lay down on the couch and set my phone alarm for six. That'll give me plenty of time to get up and get dressed before Mia wakes up.

I can't believe she's here. I never thought I'd see her again and now she's in my apartment, sleeping in my bed. I still don't know why she's here. Is she just saying goodbye, or is there more to it than that?

Chapter 9

Mia

No. Not now. This can't be happening!

I sit on the side of the bed, taking deep breaths, hoping it'll make the nausea go away. It's been a week since I got sick. I thought my morning sickness was over. But it's clearly back, at the worst possible moment.

Racing to the door, I swing it open and run across the hall to the bathroom, making it there just in time.

'Mia?' I hear Jason's voice behind me and realize I forgot to shut the door.

This is so embarrassing. I'm kneeled in front of the toilet, feeling gross, and probably looking even worse than I feel.

'It must've been something I ate,' I say to Jason as I close the lid and flush the toilet. 'You can go back to bed.'

He leans down to me. 'Can I get you something? Water? Medicine? A cold washcloth?'

He's such a nice guy. Any other guy would see me this way and get the hell out of here. I wish he'd stop doing things that make me like him even more than I already do. On my way here yesterday, part of me was hoping I'd feel nothing for Jason when I saw him again, but instead I'm finding myself falling for him even more. Like now, when he's acting so concerned for a girl who woke him up in the middle of the night, puking in his bathroom.

'Jason, I'm fine.' I rest back against the wall. 'Go back to bed.'

'You don't look fine,' he says, his eyes bouncing around my face. 'You look like you're going to get sick again.'

'I'm not. I just need a minute to breathe.'

'I'll wait with you.' He sits down on the floor, leaning against the bathroom vanity. He's not wearing a shirt, just his jeans, and damn he looks hot. I forgot how great his body is. Okay, that's a lie. I've thought about his body many times since that night. How it looked in that suit he was wearing. How it felt when I ran my hands down his chest, then lower.

'Mia?' Jason leans toward me and I quickly look up at his face.

'You can go. I just need another minute.'

'You sure you don't want some water? Or maybe some crackers? Maybe you have the flu.'

I shake my head. 'It's not the flu. I feel fine except for my stomach. I'm sure it was something I ate. What time is it?'

'Just after midnight. You want help getting up?'

'No,' I say, feeling the nausea return. 'You need to go. Now!'

'I'm not—' He's interrupted by me shoving him out of the way as my other hand yanks up the toilet lid. I get sick again, with Jason right beside me. I feel him gently pulling my hair back, holding it out of the way.

'Mia, I'm so sorry. I haven't heard of anyone getting sick from that restaurant. If I had, I never wouldn't taken you there.'

I flush the toilet and sit back against the wall. 'It's not your fault. And I liked the restaurant. The dinner was great.'

'It wasn't great. It made you sick. I'm going to tell the manager about this. A nice place like that shouldn't be getting people sick.'

'No, don't tell the manager. I'm sure it wasn't dinner. It was probably the lunch I had yesterday. I had a salad and I think the lettuce was bad.'

'What can I do?' he asks, kneeling beside me. 'Anything?'

'Can you help me up? I think I'm done now.'

'Sure.' He puts his arm behind me and gently pulls me up from the floor.

'You can go,' I tell him. 'I just need to brush my teeth.'

He leaves and I splash cold water on my face, then brush my teeth. When I leave the bathroom, Jason's waiting for me in the hall.

'I thought you might need some help getting back.'

'Thanks.' I take his arm and we go into his room and he helps me into bed.

'You think you can sleep?' he asks.

'Probably. If I don't get sick again.'

'You want some company?' he asks, then quickly says, 'I mean, as a friend. I could just wait here to make sure you're okay.'

I smile at him. 'I'd like that.' I sit up and scoot over on the bed to give him room.

He sits next to me, on top of the covers. 'I'm really sorry. I know you said it wasn't my fault, but I feel like I'm the reason you got sick.'

He IS the reason, but it's not because of the restaurant. It's because of what happened the night of the wedding. Maybe I should tell him. It's quiet. We're alone.

I almost do it, but then decide it's not the right time. I'll tell him later, before I leave.

'You sure I can't get you anything?' he asks.

'I'm good.' I laugh a little. 'I can't believe you saw that. I'm so embarrassed.'

'Don't be. I'm a teacher. I'm used to being around puke.'

I turn to him. 'Kids are puking in high school? I thought that was more of a little kid thing. I never had kids in my class puke.'

'I coach younger kids in the summer. They puke all the time, and sometimes the older kids overheat during baseball practice and puke. And I usually have one or two students a year who come into class hungover from the night before and puke either in class or in the hall. So yeah, I'm used to being around it.'

'I'm still embarrassed you saw that.' I smile at him. 'But thanks for holding my hair. That was a very gentlemanly thing to do.'

'It was, wasn't it?' he says, sounding proud of himself.

I rest my head on his shoulder. 'You're a great guy, Jason.'

'I don't know about that,' he jokes. 'You don't know me that well.'

'No, but what I know about you so far tells me you're a good guy.' I pause. 'I've really liked seeing you here, in your hometown, with your family.'

'Why?'

'Because it shows me who you are, what you're like when you're not trying to impress some girl at a wedding.'

'Who said I was trying to impress you?'

I look up at him. 'You weren't?'

'Okay, I admit it, I was, but only at first. After an hour of talking to you, it felt so natural I ended up just being myself.'

I lay my head back on his shoulder. 'It did feel natural. Like we'd known each other forever.'

'It's weird, isn't it? I've never had that happen before.'

'Me either. That's one of the reasons I had to see you again. To see if I'd still feel that way.'

'And do you?'

'Yeah, I do. How about you?'

'I feel like that even more.' He slips his hand around mine. 'I wish I could explain it.'

'Explain what?'

'Why we feel this way. Why being with you feels so familiar after only spending a night with you. Well, two nights now.'

'I think sometimes people just feel that type of connection. I don't know why. Maybe for us it's because we have a lot in common.'

'I've had stuff in common with women before and never felt this way.'

'Then I don't have an explanation. And maybe that's okay. Maybe we don't need one.'

We sit in silence a moment, my head on Jason's shoulder, his hand wrapped around mine. The nausea has passed and I feel relaxed, like I'm close to falling asleep.

'You ever fake getting sick?' Jason asks. 'Back when you were a kid?'

'No. Never. I didn't want to worry my parents.'

'I don't mean something serious. I meant like pretend to have a sore throat or put hot water on your face to fake a fever.'

'No, I never did any of that. My parents didn't think they could have kids so when they had me, they worried about every little thing. If I got sick, they acted like they thought they might lose me. So even when I really was sick, I tried to hide it from them so they wouldn't worry.'

'That's a lot of pressure for a little kid. Having to protect your parents like that?'

'It was, but I didn't know it back then. I just knew I didn't like seeing them worry.'

'Are you still trying to protect them?'

'Now it's more about not wanting to disappoint them.'

'I can't imagine you disappointing them. You're independent, supporting yourself, going to grad school.'

'They're helping me pay for grad school so I'm not really independent yet.'

'Yeah, but still, I can't see you disappointing them.'

They'll be disappointed when they find out I'm pregnant and no longer with the father. I don't even want to think about how upset they'll be, and worried. They already worry about me being single and making it on my own, but add a baby to the mix? They'll worry even more, thinking I won't be able to support both the baby and me.

'I faked being sick all the time,' Jason says.

'You did?' I look up and see him smiling. 'Why?'

'Because I didn't want to go to school. I thought it was a waste of time. I wanted to play professional baseball. I didn't need school for that.'

'If you didn't like school, how'd you end up going into teaching?'

'Mr. Anton, my seventh grade science teacher. He made the class fun, to the point I actually looked forward to going. He'd let us do experiments where we'd blow shit up or have stuff ooze all over the floor. I thought it was the coolest thing ever, and by the end of the year, I'd become a science geek. Well, maybe not a geek, but I was really into science.'

'So one teacher changed your entire life,' I say, smiling at him.

'Pretty much. I still wanted to play baseball, but I was starting to realize that playing professionally wasn't as easy as I thought. I decided to focus on playing at college.'

'Did you do it? Did you play college baseball?'

'I was supposed to, but I got injured the summer before I got there. I couldn't play and was dropped from the team. But now I get to coach and hopefully make some other kid's baseball dreams come true.'

'So after seventh grade, you stopped faking being sick?'

'Hell no. I still did it. All the damn time.' He laughs. 'If it was a nice day, I'd tell my mom I didn't feel well and had to stay home. I'd tell her it was my stomach or that I had a headache, something I didn't have to prove. And then I'd sneak out of the house and ride my bike to the batting cages.'

'And your mom didn't know?'

'I'd plan it around when she'd be gone or when she'd be out helping my dad in the orchard. I got caught a couple times, but most of the time I got away with it.'

'I couldn't do something like that. I'd be too worried my parents would find out. I wish I could be more like you and not worry so much about disappointing my parents.'

'I worry about disappointing them. I just don't let it take over my life. Or sometimes I just don't tell them stuff. If I know something might upset them, I keep it to myself.'

'Like what?'

He pauses a moment. 'If I tell you this, you can't tell my parents. Not that you would. I'm just saying, I don't want them knowing.'

'What is it?'

'I helped Brody buy a house last year. It was an old run-down house. Brody was going to fix it up and sell it and we'd split the profits. He was really excited about doing it, but he already had debt from his lawn care and snow removal business so the bank wouldn't give him a loan for the house unless I bought it with him. I put all my savings into the down payment, then had to keep making the mortgage payments because Brody didn't have money coming in. I ended up getting myself in debt trying to pay his bills and mine. We finally sold the house, but I'm still trying to pay off all the credit card debt I racked up.'

'I don't understand. You were helping your brother. Why would that disappoint your parents?'

'They'd be disappointed I let Brody get in over his head. If I hadn't helped him, he never would've bought that house and neither one of us would've ended up in debt. I'm the older brother. I'm supposed to be looking out for him, and instead I helped him to do the wrong thing.'

'I don't think it was wrong. You were supporting him in something he really wanted to do. I think your parents would be proud of you for that.'

'I still don't want them to know. They don't need to. It's over now. We got rid of the house and Brody has another one, which he bought with Kate. She used to be a financial planner so I'm not worried about Brody going broke anymore. Kate will make sure their bills get paid.'

'But what about you? Are you really in that much debt?'

'It's not as bad as I made it sound. I just need to pay off my credit cards and build my savings up again.

I really wanted to have a house by now, but I guess I don't really need one if it's just me.'

It's not just him. Soon he'll have a baby. And if we share custody, where will the baby sleep? This apartment doesn't have enough room for a crib or any of the other stuff that comes with caring for a baby.

Now I'm feeling sick again, but this time it's because I'm worried. How is this going to work? How are we going to share custody living thousands of miles apart?

'You feeling any better?' Jason asks.

'I was, but now I'm not feeling so great.'

'Lay down.' He waits until I do, then lays beside me, remaining on top of the covers.

I turn on my side and feel his arm go around me. He scoots closer and I feel the warmth of his chest on my back as he holds me. My worries fade away as I relax into Jason's arms. Soon my eyelids flutter shut and I drift off to sleep.

Chapter 10

Jason

'You don't have to get up yet,' I say to Mia as my alarm goes off. 'I set it early so I'd be up before you.'

I grab my phone from the nightstand and shut off the alarm.

Mia turns to me, shielding her eyes from the sun peeking through the blinds. They're cheap blinds and one of the slats is broken. I need to buy new ones, but I don't want to spend the money when I still have debt to pay off.

Why did I tell Mia that last night? She doesn't need to know about my financial problems. Now she probably thinks I'm irresponsible. By 28, I should know how to manage my finances, and I do, but helping Brody out really set me back. I'm in a lot better place now than I was a couple months ago, but I'm not even close to where I'd like to be. Like I told Mia, I wanted a house by now but instead I'm in this one-bedroom apartment. I don't regret helping Brody. I just wish I'd kept better tabs on him. I was trying to stay out of it and not interfere, but he needed my help and I wasn't there for him until it was too late.

'What time is it?' Mia asks.

'Just after six. You can go back to sleep. We don't have to leave until quarter to eight.'

'I'm ready to get up, unless you want to use the shower first.'

'You can use it.'

I turn to face her. 'You feeling better?'

'I am,' she says with a soft smile. She has such a beautiful smile, and beautiful brown eyes. And I love the way her voice sounds in the morning, low and raspy. I'd love to wake up like this every morning, with Mia in my bed. But I know it's not possible so I need to stop letting my mind go there.

'You want some coffee?' I ask.

'No.'

'Really? I thought you told me you can't get through the morning without coffee.'

'That used to be true, but not anymore. I cut out caffeine a few weeks ago. It was rough at first, but it's getting better.'

'No alcohol? No caffeine? Are you doing some kind of detox diet?' I laugh as I say it because she doesn't seem like someone who'd be into those things.

'I'm just trying to be healthier.' She glances down, then back up at me. 'Thanks for your help last night.'

'Of course.' I move some strands of hair off her face and tuck them behind her ear. 'Even though we can't be together, I still care about you, Mia.'

She doesn't say anything. I made her uncomfortable. Shit, that's not what I was going for. I just wanted her to know how I feel.

'I think I have some juice,' I say. 'You want some?'

'Sure.' She sits up, then squeezes her eyes shut and puts her hand on her stomach.

'You okay?'

'Yeah.' Her eyes pop open and she forces out a smile. 'I just got dizzy for a moment.'

'Maybe you're still sick. I can call my mom and tell her we can't be there.'

'No, I want to go. I just need some water, and maybe the juice would help.'

'I'll go get it.' I hurry up from the bed. 'Be right back.'

I bring her both water and juice. She takes a few sips, then slowly gets up. She says she's not sick, but she doesn't look like she feels well. I hope she's not just telling me she's okay when she's not.

By seven, we're both ready to leave so I text my mom to let her know we'll be there early.

'Jason!' a girl yells as Mia and I are walking to my truck.

I turn around and see Danielle running up to me. She moved into the building about a month ago and keeps flirting with me. She invited me to dinner last week, but I told her I was busy. I don't want to go out with her. She went out with a friend of mine and he told me she went nuts whenever he wanted a night to himself. She expected him to spend every second with her and when he didn't, she'd get angry and break his stuff, including smashing his phone. So yeah, we won't be going out.

'Hey, Danielle,' I say. 'I was just heading out.'

She glances at Mia, then looks back at me, giving me the smile she uses when she's attempting to flirt. 'I just wanted to let you know that I can go to your brother's wedding with you. I heard your mom telling someone at the grocery store that you still needed a date.'

'I don't need a date. I'm good.'

'We wouldn't have to call it that.' She steps closer to me. 'Unless you want to.'

'I don't. I mean, I don't need a date. And I really need to get going.'

'Did you already ask someone? Because if you did, I—'

'I did,' I tell her, knowing it's the only way she'll leave me alone. 'I'm already going with someone.'

'Who?' she asks, in a tone that says she doesn't believe me.

'Mia.' I put my arm around her. 'Mia is my date. Mia, this is Danielle. She lives in the building. Danielle, this is Mia.'

Danielle looks Mia up and down before looking at her face. 'Do you guys work together?'

'No,' Mia says. 'I don't live here. I live in Madison.'

'How do you two know each other?' Danielle asks.

'We met at a friends' wedding,' I say. 'We need to go, but have a good day.' I take Mia's hand and head to my truck. I look back and see Danielle watching us. She finally goes into the building when I pull out of the parking lot.

'I'm really sorry about that,' I say to Mia. 'I didn't mean to get you involved, but I didn't know what else to do. She's been trying to go out with me for weeks.'

'Why don't you just tell her you're not interested?'

'Because as you can tell, she's very persistent. And a friend of mine went out with her and said she doesn't take rejection well. She tried to set his car on fire when he broke up with her.'

'Really? That's crazy.'

'Yeah, exactly, which is why I don't want to piss her off.'

'So what are you going to do? You can't keep pretending to be dating other people. In a town this size, she's going to find out you're lying.'

'I'm hoping she'll find someone else soon. Anyway, I obviously don't expect you to go to the wedding. I'm totally fine going alone.'

'And I'll be busy that weekend. I need to get some things done before my parents arrive.'

'They're coming the following week?'

'I think on Monday, but I'm not sure.'

The rest of the drive Mia tells me more about her parents. She says her dad has a hard time getting around after having hip surgery. I see why she feels the need to care for her parents. It sounds like they have a lot of health issues.

My dad's a lot younger than Mia's, but after his heart attack last year, I don't take my time with him for granted. It's another reason why I don't want to move away. Family is as important to me as it is to Mia.

'Wow, that's a big sign,' Mia says as we drive down the country road that takes us to the orchard.

'We have them all over town. There's an even bigger one just off the highway before the exit to Haydon Falls.'

'I went a different way so I didn't see it.'

'The road you took goes past G's Brewhouse. That's the one Sawyer's girlfriend owns.'

'I wish I had more time. I'd love to see it, and that shop your other brother's girlfriend is opening.'

'Could you stay another day?'

'I could if I didn't have assignments due next week. And I have three counseling appointments tomorrow afternoon.'

'What about next weekend? Would you want to come back?'

She looks over at me. 'I could, but you'll be at the wedding.'

'You could come on Sunday and then stick around for when your parents get here.'

'I wasn't going to see them until Friday. They're flying here early so they can explore the area and make it into a little vacation. I wasn't planning on joining them.'

'It was just a suggestion.'

'I'll think about it. I just don't think I can make it work. I have so much to do. And so do you. Don't you have baseball? And you have to help with graduation.'

'Baseball's ending. We have a game next week and then we're done for the season. And the graduation planning is done. It started over a month ago. I got out of helping with it because of Nick's wedding. I spent the past couple weeks cleaning up the orchard with my brothers so it looks nice for the wedding and the pictures.'

'And here it is,' she says as I drive down the long gravel driveway to the house. 'What a beautiful home.'

'It used to look a lot better. My brothers and I kind of destroyed the place growing up. My parents fixed up the main level once we all left home but the basement and our bedrooms still need work.' I park in front of the house and turn off the truck. 'Good thing we had the orchard and all this land to play on or the house would look even worse.' I glance at Mia and see her gazing at the row of apple trees just beyond the barn. 'You want to look at the orchard before we go in?'

'I'd love to.'

We get out of the truck and I take her hand and walk her down to the orchard. I took her hand so she wouldn't trip, which is easy to do if you're not used to walking through an orchard. Or that's what I'm telling myself in my attempt to deny the feelings I'm having for her.

Those feelings are even stronger after spending last night with her. We didn't even kiss, but lying beside her, talking to her, holding her in my arms, had me wanting that, for more than just a night. I know I shouldn't, but I want to see her again. I don't want today to be it.

'It's absolutely beautiful,' Mia says, gazing out at the orchard. The apple blossoms are in full bloom, covering the trees in bright pink and white. It's really pretty, which is why Lyndsay wanted to get married here in the spring. Personally, I prefer the fall. The leaves on the apple trees are green, but when you look farther out at the countryside, all you see is fall color. Bright red, yellow, and orange. It's gorgeous, and the air has a crispness to it you don't get in the spring. If I ever get married, it'll definitely be in the fall.

'All of this is your parents' land?' Mia asks.

'They'd say it belongs to all of us, the whole family, but yes, it's technically theirs. My dad started the orchard with just a few trees and now he's got hundreds of them, along with a pumpkin patch and strawberry fields.'

Mia turns to me. 'You're really lucky to have grown up in a place like this. It had to have been a dream to a kid, having all this space to run around.'

'It was great, but we didn't know any different. Now that I'm older and see kids growing up in apartment buildings or in the middle of a big city, I realize how fortunate I was to have all this. If I ever have kids of my own, I'm going to take them here all the time so they can experience what I did growing up.'

Mia lets go of my hand and walks away from me.

'Is something wrong?' I ask, following behind her.

She shakes her head. 'I was just thinking about something.'

'Jason!' I hear Nick yell. 'You out here?'

'Yeah!' I yell back. 'We'll be up in a minute!'

Mia turns back toward the house. 'We should go. Your mom's probably waiting for us.'

I take Mia's hand as we walk up the hill. Having her here feels right, just like so many other things feel right with her. I wish I knew why that was, because if I knew, maybe I could replicate this feeling with someone else, someone who lives here that I could actually date.

'Welcome,' Mom says to Mia as we go into the house. She gives her a hug, which makes Mia smile.

'Thank you for having us,' she says. 'Whatever you're making smells delicious.'

'It's my famous apple pastries. They just came out of the oven if you'd like to try one.'

'I'd love to.'

Mom motions Mia to follow her. 'The kitchen's right through here.'

I remain behind as Nick comes up to me. 'How'd it go last night?'

'With Mia? Fine. Why?'

'I was just wondering if anything happened,' he says, lowering his voice.

'Nothing happened. I told you, she's just a friend.'

'You look at her like she's more than that.'

'I don't know what you're talking about.'

'Last night. The way you were looking at her? I've seen that look. I've had it myself. It's the look I gave Lyndsay. And now we're getting married.'

I roll my eyes. 'I know what you're trying to do and it's not going to work.'

'I'm not trying to do anything. I'm just letting you know I'm not buying the she's-just-a-friend thing.'

'I don't care if you believe me.' I glance down the hall to make sure Mia's not coming this way. 'I mean, yeah, I like her, and I could see us dating if things were different, but they're not. She's still moving away.'

'She's not leaving until the end of summer. You two could date for a few months and maybe by August she'd decide she wants to stay here.'

I shake my head. 'Her parents are getting older and need her help. She's moving back to take care of them. And I respect that. I'd do the same thing. We both put our families first. It's one of the things I like about her. I'm not going to try to change her mind about that.'

'So what does that mean? That you're done seeing each other after today?'

'I guess. I still don't even know why she's here. She hasn't given me an answer other than saying she wanted to see me again.'

'Maybe that's all it is. She wanted to see you one last time before she leaves.'

'Then why is she here now? Why not wait until the end of summer, before she goes back to Boston?'

'Why don't you just ask her this stuff?'

'I don't know. I guess because this weekend has been going so great, I don't want to ruin it.'

'You're not going to ruin it by talking.'

'I could if I don't like her answer.' I nod toward the kitchen. 'We should get in there before Mom tries to talk Mia into marrying me.'

Nick laughs. 'She was coming on pretty strong last night.'

'Yeah, and you didn't save me. What the hell?'

He pats me on the back. 'You're old enough to save yourself now.'

'You're here early,' Dad says as he comes down the stairs. He used to run down them, but he's been moving a lot slower since his heart attack. 'I thought you weren't coming until eight.'

'Mia and I were up at six,' I say, 'so I told Mom we'd be over early.'

'You show her the orchard yet?'

'I did. She loved it.'

Dad walks up to Nick and me. 'I can remember when you kids were too small to even reach the branches and now look at you. You're both taller than me.'

'Are you boys going to join us?' Mom yells from the kitchen.

'Yeah, Mom!' Nick yells back.

'What's she got cooking in there?' Dad asks as we walk down the hall. 'Smells damn good, whatever it is.'

'There you are,' Mom says as we join her in the kitchen. Mia's seated at the table, eating one of Mom's pastries, a mug of tea in front of her.

I take a seat next to Mia. 'What do you think?'

'These are amazing,' she moans, reminding me of the sounds she made when we slept together. She needs to stop doing that. I can't have my mind going back to that night when I'm having breakfast with my family.

'Jason, would you like one?' Mom asks.

'I'll wait until breakfast. But I'd take some coffee.' I get up.

'I'll get it. You stay there and entertain your guest.'

Dad joins us at the table and talks to Mia. 'Will you be coming back to visit?'

'I don't know,' she says, glancing at me. 'I have a summer job that'll keep me busy.'

'Maybe Jason could go see you in Madison.'

Great. Now my dad's trying to set me up.

'Dad, I'm teaching this summer,' I tell him. 'And I have baseball. So Nick, how are the trees looking this year?' I ask, desperate to end the conversation about Mia and me. I'd love to see her again, but I doubt it'll happen so I don't want to talk about it.

Nick had his head in the fridge, but he backs away and closes the door. 'What was that?'

'I was wondering how the trees are looking this year.'

'They're great.' He's looking at me like I'm crazy for asking. 'You were just out there. You saw for yourself how healthy they looked.'

'How many trees do you have?' Mia asks.

Nick chuckles. 'I should probably know that, but I've lost count. We planted so many new ones lately.' He sits down across from Dad. 'I'm thinking of taking out that last row this year. The one that isn't producing much.'

Dad nods. 'I think it's a good idea. We should do it soon. No use caring for trees we're just going to cut down.'

They continue talking about the orchard until it's time to move to the dining room. I really hope the matchmaking comments don't start up again during breakfast. My family needs to stop interfering. Pushing me to be with someone isn't going to make it happen.

'Mia, this is my younger brother Brody,' I say as he and Kate join us in the dining room. 'And his girlfriend, Kate.'

Mia walks over to them. 'It's nice to meet you. I hear you're opening a store,' she says to Kate.

'In a couple weeks. It was supposed to open earlier, but some of my products were delayed so I pushed the opening back. You should stop by and see it.'

'I probably won't have time. I'm leaving later today.'

'Stay until tomorrow,' Sawyer says, coming into the dining room with Gina. 'You could go check out G's tonight. Try Gina's new sour brew.'

'She's not drinking,' I remind him.

'Yeah, that's right.'

'Hi, I'm Mia,' she says to Gina. 'I drove past your place on the way into town.'

'It's not great from the outside,' Gina says. 'The inside looks a lot better. And the beer is the best in town.' She smiles at Sawyer as she says it.

'What the hell?' Sawyer huffs. 'I thought you were done insulting my beer.'

She laughs. 'I'm just kidding, although I do think my sour ale is better than yours.'

'It is,' Brody says.

'Hey!' Sawyer gives him a look to shut up.

Lyndsay walks in and goes up to Mia. 'Hi, I'm Lyndsay. Nick's fiancé.'

'Congratulations!' Mia gives her a quick hug, like she couldn't help herself.

'Thanks!' Lyndsay sighs. 'I'll be glad when it's over. It's been a lot of work planning it.'

'That doesn't sound good,' Nick says, putting his arm around Lyndsay. 'You make marrying me sound like a chore.'

She kisses him. 'Sorry. I didn't mean it that way. I can't wait to marry you.'

'Everyone go ahead and sit down,' Mom says, scanning the table to make sure she didn't forget anything.

We take our seats and pass around the food. I try to think of something to say before my family starts questioning Mia.

'So Brody, how's the house coming?' I ask.

'Good.' He passes the platter of bacon to Kate. 'We got all the major stuff done. Now we just need to do the painting and whatever decorative things Kate has planned, like putting up shelves. Hanging pictures.'

'Why are you decorating it when you're just going to sell it?' Sawyer asks.

Kate looks at Brody.

He looks back at her. 'Sorry, I wasn't thinking.'

'It's okay. You can tell them.'

'Tell us what?' I ask.

Brody gets a big grin on his face. 'We're keeping the house. Kate and I really like it and now that it's the way we want it, we decided just to live there ourselves rather than sell it.'

'Does this mean something?' Mom asks with a hopeful tone.

'We're not engaged, Mom,' Brody says. 'Not yet.'

She gets an excited look on her face, knowing it won't be long until they're engaged. Sawyer will be next, or maybe he'll propose before Brody. Either way, all my brothers will soon be engaged or married and I'll still be single.

I never would've guessed this is how it would turn out. I thought for sure I'd be married by now with two or three kids. But instead I'm single and can't even find a girlfriend.

Chapter 11

Mia

Jason has such a wonderful family. They're kind and welcoming and I love watching them interact. Growing up, I always wondered what it'd be like to have siblings. It's fun watching Jason with his brothers. They bicker and tease each other, not in a hurtful way, but more to rile each other up. It's clear they love each other and look out for each other.

Hearing what Jason did for his younger brother made my heart melt. He wanted Brody to follow his dream of fixing up old houses so he made it happen by going into debt to buy the house with him, and then went into more debt when Brody couldn't pay the mortgage. A lot of siblings wouldn't do that.

'Did you hear about the caterers?' Nick asks Jason.

'No, what about them?'

'They called last night and said their kitchen flooded from a burst pipe. They won't have it fixed in time for the wedding.'

'So what are you going to do?'

'Luckily, we found another caterer,' Lyndsay says. 'They just confirmed this morning that they'll be able to do it.'

'It's that place outside of town,' Nick says. 'Rita, the catering manager, said her daughter lives in your building. Deidre? Dylan? Something like that.'

'Danielle?' Jason says.

'Yeah, that was it,' Nick says. 'Her mom's handling the catering for us.'

'Wait, so you're saying Danielle's mom will be at the wedding?' Jason asks Nick.

'She'll be there all day, setting up in the morning and staying late to clean up. Why?'

Jason sighs. 'Danielle stopped me in the parking lot this morning and invited herself to the wedding with me. I told her no, but from what I've heard, she's crazy and doesn't take no for an answer.'

Brody laughs. 'So you're bringing some crazy chick to the wedding?'

'No, I told her I was taking Mia.' He shakes his head. 'Shit. Now what am I going to do? Danielle's mom is going to tell her I was at the wedding alone.'

'Maybe Mia would agree to go with you,' Martha says. 'If you asked nicely.'

Jason turns to me. 'You don't have to do this, but if you do, I'll totally owe you. You can ask me to do whatever you want. I'll even go pick you up in Madison so you don't have to drive here or pay for gas.'

'That's not really asking her,' Brody says.

Jason gives him an annoyed look before turning back to me. He takes my hand and looks in my eyes. 'Mia, would you go with me to the wedding?'

Everyone's quiet as they wait for my answer. If I do this, I can't tell Jason about the baby, not today. I'll have to wait until after the wedding. I should wait even if I don't go to it. I don't want to take attention away from Nick and Lyndsay the week of their wedding, and news that Jason's going to be a dad will definitely do that.

What's one more week? I could wait a week if it means giving Nick and Lyndsay their perfect day that's focused just on them.

'Sure, I'll go,' I say.

'Thank you,' Jason says, sounding relieved. 'I'll pay you back. I promise.'

We finish breakfast, then go to the barn with Nick. He gives me a tour of the place, then takes me out to the orchard, where he tells me about all the different types of apples they grow. I'd love to stay and learn more, but Jason needs to be at the baseball field soon to meet up with his team.

'So that's my family,' Jason says as he drives down the gravel road that leads away from the house.

'They're great! You're lucky to have them.'

'Yeah, we fight now and then, but most of the time, we get along.' Jason glances at me. 'Thanks again for agreeing to go to the wedding. And I wasn't kidding when I said I'd go to Madison and pick you up.'

'I can drive myself. I'll have to figure out what to wear. I assume you're wearing a suit?'

'Yeah, all the groomsmen are wearing black suits with white shirts and pink ties.'

'Pink is the wedding color?'

'Pink and white to match the apple blossoms. We're doing the pictures in the orchard.'

'That'll be pretty. Maybe I'll look for a pink dress, unless you don't want us matching.'

'We can match. And whatever you buy, give me the bill. I'll pay for it. You shouldn't be paying for a dress for a wedding you didn't even want to go to.'

'I don't mind going. I love weddings.' I smile at Jason. 'We had fun at the last one.'

'Yeah.' He clears his throat. 'Maybe too much fun.'

'Do you regret it?'

'I don't regret it. I just didn't want it to end.'

'I didn't either,' I whisper, gazing out the window.

Jason reaches over and takes my hand. 'I wish we could've found a way to make this work. But I can't move to Boston, Mia. I have a life here, and my family. I can't—'

'I know. I never expected you to.'

We continue the drive in silence until we reach Jason's apartment. We go inside so he can change clothes, then leave again to go to the game.

* * *

'Which one is yours?' the woman next to me asks as we sit in the bleachers, watching the game. It just started, but the other team already scored.

'Oh, I'm not a mom,' I tell her, wondering how old she thinks I am. I hope I don't look old enough to have a kid in high school.

She laughs. 'Sorry, I said that wrong. I meant which one is your brother? I assumed you're an older sister. You're far too young to be a mom.'

'I don't actually know any of the players. I'm friends with Jason, the coach.'

She turns to me, smiling. 'So Jason finally got himself a girlfriend? It's about time. That man is so picky I was starting to think he'd never settle down. He's dated just about every girl in town.'

'Really?' I ask, wanting her to tell me more.

'He doesn't date as much now, but when he was younger, he was going out all the time. It was like he was on a mission to find a wife. We all thought for sure he'd be married by now. But he just didn't click with anyone I guess. Well, except you. How long have you two been seeing each other?'

'We're not dating. We're just friends. I live in Madison. I'm only here for the day.'

She leans over to me, her eyes on the field. 'If I were you, I'd snatch him up while you have the chance. He's a great catch. I mean, look at him. Those muscles. Those eyes. That smile. And he's great with the kids. They all love him. He'll make a great father someday.' She nudges me. 'Friends can become more, if you know what I mean.'

'I do. It's just that I'm not staying here. I'm moving back to Boston in a few months.'

'Oh, that's a shame. Jason will never leave here. He loves Haydon Falls. Loves his students. His family. I'm sure he'll find someone eventually. A man like that doesn't stay single forever.'

My heart sinks hearing her say that. But she's right. I'll move away and Jason will find someone else. Someone he'll marry and have children with, but what does that mean for *our* child? Will he still want to see him or her? I can't imagine Jason not wanting to be part of his child's life, but what if that changes when he has children with someone else?

The woman next to me jumps up. 'Andrew, go! You're almost there!'

I look up and see a kid trip and fall before reaching home base. That must be Andrew because the woman next to me, who must be his mom, slumps back down on the bleachers.

'He trips every time,' she says. 'I love the kid, but baseball isn't his sport.'

I watch as Jason goes over to the kid and consoles him. The kid looks at Jason like he's the coolest guy ever. He's right. So is the lady next to me who said Jason's a great catch. I bet everyone in town would say Jason is great, but I still can't have a future with him. Not when I'm moving away.

* * *

'Did you really like the game or were you just being nice?' Jason asks as we walk along the trail that leads to the falls. It's a short walk, and when we get there we can't stay. We don't have time. We'll see the falls, then go to an early dinner before I have to leave.

'I liked the game,' I say, 'but I liked seeing you coach it even more. You're really good with the kids.'

He shrugs. 'I try, but I'm not always sure I'm getting through to them.'

'I wasn't either back when I was teaching. But I think we make a difference in their lives even if we don't always know it. Just think about your science teacher, the one you said made you like science. Did you ever tell him how much he meant to you?'

'No, but I would now if he was still around. He moved away when I was a senior in high school.'

'That's what I mean. We don't always know the effect we have on our students.'

'Yeah, I guess.' He stops and looks up. 'What do you think?'

My eyes follow his gaze to a large waterfall, the water crashing down on big boulders underneath.

'I was thinking it'd be smaller. This is impressive. I can't believe we're the only ones here.'

'It gets busy during the summer and fall when the tourists come through town. This time of year it's just locals and they've seen it enough times to not feel the need to come back.'

'I would. If I lived here, I'd come here all the time.' I close my eyes and listen to the water crashing down. 'I love that sound. It's so powerful but also calming.'

'Mia.'

I open my eyes and see Jason in front of me, looking at me like he did the night of the wedding. I gaze back at him, feeling the heat between us bubbling up, trying to ignore it, wishing I could.

Jason wraps his hands around my face. 'I know I shouldn't do this, but fuck . . . I want to. It's been torture being around you the past day and not being able to kiss you.'

'Then do it,' I say, my heart thundering in my chest. 'Kiss me.'

He leans down and gently presses his lips to mine. He's being cautious, unsure if we should be doing this. Maybe we shouldn't, but it feels too good to stop. My lips part and his tongue slips past them as his arms lower to around my waist, pulling me closer.

We kiss for several minutes, maybe longer, the sound of the rushing waterfall surrounding us. It's romantic, and getting me all tingly inside.

I slowly pull away. 'We should go.'

'Yeah.' Jason takes a step back, then motions me to go ahead of him on the trail that leads back to the parking lot.

I didn't want to leave, but being in that romantic spot, kissing Jason, was bringing back all the feelings I have for him that I'm trying to ignore.

We're both quiet as Jason drives back to his apartment. Neither one of us wants to say goodbye, but we have to. I need to get home, and away from Jason before I fall for him even more.

'Did you get everything?' Jason asks, coming into the bedroom where I'm zipping up my overnight bag.

'I think so.'

He walks up to me. 'About what happened at the falls.'

'We don't need to talk about it.' I smile a little. 'I think it's fair to say we're both still attracted to each other. Honestly, I'm surprised it didn't happen sooner.'

His hand cups the side of my face as he looks into my eyes. 'What I feel for you is more than just attraction.'

'Jason, we shouldn't—'

His lips press to mine before I can finish my thought. I was going to tell him we shouldn't be talking about what we feel for each other, or acting on it. And that we shouldn't kiss because it might lead to us doing more.

So why am I still kissing him? And why am I willingly going with him as he leads me to the bed? Why am I letting him take off my shirt, my bra, my jeans, my panties? Why am I desperately trying to get his belt off?

'Oh God,' I moan as he sinks into me.

I don't know how we ended up here, but we've gone too far to go back. He's buried inside me, stretching me, filling me, in the most wonderful way. I've dreamed about this, relived that night, for months now. I haven't been with a man since Jason because he's all I've been able to think about.

'Don't go,' he whispers in my ear, slowly pulling out before thrusting back inside me. 'Stay with me tonight.'

'I can't. I have to—'

Jason's lips press to mine, stopping me from telling him I have to go. I'd love to stay, but I can't. I have too much to do, and staying with him would just bring us closer, which we both know is a bad idea.

What we're doing now is a bad idea, but God, it feels good. He's rocking into me in a slow, steady, intoxicating rhythm. My hips rise and fall, moving with him as I rake my fingers down his back.

'You feel so fucking good,' he groans. He speeds up a little, then a little more.

I suck in a breath as his hand slips between us, rubbing over my clit as he moves in and out of me.

'Yes,' I pant. 'Keep going.'

I feel it building, the sensations getting stronger. I hold onto him as he thrusts harder, deeper, his body tensing up.

'Shit,' he mutters, like he can't hold back a second longer. He comes, but so do I, waves of pleasure shuddering through me, reminding me of that night we shared. But this time feels even better, maybe because my sensations aren't numbed by alcohol. Or maybe it's because spending time with Jason and meeting his family, I feel closer to him than I did that night.

Jason pauses a moment, then gently pulls out of me.

'I didn't plan that,' he says, laying back on the bed. 'I swear.'

'I did.'

He looks at me. 'What?'

'It was my fault. I lured you to the bedroom, made you kiss me, then had my way with you.'

He smiles. 'I don't think it happened that way.'

'Maybe not, but I'm not sorry we did it. Are you?'

'No. But that's the problem. I want this, Mia. Not just the sex, but you.' He looks up at the ceiling. 'I don't want you to leave. I know you have to, but I don't want you to.'

I rest my head on his chest. 'Let's not talk about it. Let's just be happy in the moment.'

We lie there for several minutes, then Jason suddenly sits up. 'Fuck.'

'What's wrong?'

'We didn't use anything. You're still on the pill, right?'

'Um, yeah,' I lie. I should tell him the truth, but I can't. Not yet. I need to wait until after his brother's wedding.

Jason lets out a sigh of relief. 'Sorry, I was panicking for a minute there. I'm always lecturing the guys on the team to be safe, and here I am, forgetting to use a condom.'

'We should get up,' I say, wanting to get off that topic.

He turns to me. 'Where do you want to go for dinner?'

'We'll have to skip it. I need to head home.'

'It won't take long, and you need to eat. You didn't have lunch.'

'I'm still full from your mom's breakfast. And I really should start driving.'

He places his hand along the side of my face and looks in my eyes. 'I'm not ready for you to leave.'

I look back at him, my heart aching, wishing I could be with Jason. Wishing things were different. Wishing there was a way for us to be together, or at least have a chance to try.

'Jason, we can't—'

'Yeah, I know,' he says, looking down. He pulls away from me and gets out of bed.

'It's not that I don't want to stay. It's just—'

'You don't have to explain,' he says. 'I shouldn't have said it. I know you have to go.'

He says it without any emotion, like he just flipped a switch and turned off the feelings he was expressing just moments ago. I understand why. I'm trying to shut off my feelings too. I've been trying to all day, without success. The more time I spend with Jason, the more I feel for him.

We get dressed and Jason walks me out to my car.

'Call me when you get there,' he says as he puts my suitcase in the trunk. 'So I know you made it.'

'I will.' I open the car door.

'Mia, wait.' Jason pulls me in for a hug. 'I'll see you next weekend, right? You're not going to change your mind, are you?'

'No, I'll be here.' I smile and pull away from him. 'I'll see you Saturday.'

'Why don't you come on Friday? I need a date for the rehearsal dinner.'

'A date?' I ask, my brows rising.

'Not a date. Someone to go with. Will you do it?'

'Can I stay with you again?'

'Of course.'

'Then yes, I'll go to the rehearsal dinner with you.'

'Thanks.' He gives me another hug. 'Have a safe trip. And remember to let me know you're home.'

'I will. Bye, Jason.'

On the drive back, I keep thinking about what we did, telling myself we shouldn't have done it but not regretting that it happened. I'm so confused right now. I thought seeing Jason again would convince me that the night we shared was nothing more than two strangers having a fun time at a wedding followed by a night of great sex. But the truth is, Jason and I really are good together, even outside the bedroom. We have similar values, similar goals, and we're comfortable with each other.

Jason's a great guy and he'll make a great father for our baby. I just wish he could be more than that. I wish we could try being a couple, but since we can't, I'll just be grateful he's a good person with a good family who I know will be the best father he can be.

Chapter 12

Mia

'You didn't tell him?' Nora says, her voice so loud that the people around us heard and are now staring at us.

It's Sunday morning and we're having brunch at our favorite place by campus.

'Would you keep your voice down?' I whisper.

She glances at the table next to ours and smiles at the older couple. 'Sorry. My friend's hard of hearing.'

They give me a sympathetic look, then go back to eating their breakfast.

'Why didn't you tell him?' Nora asks.

'Because his brother is getting married next weekend and I didn't want to take attention away from the wedding. I'll wait until it's over and then I'll tell him.'

'Over the phone? Don't you want to tell him in person?'

'I will. When I go back there.' I pop a piece of cantaloupe in my mouth so I'll be too busy chewing to answer the million questions I know are coming.

She leans toward me across the table. 'Please tell me you are not going to the wedding with him.'

I point to my mouth as I eat the cantaloupe.

She leans back, folding her arms over her chest and stares at me. 'You're leaving, Mia. You're going back to Boston. Why would you get involved with this guy knowing it'll never work out? You were supposed to go there, tell him about the baby, and discuss what to do going forward. That's it. And now you're going to be his date for his brother's wedding?'

After dabbing my mouth with my napkin, I lean toward her and lower my voice. 'It's not a date. I'm going to the wedding as a favor to Jason. Some crazy girl at his apartment was pressuring him to take her to the wedding so he told her he was going with me. Then when we were having breakfast with Jason's family, his brother said the crazy girl's mom would be catering the wedding, so obviously, she'd know Jason lied if he showed up alone.'

'Okay, wait.' She puts her hand up and takes a deep breath. 'You had breakfast with his family?'

'Yes, and it was so good. His mom is the best cook. Her food is even better than here, and you know how much I love this place. Jason's parents live in this adorable farmhouse way up on a hill next to the orchard. His brother Nick runs the orchard and gave me a tour of it and the barn where they host events.'

'Wait.' She puts her hand up again. 'We'll go back to the whole barn-breakfast thing. First, let's talk about this girl at his apartment. Were you there? At his apartment?'

'I stayed there,' I say like it's not a big deal, but I know Nora will make it one.

Her brows rise. 'You stayed at his apartment? You said you were getting a hotel.'

'There's only two hotels in town and one of them was doing renovations, which could've been loud. So Jason offered to let me stay at his apartment.'

'You had sex with him, didn't you?' she says, raising her voice again. The older couple next to us gives us an annoyed look.

'Sorry,' Nora says to them, pointing at me. 'She's practically deaf. I have to shout for her to hear me. She has a hearing aid, but she refuses to wear it.'

'They make ones you can barely see,' the old man says to me. 'Show her, dear.'

The old lady moves her gray hair aside to show me her hearing aid. 'I got it at the place at the mall.' She says it's really loud and enunciates each word.

'I'll take her there later today,' Nora says. 'Thank you.'

They nod, then get up from the table to leave.

'Are you done?' I point to Nora's plate. 'We need to get out of here before you embarrass me even more.'

'We can go, but we're not done talking about this.'

When we're back at my apartment, Nora starts in again. 'You said you wanted to keep your distance from this guy. And I agree. That's the best thing for both of you. If you start having feelings for each other, it'll be that much harder when you leave.'

I sink down on the couch. 'I already have feelings for him. I had feelings for him the night of the wedding.'

'You said it was just sex.'

'Yeah, well, I might've lied about that.'

She sighs. 'Mia, why are you doing this? Staying at his apartment? Hanging out with his family?' She sits beside me, facing me. 'You know this isn't going to end well.'

'I'm not just doing this for me. I'm doing it for the baby. I have to get to know my baby's father. He or she is going to be spending time with him and I have to know I can trust him and that he'll be a good dad.'

She pauses a moment. 'Okay, you make a good point. But you can get to know him without having sex with him.'

'I didn't—'

'You did. Don't even try to lie about it. You don't have the hots for some guy and spend the night at his place and have nothing happen.'

'It didn't happen at night. I got sick during the night. Jason woke up and found me in the bathroom. It was disgusting. Trust me, we were not having sex that night.'

'You got sick? How'd you explain that?'

'I told him it was food poisoning.' I smile. 'He was so sweet. He helped me back to his room, then stayed there with me and we talked until I fell asleep.'

'And he didn't try anything?'

'No! Gross! Did you not hear the part about me puking?'

'I'm just asking. Some guys wouldn't care.'

'Jason's not like that. He felt really bad that I got sick. He kept offering to get me stuff, like water or crackers. He's going to make a great dad,' I say, in a dreamy voice as I imagine him with our baby.

'So when did you have sex?'

'Right before I left.' I tell her how we went to the falls and kissed, which sparked what happened later at his apartment. 'The sex was even better than last time.'

'Guess I know what you'll be doing this weekend,' she says, sounding annoyed with me.

'We're not going to do that, not after I tell him my news. I'm worried he's going to be mad that I'm still planning to move away.'

'He can move to Boston.'

'He won't. Seeing how close he is with his family, I can't see him ever leaving there. And I get it, because I'm the same way. We both want to be with our families.'

'When are you going to tell your parents?'

'Right before they fly home. I want them to be happy at my graduation, not disappointed and sad.'

'They're not going to be sad. They're getting a grandchild.'

'Who came from a one-night stand,' I say with a sigh.

'They don't need to know how it happened. And it wasn't a one-night stand. You're still seeing him.'

'But for how long? This weekend will probably be it.'

'Wait.' She gets up. 'Didn't you say your parents are going to Haydon Falls?'

'Yeah, they're coming here the week before I graduate to drive around and see the area. Why?'

'What if they meet Jason?'

'It's a small town, but not that small. I doubt they'll run into him. And if they did, they wouldn't know who he was. I'm not ready to tell them who the father is.

I want to wait until Jason and I have had time to figure out how this is going to work.'

'You know they won't accept that, especially your mom. No offense but she's kind of nosy, and persistent. Remember when she kept asking how I got that bruise on my neck?'

'And you told her you got hit by a tennis ball when it was really a hickey? That was quick thinking. I'm impressed you came up with that so fast.'

'Can you believe that guy gave me a hickey? Like we're still in high school?' Nora goes to the fridge and takes out a bottle of water. 'I was so pissed. I'm a professor. I can't be showing up to class with a hickey. This is why I got off the dating apps.'

I get up and meet her in the kitchen. 'So what's your point? About Jason?'

'Oh! Yeah.' She takes a sip of her water. 'Why don't you introduce your parents to Jason?'

'Why would I do that?'

'Because your nosy mom is not going to wait months to find out who her grandchild's father is. If they're going to be in Haydon Falls, you might as well introduce them.'

'And what am I supposed to say? This is the guy I had sex with last January, resulting in your grandchild?'

'Tell them he's your boyfriend,' she casually says as she goes back to the couch.

'Wait—what?' I join her on the couch. 'You want me to lie to my parents and tell them Jason's my boyfriend?'

'It's not really a lie. You're staying with him, having sex with him, going to his brother's wedding. Sounds like a boyfriend to me.'

'But he's not. And there's no way he'd agree to that unless it was actually true.'

She turns to me, her eyes getting big. 'You know what would be even better?'

'What?' I ask, not sure I want to hear this.

'If you told them he's your fiancé.'

I burst out laughing. 'Yeah, right. That's funny. I needed a laugh.'

'I'm serious. You tell your parents he's your fiancé, then later, in a few months or whatever, you tell them you guys broke up. That way it looks like you tried to make it work with Jason, but then found out you two weren't a good match. They can't be mad about that. And if you're engaged to him, they'll assume you've been dating Jason for months instead of it being a one-night fling. '

'No.' I shake my head. 'Absolutely not. I'm not making up some crazy story about being engaged. Even if I wanted to, there's no way Jason would go for that. If he did, he'd be lying to his family too.'

'Why? They don't have to know.'

'My parents will insist on meeting Jason's family if they think I'm marrying him. And it's not like I can lie and say they don't live there. The Kanfield name is all over town. Everywhere you go there's signs for Kanfield Orchard and if they go downtown they'll see Kanfield

Brewery. My parents could easily find out where Jason's parents live.'

'Okay, so he lies to his family about your engagement. So what? It's probably a good thing since he knocked you up.'

'He's not going to agree to it. And his family knows we've barely spent any time together. It wouldn't make sense to them that he's engaged.'

'You said he's a good guy, right?'

'Yeah. Why?'

'Guys like that want to marry the girl. They feel it's their duty after knocking her up.'

'Would you please stop saying he knocked me up? I never liked that phrase.'

'What do you like better? Planted his seed? Made a deposit? Put a bun in your oven?'

'Stop!' I laugh. 'Those are all horrible. Just go with he got me pregnant.'

'He got you pregnant and asked you to marry him. Done. That's your story. Your parents will be thrilled and so will his. Problem solved.'

'It's not solved because we're not engaged. And I'm telling you, Jason would not agree to make up a story like that.'

'He might. Didn't you say you were doing him a favor by going to his brother's wedding?'

'Yeah. Why?'

'If you're doing him a favor, he owes you. And now it's time to pay up, in the form of a fake engagement.'

'Jason doesn't owe me. And I want to go to the wedding. I think it'll be fun.'

'But he thinks you're doing him a favor, right?'

'Well, yes.' I think back to what he said at breakfast. 'I guess he did mention he'd do anything I want if I agreed to go with him.'

'There you go.' She shrugs. 'He has to do this. He owes you. It's as simple as that.'

'Nora, I don't think this is a good idea. I hate lying to my parents.'

'You'd rather have them think their grandchild was conceived during a drunken one-night stand with a stranger?'

'Well, no, but . . . I don't know. I have to think about it.'

'You've got a week to decide, but if you want to please your parents, a fake engagement is the way to do it. And hey, it's not like you're actually committing to anything. You let them think you're engaged, then tell them it didn't work out.'

Maybe she's right. It's a crazy idea, but it would save my parents the heartache of knowing their daughter got pregnant from a random hookup. And I know they'd love Jason if they met him.

I just don't think Jason would go along with it, even if he owes me. But who knows? Maybe he would.

* * *

Friday night, I get nervous as I drive to Jason's apartment. I only talked to him once this week and it was quick. We just confirmed the details for tonight, like when I'd be arriving and what I should wear, and that was it. He hurried me off the phone. He didn't seem like himself, but maybe he was just tired.

'Hey.' Jason opens the door and gives me a quick hug, then steps aside to let me in. 'We need to leave in a few minutes. Mom just called. The place she ordered the food from screwed up. They thought the dinner was at six, not seven, so Mom moved the dinner up. Everyone's there. I told her we'd leave as soon as you got here.'

'Oh. Okay.' I set my suitcase down. 'Do I have time to change?' I point to my shorts and t-shirt, which are wrinkled from the drive. 'I don't want to show up in this.'

'Go ahead. I'll get your suitcase.' He picks it up and takes it to his room. 'I'll just wait in the living room.'

He's acting strange. He barely even smiled when he saw me. And that hug he gave me was like one you'd give a person you just met, not someone you slept with and claim to care about.

I change into a sundress, then go into the bathroom to freshen up my makeup and fix my hair. When I come out to the living room, Jason's on the couch, watching a baseball game.

He sees me and gets up. 'Ready?'

I walk up to him. 'Jason, is everything okay?'

'Yeah. Why wouldn't it be?'

'You seem kind of off tonight, like maybe you're in a bad mood.'

'I'm not. I'm just tired. It's been a long week.' He goes around me to the counter to get his keys, then heads to the door and opens it. 'After you.'

We walk down the hall and get on the elevator. He stands a few feet away and doesn't even try to hold my hand. This is a totally different Jason than the one I was with last week. That Jason kept smiling at me, complimenting me, and couldn't keep his hands off me.

Did he meet someone? Maybe that's it. Maybe he has someone else. If so, why isn't he taking her to the wedding instead of me?

'How was the drive?' he asks on our way to the brewery.

'Good. It went faster this time.'

'How was your week? Did you get everything done? All your assignments?'

'Yes. I'm officially done with school.' I smile at him, but he doesn't even look at me, and he doesn't say anything.

There's definitely something going on with him and I think it's more than him being tired. This is not the Jason I know. He's acting like a different person. Cold. Distant. Quiet.

We don't talk the rest of the way there. He parks in front of the brewery, which is closed tonight for the rehearsal dinner. He comes around the truck to help me out, but once I'm safely on the ground, he lets go of my hand.

'Mia, welcome!' Martha says as Jason and I walk into the brewery. She comes up to me and gives me a hug. 'It's so nice that you could join us.'

At least Jason's mom is acting like she wants me here. The rest of his family seems to feel the same. They all come up and greet me. Gina, Kate, and Lyndsay give me a hug. Jason goes straight to the bar to get a drink.

'Mia,' he yells from the bar. 'You drinking tonight?'

'No. I'll just have water.'

'We have wine,' Sawyer says to me. 'And Brody brought some whiskey.'

'You'll need something to toast with,' Nick says, holding up his beer glass.

'Try this,' Lyndsay says, offering me her wine glass. 'It's my favorite Chardonnay.'

'Really, I'm fine.' I back away from the glass. 'I have a headache and wine will make it worse.'

'A headache?' Martha says with concern. 'Do you need something? I have aspirin in my purse.'

'Oh, no, it'll go away.'

'Martha, we need to eat,' Carl, Jason's dad, says, as he stands by the long table where the food is set up. 'It's starting to get cold.'

'Just so everyone knows,' Martha says. 'The rehearsal has been moved to seven since the food showed up early.'

The rehearsal is at the orchard, where Nick and Lyndsay are getting married. Jason said they were going to have the rehearsal dinner at the barn but decided not to since it's already set up for the reception tomorrow.

Maybe I'll ask Jason to drop me off at his apartment on his way to the rehearsal. I don't need to be there, and given how he's acting, he'd probably rather go alone.

'I love your dress,' Kate says to me during dinner. 'Where'd you get it?'

'At a store back in Boston. I've had it forever.'

'It's really cute. Hey, while you're here, do you want to come check out my store?'

'I don't know if I'll have time. I might head home after the wedding tomorrow.'

'Wait—what?' Jason looks at me. 'You're leaving after the wedding? It'll be dark and late. It's not safe.'

'I'll be fine. It's not that far.'

I'd planned to stay until Sunday, but I'd rather leave tomorrow if things between Jason and me continue to feel awkward and uncomfortable.

'You can't leave.' Brody laughs. 'If you do, the crazy girl will show up to be Jason's date.'

'Who's leaving?' Martha asks from the other end of the table.

'Mia,' Sawyer says. 'She said she might leave after the wedding.'

'Oh, honey, you don't want to do that,' Martha says in her motherly tone. 'It's dangerous to be on those country roads at night.'

'A buddy of mine hit some deer on that road to Madison,' Carl says. 'The force was bad enough to land him in the ditch. He hit his head on the window and laid there unconscious until someone drove by the next morning.'

'You see?' Martha says. 'It's always safest to drive during daylight, especially with all the critters that come out at night.'

Jason leans over to me. 'This will keep going until you agree to stay.'

I smile. 'Okay, I'll leave on Sunday.'

'Isn't that when your parents are coming?' Jason asks.

'They're coming on Monday, and I'm not planning to be here with them. They have a list of things they plan to do. And they're not spending all their time in Haydon Falls. They'll stay here overnight, but during the day they plan to drive to the other towns in the area.'

'Tell them to come by the orchard,' Nick says. 'I'll give them a tour.'

'Okay,' I say, but I'm not going to tell them to go there. I'm going to tell them the orchard is closed for the season, which is true until they reopen in a few weeks for strawberry picking. I don't want my parents to meet Jason's family. I'm not even going to tell them about Jason.

I thought about Nora's fake engagement idea and decided I'm not doing it. Even if I wanted to, Jason would never agree to be my fiancé. He isn't even acting like we're friends anymore. Given how things are going, I think this is it for Jason and me. We'll be connected by our child, but that's where our relationship will end.

Chapter 13

Jason

It's the day of Nick's wedding. I should be happy, but instead I feel like shit for how I've been treating Mia. I haven't been mean to her. I just haven't been like I usually am around her. I'm not holding her hand. I'm not complimenting her. I'm not putting my arm around her or giving her a hug. It's been hard not to do that stuff, but I made a commitment to treat her like a friend, nothing more, and I'm keeping that commitment.

All last week I thought about Mia, about how much I like her and how much I miss her when she's not around. And then it hit me that I was doing it again. I was letting myself fall for her just like I did the night of the wedding. I was dreaming about her, imagining a future with her, forgetting the fact that she'll be gone soon.

Last weekend I treated her like a girlfriend and started to believe that she was, but I can't do that. It's not fair to either of us. Mia's not my girlfriend and never will be, so I can't play this game where I pretend that she's mine. And yet whenever she's around me, I find myself wanting to hold her hand and put my arm around her. It feels natural to do those things and unnatural not to, which is why I'm struggling to stay away from her.

I did okay last night. Mia didn't want to go to the rehearsal so I dropped her off at my apartment. When I got home, she was already in bed. I was on the couch all night, but I couldn't sleep. I laid awake thinking about her in my room, wanting to go in there and apologize for being cold and distant. I wanted to hold her in my arms and tell her how she makes me feel and how she's on my mind every second of the day. But instead I remained on the couch until morning.

When she got up, I was already dressed and ready to take her to breakfast. After we ate, I drove around, showing her the town. I was really just killing time until we had to leave for my parents' house. The less time we have alone together at my apartment, the better. I keep thinking about last weekend, before she left. We went to my apartment so she could get her things and ended up having sex. I had no intentions of doing that. It just happened, but it can't happen again.

'You waiting for someone?' Dad asks, coming down the stairs.

'Yeah, Mia. I was just going to let her know I'd be upstairs changing.'

He nods. 'She's up with the girls. I need to go check on some things in the barn.' He goes down the hall.

Mia and I arrived at my parents' house an hour ago to help with whatever last-minute things needed to be done. Turns out they didn't need our help. Mom just told me they did so I'd get here early. She was worried I'd show up late. She should've been worried about Brody. He's the one who's never on time.

Maybe I'm imagining it, but I feel like my parents are starting to see me as being less mature and responsible than my brothers. I think it's because I'm still single, which is completely unfair. Being single doesn't mean I'm irresponsible. It just means I haven't found the right girl. But my parents equate settling down with maturity, so to them, my single status means I need to grow up.

'Lyndsay looks gorgeous,' Mia says as she runs down the stairs. 'I absolutely love her dress!'

Mia's been hanging out with my brothers' girlfriends since we got here. I'm not even dating Mia and yet she's like part of the family. I'm not surprised everyone loves her. She's got a bright and sunny personality that makes you want to be around her. And she's a hugger so she fits right in with the rest of us.

'Is Lyndsay almost ready?' I ask.

'Yeah, she's just finishing her hair and touching up her makeup.'

We walk to the living room and sit down on the couch.

'How's Nick doing?' Mia asks.

'Good. He's not even nervous. But he's wanted to marry Lyndsay since high school so it's not like he has any doubts.'

'I'm really happy for them. They're a great couple.'

'They are. They remind me of Mom and Dad. Always looking out for each other. Hardly ever fighting.'

The front door swings open and Gina storms into the house, with Sawyer following behind her.

'What the hell did I do?' Sawyer yells.

'Are you serious right now?' Gina stops behind the couch where Mia and I are sitting and glares at Sawyer across the room. 'I heard you! You asked that girl out!'

'I did not ask her out!' Sawyer goes over to Gina. 'Why were you even there? You were supposed to be here, helping Lyndsay get ready.'

'She didn't need help. She has like ten girls up there. And stop changing the subject. Why was that girl at the brewery with you? And why were you telling her to meet you at your apartment Monday night?'

'Because I . . .' Sawyer looks down, shaking his head. 'Let's not do this right now.'

'Oh, we're doing it. I'm not waiting. If we're through, just tell me. I'm not going to be your girlfriend all night only to be dumped tomorrow for some blonde with fake boobs. Is that really what you want? Because if it is, why'd you ever date me?'

'Guys,' I say. 'Why don't you take this outside?'

'Stay out of this, Jason,' Sawyer says, keeping his eyes on Gina.

'I'll just go,' Gina says. 'I can't watch people get married after finding out my boyfriend's cheating on me.'

Sawyer throws his hands up. 'I wasn't cheating on you!'

'Then how do you explain what I heard at the brewery?'

'You heard me making an appointment, not a date.'

'Since when do you have appointments in your apartment?'

He sighs. 'Gina, please, I'm begging you. Just end this. It's not what you think.'

'We should go,' I say to Mia.

'No, wait!' Gina says, looking at us. 'Mia, what would you think if you heard Jason asking some girl to come to his apartment on a night he knew you had to work?'

'Oh, I don't think I should be getting involved in this,' Mia says, sounding flustered. 'And I'm not dating Jason so it's really not the same.'

'But if you *were* dating him, and you found him making plans with some girl, would you just assume it was nothing?'

Mia looks at me. 'I'd talk to him after she left and ask him to explain. I'd want to believe he wouldn't do something like that to me.'

'I want to believe that about Sawyer, but why would he invite a girl up to his apartment if it was just something innocent? He could just talk to her in the bar or in his office.'

'Gina, for the last time,' Sawyer says. 'There is nothing going on with her. I love you. Why would I mess around with some other girl?'

'Because you can,' she huffs. 'Like I don't notice all the girls hitting on you at the brewery?'

'Yeah.' He takes Gina's hand. 'And when they do, I tell them I'm taken. I tell them I have a girlfriend I'm going to marry someday.'

Gina rolls her eyes. 'You don't tell them that.'

'Maybe not the marrying part, but I tell them I have a girlfriend. And I do plan to marry her.'

Gina yanks her hand from Sawyer's. 'I know what you're doing and it's not going to work. You can say all the sweet things you want, but it's not going to change what I heard.' She folds her arms over her chest. 'Just tell me the truth. How long have you been seeing her?'

'About three weeks.'

Gina's jaw drops. She looks like she wants to kill Sawyer.

'But it's not what you're thinking.' He steps closer to her. 'You really want to know the truth?'

'Just hurry up and tell me,' she says, blinking really fast like she's trying to hold back tears.

'That girl, the one you saw me with, makes jewelry. She does custom pieces. I heard about her from the jewelry store in town. She lives about an hour away. The first time I met with her I drove to her shop. We talked about what I wanted and she said she'd work up some ideas. I went back a week later and saw her drawings. They were good, but I wanted this piece to be perfect. So I invited her to come to my apartment this week to show her some of the clothes you have there, along with some of your jewelry, so she could see your style. That's why she was at the brewery today. She's in town working with some other clients and will be here for a few days. The only time I could meet with her is Monday night, before she heads home.'

'I don't understand,' Gina says. 'Are you saying you hired this woman to make me jewelry?'

'Not just any jewelry.' He pauses. 'She's making your engagement ring.'

'Shit,' Gina mutters.

'Yeah.' Sawyer laughs a little. 'You just ruined the surprise.'

'But I thought we were going to wait.'

'I didn't say I was proposing. I said I'm getting your ring. It's handmade. It's going to take awhile to make. I knew you didn't want a traditional ring so when I heard about this girl and saw her designs, I hired her. I guess now that you know, we could work with her together if you want.'

'No.' Gina cracks as smile. 'I want you to do it. I want the ring you designed.' She hugs him. 'I'm sorry. I got jealous and ruined your surprise.'

'So we're good?' Sawyer says. 'Because I need to go change.'

'Go ahead.' Gina lets him go. 'I'm going to go check on Lyndsay.'

They leave and I'm alone with Mia again.

'Another one of your brothers is getting married,' Mia says. 'That's exciting.'

'I worry about those two. They fight constantly.'

'I think they're just both really passionate. They seem perfect for each other.'

I stand up. 'I need to go get ready.'

'Okay.' Mia smiles at me and I feel a pain in my chest. She's being so nice and I'm being cold and aloof. But I don't know what else to do to keep myself from falling for her even more. Just looking at her, at her deep brown eyes and long dark hair and that beautiful smile, has me wanting to take her in my arms and kiss her.

Then I see her with my family, how well she fits in, and my mind starts going again, dreaming of a future where we're together.

'Are you coming back?' she asks. 'Or will I just see you after the wedding?'

'I'll come down after I'm dressed. Mom wants my brothers and me to meet her and Dad in the barn before we go out to the orchard for the ceremony. She wants to do some family pictures. If you want to wait there while we take photos, you can. Or you can go upstairs with the girls.'

'I'll think about it.'

I go up to Sawyer's old room where my brothers are getting ready.

'There you are,' Nick says when he sees me. 'Where the hell have you been? We're supposed to be in the barn in five minutes.'

'I can be ready in five minutes.' I yank off my t-shirt and grab my dress shirt from the hanger.

'He was downstairs talking to Mia,' Sawyer says, standing in front of the mirror, messing with his hair.

'What's up with you two?' Nick asks. 'You almost seemed angry at her last night. You two not getting along?'

'I don't know what you're talking about. I was acting normal last night.'

'You wouldn't even look at her,' Brody says. 'Kate and I thought you guys had a fight.'

'Why is everyone watching me with Mia? We spent a night together. That doesn't make us a couple. We're just friends. Not even that.' I finish buttoning up my shirt and put on my tie. 'And before you ask, nothing happened last night. I slept on the couch.'

'What about last weekend?' Brody asks, leaning against the wall. Mom told us not to sit down or we'd wrinkle our suits and ruin the pictures. But there's no way we're all going to stand for the next two hours or however long the ceremony and pictures take.

When I don't answer Brody's question, Sawyer turns away from the mirror and looks at me. 'Did you do it or not?'

'It's none of your business.'

'He did it,' Nick says.

'Why the hell are we talking about this?' I quickly take off my jeans and toss them on the bed. 'Nick's the one getting married.' I pull on my dress pants. 'We should talk about him. Or Sawyer. He just proposed to Gina.'

'You did?' Nick and Brody say at the same time.

'I didn't propose to her,' Sawyer says, turning back to the mirror. 'She caught me talking to the jewelry designer and thought I was cheating. I had to fess up and tell her I'm having her engagement ring made.'

Nick chuckles. 'So you're next, huh? I thought it'd be Brody, now that he and Kate got a house.'

Sawyer looks back at Brody. 'When are you asking her?'

He shrugs. 'I don't know. I haven't decided.'

'Tell me before you do. We can't be doing it at the same time. You know how girls get when someone takes away their special moment. Actually, Gina probably wouldn't care, but Kate might.'

'Okay, am I good?' I ask, desperate to get off the topic of marriage. How did all these idiots get girlfriends and I'm still single? I must be doing something wrong.

'Yeah, you're good.' Nick walks up to me. 'Be nice to Mia. She drove all this way to help you out.' He continues to the door and we follow him out to the hall and down the stairs.

Nick doesn't understand what's been going on with Mia. None of my brothers do, which is why they shouldn't be giving me advice. They get to be with the girl they want, the one they can see a future with, the one that makes them feel that spark. I'm not that lucky. The girl I want I can't have, so why would I keep acting like she and I are anything more than two people who shared a night together?

When we get to the barn, my parents are there, along with Uncle Mitch and my four cousins. I look for Mia and see her standing off to the side, looking like she feels out of place. I head over to her, but Nash gets there first.

'Hey,' he says, smiling at her. 'You look kind of lonely over here.'

'She's with me,' I say, coming up next to him. 'Mia, this is Nash, my cousin from Chicago.'

Nash shakes her hand. 'It's good to meet you.'

'You too.' She smiles at him.

Nash turns to me. 'I didn't know you had a girlfriend.'

'Mia is just a friend. We met a few months ago at a wedding.'

'Your brother played in the band,' Mia says to Nash. 'He's really good.'

'Austin was there?' Nash asks me.

'Yeah, I didn't know until I saw the band warming up. We talked when they had a break. I'm surprised he didn't tell you.'

'Nash.' Callie walks up to him, holding the baby. 'Can you take her? I need to use the bathroom before the ceremony starts.'

Nash takes the baby, who's all dressed up in a pink dress and little white shoes. 'Babe, this is Mia,' he says to Callie. 'Jason's girlfriend.'

She's not my girlfriend, but hearing Nash call her that is making me have those feelings again, the ones I'm trying to stop.

Mia smiles at Callie. 'Your baby is adorable.'

'Thanks! You can hold her if you want. Sorry to run off, but I really have to go.' She takes off for the bathroom.

'Here.' Nash hands Mia the baby.

'She's beautiful,' Mia says, smiling at the baby. She rocks her side to side. 'What's her name?'

'Addison,' Nash says. 'But we've started to call her Addie.'

'What a pretty name.' Mia's eyes haven't left the baby and she can't stop smiling.

Mia and Nash continue to talk about the baby until Callie returns.

'Okay, I'm back,' Callie says, racing up to Nash. 'We should go take our seats. It's filling up out there.'

Mia hands Callie the baby. 'She's really sweet. Thanks for letting me hold her.'

'Sure! You can hold her again later so I can get a dance or two in with Nash.'

'Two?' He smiles at her. 'We're doing more than that.'

They go out the door to the orchard.

'I should go grab a seat,' Mia says.

'Mia, wait. I need to say something.'

I can't take this any longer. I can't take seeing her sad because of me. I at least need to explain.

'Jason, we need you over here,' Mom says. 'Your Uncle Mitch is taking a few photos for us.'

'Wait there,' I say to Mia.

I hurry over to where my family's lined up and stand between Brody and Sawyer. Mom insists we line up by our ages.

'I thought photos were after the ceremony,' I say to Brody.

'Those are with the photographer. These are just Uncle Mitch taking pictures with his phone.'

'Okay, give me some big smiles,' Uncle Mitch says.

He takes like 30 photos before Mom finally tells him it's enough.

'Well,' Mom says, a big grin on her face. 'I guess it's time.'

'Brody,' Nick says. 'You got the rings, right?'

'No. I thought Jason had them.'

I look at him. 'Why would I have them? The rings were your job.'

'Didn't I give them to you?'

'No.'

Brody searches his suit pockets. 'I don't have them.'

'What the hell?' Nick races up to Brody. 'Are you telling me you lost the rings?'

'What's happening?' Dad says, walking over to us with Mom.

'Brody lost the rings,' Nick says.

'Brody!' Mom says in her scolding tone.

'It's not like I did it on purpose,' he says.

'Okay, everyone just calm down,' Dad says. 'We'll find them. They gotta be around here somewhere.'

'Sawyer,' Nick says. 'Could you go tell the minister we need a few minutes?'

'Sure.' He takes off.

'I'll text Lyndsay to let her know,' Nash says, getting his phone out.

'You're telling her you lost the rings?' I ask. 'You sure you want to do that?'

'I'm telling her people are still being seated and we need more time.' He sends the text, then looks back at Brody. 'Where were you the last time you had the rings?'

'I don't know. I can't remember.'

'I'll check the house,' I say, but instead I go over to Mia.

'What's going on?' she asks.

'Brody lost the rings. They're trying to find them. Can we go in the house for a minute? I need to talk to you.'

'What about the wedding? We're supposed to be out there.'

'It's delayed until we find the rings.'

'Don't you want to help look for them?'

'My brothers can handle it. Come on.' I take her hand, something I haven't done since she got here. She glances at me, like she's not sure what's going on or what I'm going to say. I haven't figured that out myself, but I'm hoping it'll come to me when we get inside.

We go into the house and I take her to the kitchen.

'Mia, I need to apologize.'

'For what?'

'For how I've been acting. You did a really nice thing for me coming to the wedding and making the drive here and I've been treating you like shit.'

'Jason, I don't expect you to treat me like we're dating. I know you just want us to be friends.'

'That's not what I want.' I look her in the eye. 'When I said that, I wasn't being honest. I want us to be more than friends. But we can't. And that's the part I'm struggling with. I finally find the perfect girl and I can't be with her.'

She looks down. 'I'm not perfect.'

'You're perfect for me. You're smart. Kind. Beautiful.' I pause. 'I've been pulling away from you because I don't know how else to deal with these feelings I have for you, how to make them stop.'

'Oh God.' She holds her stomach and runs to the sink.

'What's wrong?'

'I think I'm going to be sick. Could I get some water?'

I race to the cupboard, grab a glass, and meet her at the sink. I fill the glass with water and hand it to her.

'Was it because of what I said?' I ask as she drinks the water.

'No.' She shuts her eyes and takes some deep breaths.

'This is the second time this has happened in a week. Maybe you should go see a doctor.'

'I'll be fine. I just have to wait for it to pass.' She was leaning over the sink but slowly straightens up. She grabs hold of the counter and takes another deep breath.

'Are you okay?'

'Yes. I just felt lightheaded for a moment.'

'Mia, I'm worried. I think I need to take you to a doctor.'

'I don't need a doctor. Just go. Go back to your family.'

'After you almost passed out? Yeah, I don't think so.'

She looks at me. 'Jason, I'm fine. I promise. Just go.'

'I'm not leaving you. Not when you're sick.'

'The wedding's about to start. You have to get out there.'

'Stop worrying about the wedding. Something could be seriously wrong here. When's the last time you felt like this?'

'Jason, please. I don't want to do this now.'

'Do what?'

'Tell you this.'

'Tell me what?'

She looks down.

'Mia, what is it? What are you not telling me?' I put my hand on her arm. 'You're sick, aren't you? It's something serious.'

She doesn't answer, which makes me start to panic.

'Dammit, Mia, just tell me!'

She looks up at me. 'I'm not sick. I'm pregnant.'

'You're what?' I hear Brody's voice and turn back to see my whole family standing there.

'She's pregnant,' Sawyer says.

My family's staring at me, looking as shocked as I feel.

Chapter 14

Jason

'You're pregnant?' I say to Mia.

'Yes.' She glances at my family.

'When?' I say. 'When did you find out?'

'A few weeks ago.'

I back away. 'Mia, what's going on here? Why are you with me when you're pregnant with some guy's baby?'

'Jason, I—'

'What happened to the father? Are you still with him? Does he know?'

'Jason,' Nick says. 'She's telling you—'

'Stay out of this, Nick.' I keep my eyes on Mia. 'Why are you doing this? Why'd you call me up and say you want to see me again when you're having some other guy's kid?'

Mia sighs. 'Jason, I'm four months pregnant, almost five.'

'Yeah? So?'

'Dude, seriously?' Brody says.

I look at him. 'Would you shut up? I'm trying to—'

'It's yours,' Brody says. 'She's telling you the kid is yours.'

I look back at Mia. 'That's not possible. We were together last year. It was last . . .' I stop to think.

'Last January,' Mia says. 'Four months ago. It's yours, Jason. The baby is yours.'

I'm silent. I have no words. I'm too shocked.

Mom races up to us and gives Mia a hug. 'Congratulations! That's wonderful news.' She turns to me. 'Isn't it, Jason?' She's giving me a look like I better respond the right way or she'll yell at me later.

'Yeah. It's good. I just need a minute.' I turn toward the sink, my back to my family as I try to process this. I'm going to be a father. Mia and I are having a baby.

'Let's give them some time alone,' I hear Dad say.

'We can talk later,' Mia rushes to say. 'I don't want to delay the wedding.'

I hear someone coming down the stairs and then Gina's voice. 'I've got the rings. Kate said to give them to you.'

'Shit, that's right,' Brody says. 'I forgot I gave them to her.'

'What's everyone doing in the house?' Gina asks. 'I thought you guys were waiting in the barn.'

'We were looking for the rings,' Nick says.

'And found out we're going to be uncles,' Brody says.

Gina gasps. 'Lyndsay's pregnant? Why didn't she tell me?'

I turn to face my family. 'Lyndsay's not pregnant.'

'I am,' Mia says.

Gina's eyes get huge. 'You and Jason? So this happened when you two—'

'We don't need to get into details,' I say, not wanting to tell my parents their grandchild is the result of a night of too much drinking. They'll figure it out.

'We need to make a decision here,' Dad says. 'We've got people waiting.'

'What do you want to do?' Nick asks me. 'You need some time?'

'No. It's your wedding. We need to get out there. Mia and I will talk later.'

'I'm sorry,' Mia whispers.

Mom hugs her again. 'Honey, you don't need to be sorry. Everything will work out. It always does.' She lets Mia go and turns to me and straightens my tie. 'Go join your brothers.'

My eyes go to Mia's. She's looking at me like she's pleading with me to be okay with this, but I don't know how I feel. I'm mad that she knew all this time and didn't tell me until now. And she only did because I thought she was sick. When was she planning to tell me? Maybe she wasn't going to tell me at all. She could've moved to Boston, had the baby, and never told me it was mine.

'You okay?' Nick asks as we wait in the barn for the ceremony to start.

'Not really, but I don't want to ruin your day.'

'You're not ruining it. You're in shock. I would be too.'

Brody pats me on the back. 'Congratulations. I always knew you'd be first to have a kid.'

'It wasn't supposed to happen this way. I'm not even dating Mia. And she's moving away.' I pause. 'Shit. She's moving away.' I look at Nick. 'When the hell am I going to see my kid?'

'Calm down,' Dad says, coming in front of me. 'Like your mother said, everything will work out. It always does.'

Mom comes into the barn. 'The girls are ready. You boys need to go take your places outside.'

The ceremony is right outside the barn at the top of the hill, overlooking the rows of pink-and-white blooming apple trees. Nick and Lyndsay will say their vows under a wooden arch that Dad made and Mom covered with flowers.

'Jason.' Mom stops me before I go outside. 'This will all work out. I know you might be upset right now, but don't take it out on Mia. Remember it took both of you to make this baby.' She smiles at me. 'I'll see you out there.'

I follow Nick, Sawyer, and Brody outside. The bright sun feels hot beating onto my dark suit. I'm already starting to sweat, or maybe it's my nerves making me sweat. I'm going to be a dad. Holy shit. How did this happen?

We didn't use protection that night, but I assumed Mia was on the pill. She must not have been if she got pregnant. Why didn't she tell me she wasn't on birth control? Why didn't we talk about this? We're both responsible adults, so how could we be so careless?

'And now, for the first time,' the minister says, 'I'd like to present to you Nicholas and Lyndsay Kanfield.'

Shit. I missed the whole ceremony. I was too wrapped up thinking about Mia and the baby and the fact that in a few short months, I'm going to be a dad.

The wedding guests go into the barn where we're serving appetizers and cocktails. The rest of us remain outside for the pictures. I hope it doesn't take long. I really need to talk to Mia.

Just as I'm thinking that, she walks up to me, looking beautiful in her light pink dress, her long dark hair blowing in the breeze. She's the mother of my child. I can't believe this is happening.

'Jason, I think I'm going to go,' she says.

'Go? Mia, no, you can't leave. We need to talk.'

'We can talk later. This is a special day for your family. I don't want them feeling awkward having me here. This should be a celebration.'

'It is, and you being here isn't making anyone feel awkward. My family loves you. Just look at how my mom reacted to the news. She couldn't stop hugging you.'

'And what about you? You haven't said or done anything to let me know how you feel about this.'

'Because I'm not sure. I'm still trying to process it.'

Mia glances behind me. 'The photographer has everyone lined up. You need to get over there.'

I hold her arm. 'Don't leave. You can't. You don't even have your car here.'

'Kate offered to give me a ride back to your apartment.'

'And then what? You're going back to Madison?'

She nods.

'No. Mia, we have to talk about this.'

'You need more time. There's no use talking about it if you haven't accepted it.'

'Jason,' a guy says. I turn and see the photographer coming up to me. 'We're ready for you. If you could just go stand by your brothers?'

'Yeah, I'm coming.' I turn back to Mia. 'Please don't leave. When I'm done with this, we'll go in the house and talk.'

She doesn't agree to it, but she doesn't say no. As I'm walking over to my brothers, I look back and see Mia going into the barn.

'Hey,' I say to Brody. 'Text your girlfriend and tell her not to give Mia a ride.'

'She's leaving?' Brody asks.

'She can't unless someone gives her a ride. Kate told her she would, so you need to stop her.'

'Maybe you should let her go,' Nick says. 'You're not in a good place to be talking to her right now.'

'It can't wait. We're having a baby. We have decisions to make.'

'They don't have to be made today,' Sawyer says.

'Okay, everyone look this way,' the photographer says.

I force a smile on my face, hoping it doesn't look fake. I don't feel like smiling right now, which I know is wrong. I should be happy I'm going to be a dad. I'm just not there yet. All I can think about is how I'm going to see my kid when Mia moves to Boston.

When the photos are done, I go up to Nick. 'Congratulations.' I give him a hug. 'I should've said that sooner.

Sorry, I'm kind of out of it right now. But this is your day and I don't want what happened earlier to take away from it.'

'Don't worry about it. Is Mia still here or did she leave?'

'I don't know. I need to go find out.'

Lyndsay comes up to me, smiling. 'I heard the news. Congratulations!'

'I should be saying that to you.' I give her a hug, then motion to Nick. 'Then again, you're stuck with him for the rest of your life so maybe I shouldn't congratulate you.'

She laughs and goes over to Nick. 'I'm thrilled to be stuck with him.'

He kisses her and doesn't stop.

'Okay, well, I need to go. I'll see you guys inside.'

I leave them in their wedded bliss and hurry to the barn, hoping Mia's there. When I get inside, I look around but don't see her.

Mom notices me searching for her and waves me over to the table where she's sitting with Dad.

I go over there. 'Did Mia leave?'

'She's in the house,' Mom says. 'She wasn't feeling well so I had her lay down in the guest room.'

'What's wrong? Did she get sick again?'

'I think she's just worried she upset you. You need to talk to her.'

'And when you do,' Dad says, 'don't be getting ahead of yourself. You don't need to have everything figured out today. There's plenty of time for that later.'

He's saying that because he knows I have a hard time living in the present. I'm always looking forward, worrying about the future. Like during the wedding, I kept imagining my child growing up without me, being raised by whoever Mia ends up with. It made me angry, and worried that I'd never see my kid. But my dad's right. I shouldn't be thinking that far ahead. I need to focus on what's happening right now.

When I get to the house, I go to the guest room and knock on the door.

'Mia?'

She doesn't answer.

'Mia, are you in there?'

'Yes,' she says in a happy tone that sounds fake. 'I'll be out in a minute.'

'Are you feeling better?'

When she doesn't respond, I open the door. She's lying on the bed, curled up in a ball, crying.

'Mia.' I race up to her. 'What's wrong?'

'Everything.'

'Mia, I'm sorry for how I reacted earlier. I just needed some time.' I wipe the tears from her cheek. 'I'm happy about being a dad.'

'You are?' she asks, sniffling.

'Of course. You know how much I love kids. And now I'm getting my own.'

She sits up. 'But this isn't how you wanted it to happen. It's not how I wanted it either.'

I sit beside her. 'Sometimes life doesn't work out that way. Nash and Callie weren't planning on having kids for a few more years and now they have a daughter.'

'But they're married. That's different.'

'It still wasn't what they planned. And because of the baby, they moved up their wedding. They weren't supposed to get married for another year. The point is, plans change. And I admit, I'm not good with that. I tend to stress out when things don't go the way I was hoping, but I'm going to work on that.'

Mia wipes her eyes. 'Sorry. I cry all the time now. It's the hormones.'

I grab the tissue box from the nightstand and hand it to her.

'Thanks.' She takes a tissue and dabs her eyes.

'Can I ask you something? About that night?'

'I know what you're going to ask, and yes, I was on the pill. But it was a new one I was trying. The doctor said to use a backup method for the first month, but I'd been on it for almost a month when we slept together. I thought I'd be okay.'

'And you really didn't know until a few weeks ago?'

She shakes her head. 'At first, I thought the pill was making me sick so I went off it, but I still didn't feel right. I thought maybe I was tired or stressed. I've never had regular periods so I didn't think anything of it when I missed a few. The reason I finally saw the doctor is because I was really tired and feeling nauseous. I thought I might have the flu. But instead I found out I'm pregnant.'

'Why did you wait to tell me?'

'I only waited a couple weeks. And I needed those weeks to accept that it was really happening. When I finally called you and asked if I could come here, I was ready to tell you.'

I sigh. 'And I made you wait another week. But why didn't you tell me last weekend?'

'I didn't want to take attention away from Nick and Lyndsay's wedding.' She looks down. 'But then I ended up doing it anyway. On their wedding day. I feel terrible about that.'

'You shouldn't. It's not your fault they walked in on us.'

'I didn't want you to know either. I wanted you to have this time with your family before I told you.'

'They're your family too now. We're having a baby.'

Her eyes lift to mine. 'Are you really happy, or are you just saying that to make me feel better?'

'I'm happy. There's just a lot going on in my head right now.'

'Like what?'

'Like what happens when you move away. I don't want to only see my kid once or twice a year.'

'I know you said you'd never leave here, but now, with the baby, would you consider moving?'

'I can't answer that. I need more time to think.' I pause a moment. 'My dad just gave me some good advice. Something I think we could both use.'

'What is it?'

'He said not to look too far into the future. If we do, we'll just worry about stuff we don't need to worry about yet. Why don't we just try to take it a day at a time for now?'

She smiles a little. 'I'd like that.'

'Let's start now. My brother just got married. There's a party going on.' I stand up and offer her my hand. 'Will you join me? You did kind of agree to be my date tonight.'

She takes my hand and gets up from the bed, straightening her dress. 'Do I look okay?'

'You look beautiful. How do you feel?'

'Better. I just need to eat.'

'Let's go.' I take her hand and we walk back to the barn.

Mom smiles when she sees me walking up to the table with Mia.

'Have a seat,' Dad says to us. 'Sawyer and Brody just went to get drinks. The food will be served in a few minutes.'

'Whatever it is, it smells good,' Mia says as we sit down at the long table reserved for the family.

'It's barbecue,' Mom says. 'Nick and Lyndsay's favorite. There's smoked brisket, chicken, pork and all the usual sides. I made the desserts. A little of everything.'

Sawyer and Brody return to the table, each holding a cup of beer.

'Where's mine?' I ask.

'What do you want?' Sawyer says.

'I'm joking. I'll go get it.'

'I can do it. I'm going back there anyway to get Dad's.'

'I'll have the lager.'

He takes off.

'So did you decide when you're heading back?' Mom asks Mia.

She looks at me. 'I'm not sure yet.'

What does she mean? Did she change her mind about leaving tomorrow? I hope she did. Now that I know about the baby, I don't want her to go. I want to spend more time with her. I need more than a couple days with the woman having my baby.

She asked if I'd move with her. It's not what I want. I have a life here, a job, and my family. But if moving means being there for my kid, I might have to consider it.

Chapter 15

Mia

My alarm goes off at seven, the time I set it for when I thought I was going home today. Now I'm considering staying another day. Jason and I need more time to talk and I really like spending time with him.

We had a great time at the wedding reception last night, which I almost didn't go to after accidentally dropping the bomb that I'm pregnant. I still can't believe I did that, that I just blurted it out—and that Jason's whole family heard me say it! The entire scene was a nightmare that could've been even worse if Jason's family wasn't so kind and understanding. Even his parents seemed okay with it, although I'm sure they're not thrilled their son's having a baby with a girl he's not dating who's moving away.

That's what Jason's most upset about—me moving away. I can tell he's excited about being a dad, but he's worried he won't see the baby as much as he wants. I agree that's a problem, but I don't know how to solve it. We're both committed to living in our hometowns, close to our families.

A text pops up on my phone from Nora. *What time are you leaving? Are we still going to brunch?*

I text her back. *I think I might stay.*

My phone rings. It's Nora.

'Hey,' I say, answering the call. 'I probably won't make it to brunch.'

'Why? What happened?'

'I told Jason.'

'And? What did he say?'

'Not much. I think he's still in shock. His brother's wedding was last night so we didn't have much time to talk. That's why I'm thinking of sticking around today.'

'You told him at the wedding?'

'I didn't mean to. You won't believe what happened.' I tell her the story, then wait for her to respond.

She starts laughing.

'Why are you laughing? It's not funny. It was horrible.'

'Sorry, but the part about Jason not figuring out the baby was his? That's funny. I mean, really, why else would you be stalking the guy the past few weeks?'

'I wasn't stalking him.'

'You know what I mean. You've been calling him, asking him to dinner, inviting yourself there. You wouldn't do all that if the kid was someone else's. I thought you said this guy was smart.'

'He is. He just didn't put it together. Or maybe he didn't want to believe it. I didn't either when I found out. He wasn't ready to talk about it last night so we just went on with our evening and had a great time. We danced. Talked to his family. I met some of his friends. It was a perfect night, despite his whole family finding out I'm pregnant.'

'Mia, seriously?' she says, sounding annoyed.

'What?'

'We've been over this a million times.'

'Over what?'

'You can't be falling for this guy. You're supposed to be getting over him and focusing on the baby and getting a job.'

'I have a job.'

'A job in Boston, for when you move.' She pauses. 'You're still moving, right?'

'I have to. My dad keeps having falls at the house and it's only going to get worse the older he gets. Mom can't help him and I don't want some stranger taking care of him. I asked Jason about moving with me, but he didn't want to talk about it. I can't see him leaving. This town and his family are his life.'

'Maybe that'll change now that he's having a kid.'

'I don't think so. I can't see him living in a big city. Anyway, we can talk later. I just wanted to let you know I wouldn't be there for brunch.'

'So if you're staying there, does that mean you're going to introduce Jason to your parents? Do the whole fake engagement thing?'

'No. I'm not going to do that. It's crazy. I don't even think I could pull it off. You know what a terrible liar I am.'

'Don't think of it as lying. Think of it as pretending, or acting, like you're in a play. Didn't you used to act?'

'Yeah, in grade school, and I wasn't very good.'

'I'm sure your acting skills are good enough to convince your parents you're engaged to Jason, especially since you're crazy about the guy.'

'I never said I was crazy about him.'

'You didn't have to. It's obvious just hearing you talk about him.'

Another call pops up on my phone.

'Nora, I have to go. My mom's calling.'

'Okay, talk to you later.'

I switch over to my mom's call. 'Hey, Mom.'

'Hi, honey. We're here!'

'Where?'

'In Wisconsin. We went to—'

'Wait. Hold on. I thought you were getting here tomorrow.'

'No. Today. Didn't you see the email I sent you with our itinerary?'

'Yes, but it was supposed to be tomorrow, the 16th.'

'Honey, today is the 16th.'

'It is?' I quickly check the calendar on my phone. 'Shit. I mean, I guess I got the days mixed up. So where are you right now?'

'On our way to Haydon Falls. After we left the airport in Madison, we went to your apartment but you weren't there. That nice neighbor lady of yours heard us knocking and came out and told us you were in Haydon Falls this weekend. It's so sweet of you to surprise us like this! Your father and I are thrilled you decided to join us on our little getaway! It's been so long since we had a family vacation.'

'Wait. Mom, I wasn't planning to—'

'Are you staying at the same hotel as us? That cute little historic one near the downtown?'

'Um, Mom, could we talk later? I just got up and really have to use the bathroom.'

'Of course! So should we meet somewhere, or what would you like to do?'

'We'll meet somewhere. A restaurant. I'll text you the name.'

'Sounds good! Can't wait to see you!' She ends the call.

What am I going to do? They're on their way here. They think I'm spending the week with them. In Haydon Falls!

'Mia?' Jason knocks on the door. 'Are you up?'

'Yes! Just a minute.' I race to the door and open it.

'Good morning.' He smiles. 'I assumed you were up. I heard you talking.'

'I was on the phone.' I race over to my suitcase and pull out some clothes.

'What's going on?' Jason asks, coming into the room. 'You're leaving already? I thought we'd go to breakfast.'

'I can't. I mean, not with you.'

'What do you mean?'

I toss the clothes I was holding on the bed. 'Where's my phone? I just had it.'

'You just threw it on the bed.'

I look down and see it on top of my clothes. 'Oh.' I pick it up, along with the clothes. 'I need to go shower.' I walk past him, then stop. 'Hey, how much is that historic hotel you told me about? The one near downtown?'

'I don't know. A couple hundred a night?'

'Wow, that's a lot.'

'Why are you asking about the hotel?'

'No reason.' I leave his room.

'Mia, wait.' Jason catches me before I go into the bathroom. 'What's going on?'

'My parents are coming.'

'Yeah, you told me. But why are you in such a hurry?'

'Because they're coming here now. They're on their way. They'll be here in less than an hour.'

'You said they were coming tomorrow.'

'I know. I messed up. I got the dates wrong. Jason, I really need to get ready. I told them I'd meet them for breakfast.'

'Where?'

'I don't know. What's a place that serves breakfast around here?'

'Maury's Chicken Roost.'

I start to text my mom, but stop and look at Jason. 'Did you say Chicken Roost?'

'Yeah. Maury's. They have the best breakfast in town.'

I text the restaurant name to my mom.

'Would you care if I came with?' Jason asks. 'I'd like to meet your parents.'

'No!' I yell it, then smile. 'I mean, I told them it would just be me joining them.'

'Do they know about me?'

'No.'

'And you don't want them to. Is that why you're acting so strange?'

'I'm not acting strange. I'm just in a hurry.' I go into the bathroom and shut the door.

When I'm in the shower, I try to think how to handle this. Do I go to the restaurant and tell my parents I have to go back to Madison? I could say I have to work, although that would be lying since my job doesn't start for another week.

I'm conflicted. I thought my parents wanted to have this time to themselves. I didn't think they wanted me tagging along. But now they're all excited about me being here with them. I hate disappointing them, but how can I be here without running into Jason and his family? It's not possible, and if I see them, I can't just pretend not to know them.

Maybe I should do it. This could be the last vacation I'll have with my parents. But if I do this, I'll have to introduce them to Jason, which means explaining who he is and telling them I'm pregnant. I don't know if I can do that. Telling them I'm pregnant and not even dating the father is going to ruin their trip. It'll ruin the whole week, which was supposed to be a celebration for my graduation.

When I get out of the shower, I get dressed and go to the kitchen where Jason is pouring himself some orange juice.

'You want some?' he asks.

'No, thanks.' I walk up to him. 'Remember how you said you owed me a favor for going to the wedding?'

'Yeah. What about it?'

I can't believe I'm doing this. I'm still not sure I can.

'You said you'd do anything, right?'

'Within reason. Why?'

'You didn't say within reason. You can't add that part now.'

He laughs. 'Mia, what is this about?'

'My parents don't know that I'm pregnant. I was going to tell them after my graduation, but I don't think I can wait. They'll want to know who the father is and since you're here, and they're here, and I'm here, I thought I'd introduce you to them.'

'Okay. But that's not doing you a favor. I'm happy to meet your parents. I want to.'

'Yeah, um, that's not really the favor part.'

'Then what is it? What do you want me to do?'

'I need you to pretend to be my fiancé.'

'Fiancé? We're not even dating.'

'But my parents don't know that.'

'Why would you lie to them?'

'Because they're old-fashioned. They grew up during a time when people got married and then had kids. They expected me to do the same. I don't want them knowing I hooked up with you at a wedding and haven't seen you in months. I was going to tell them we've been dating this whole time.' I pause. 'And maybe part of last year.'

Jason laughs. 'You're kidding, right? This is some kind of joke?'

'It's not a joke. I need you to do this.' I clutch his arm. 'I'm begging you to. If you knew my parents, you'd understand.'

'I'm sure they know things have changed since they were our age. People have kids outside of marriage all the time.'

'Yes, I know, but it's not what they wanted for their only daughter. Jason, you said you'd do anything if I went to your brother's wedding. I did my part of the deal. I'm asking you to do yours.'

He goes past me to the living room, rubbing his jaw. 'So what happens when you leave at the end of the summer?'

'I'll tell them we broke up. I'll say we tried to make it work but it didn't.'

He shakes his head. 'I don't know, Mia. I don't like this. I think you should just tell them the truth.'

'And break their hearts?' I walk over to him. 'Jason, I've seen how much you love your parents. If you knew something would hurt them and disappoint them, but there was a way to avoid all that, wouldn't you do it?'

'Maybe. But I'd be more likely to tell them the truth.'

'Think about that house you bought with Brody. You said you didn't tell your parents you helped your brother buy it because you didn't want them finding out he couldn't buy it on his own. Because you knew it would upset them to know he was in a lot of debt. You were protecting them.'

He sighs. 'Okay, yeah, but it's not the same as making up some fake engagement.'

'It's not that different. I'm trying to protect my parents because I know how they'd feel if they knew the truth.'

He looks down and doesn't say anything.

My phone dings with a text. 'My mom says they'll meet me there in a half hour. I'm going to go finish getting ready, then pack up.'

'You're leaving?' Jason looks up. 'You're going back to Madison?'

I nod. 'After breakfast. My parents want me to stay and spend the week with them but it's too risky. I'd end up running into your family and then I'd have to tell my parents everything. I'm just going to go with my original plan of telling them I'm pregnant right before they leave.'

'What are you going to tell them about the father?'

'I haven't decided, but I'll figure it out.' I go back to the bathroom to dry my hair and do my makeup. Then I go into the bedroom and pack up my things. I take my suitcase out to the living room and see Jason sitting on the couch.

'Bye, Jason.' I walk to the door.

'Wait.' He jumps up. 'I'll walk you out.'

'You don't have to.' I don't want him to because I'm pretty sure I'll burst into tears when I get past the door. I really thought he'd do this for me. But he won't, and now I have to tell my parents I'm leaving and can't spend the week with them.

Jason goes with me to my car. He puts my suitcase in the trunk, but doesn't close it.

'Jason, I need to hurry. I'm going to be late.'

He closes the trunk and walks up to me. 'What would I tell my family? If we did this?'

'You don't have to tell them anything. My parents don't live here, and as long as we keep them away from your parents this week, they never have to know.'

'What if your parents want to meet mine?'

I take a moment to think. 'We could tell them we haven't told your parents yet. We could say we just got engaged and that you wanted to wait to tell them about the baby.'

'They might still want to meet them.'

'Then we'll say they're sick and aren't up to entertaining.'

'This is never going to work.'

'My parents aren't going to be here that long. Their hotel is here, but during the day they'll be driving to other small towns. They're only planning to spend a day here. And on Friday, they're going to Madison. They sent me their itinerary. They've got every day already planned. There's very little chance they'll run into your parents.'

He checks his watch. 'I need to clean up. I'll meet you there.'

'Really? You'll really do this?'

He shrugs. 'I owe you. I have to pay you back.'

'Thank you!' I hug him, then get in the car. 'I'll see you soon!'

Driving there, I get nervous, still not confident in my acting skills. And I'm not sure if Jason's a good actor. But there's no turning back now. We're doing this.

When I get to the restaurant, I wait in the car and get out my phone to text my mom.

Someone taps on my window. 'Mia!'

I look up and see my mom there, a huge smile on her narrow face. She's lost weight the past couple years, worrying about my dad. She's almost too thin now. It makes her look older.

'Mom!' I get out of the car and give her a hug. 'Where's Dad?'

'In the restaurant. He thought you might be waiting in there.'

My mom looks me up and down. 'You look good, honey.'

'Thanks! Let's go find Dad.'

We go into the restaurant and I see my dad sitting at one of the tables. He waves us over as he slowly gets up from his chair. He looks the same as he did at Christmas, which is good. I thought he might've lost weight after the hip surgery.

'Hey, Dad.' I give him a hug. 'How's the new hip?'

'Good enough that I walked in here without a cane.'

My mom huffs. 'I told him to use it, but you know how your father is. He never listens to me.'

The waitress comes by as we take our seats. 'Can I get you some coffee? Juice?'

We give her our drink order.

'Oh, and one more person is coming,' I say.

She nods and walks off.

'Someone's joining us?' my mom asks.

'Yes.' I smile. 'I'll explain when he gets here.'

'He?' My mom looks at my dad. 'I think Mia might be courting someone.'

Courting. If Jason heard that, he'd get what I mean when I say they're old-fashioned.

'The boy lives here?' my dad says in a loud voice. 'Why would you be seeing someone who lives an hour away?'

My mom pats his hand. 'Quiet down. She said she'll explain when he gets here.'

'How was your flight?' I ask, knowing that topic can fill at least 20 minutes. My parents can take something as simple as an airline trip and talk about it forever.

They're just finishing up telling me about the lady who was seated next to them when Jason arrives. He's all cleaned up and looks extremely handsome in a pair of dark jeans and a light blue dress shirt with the sleeves rolled up. And he wore a nice pair of brown leather shoes.

'You made it,' I say, smiling at him.

He smiles back, then smiles at my parents. 'Hi, I'm Jason Kanfield.'

He used his last name. That's good. My parents like it when people introduce themselves with their full name.

'Walter Daniels,' my dad says, rising up to shake Jason's hand.

'And I'm Harriott,' my mom says, shaking Jason's hand. 'Mia's mother.'

'It's nice to meet you.' Jason sits down beside me, giving me a look like he's not sure what to do next.

'I was waiting until you got here to tell my parents about you,' I say.

My mom's brows rise. 'And what is it you'd like us to know?'

I smile at Jason, then look back at my parents. 'Jason and I are dating. We have been since last fall. I didn't tell you because I didn't want to get your hopes up.' I laugh a little. 'You two always think I'll end up marrying whoever I date so I thought it'd be better if I waited until Jason and I became more serious.'

He puts his arm around me and I scoot closer to him.

'So you two are serious?' my mom asks.

'We are,' Jason says.

'I don't understand,' my dad says. 'How does this work with you living here and her living in Madison?'

'We've made it work,' I say, gazing lovingly at Jason. 'When you really love someone you find a way.'

'Walter, did you hear that?' my mom says. 'Our daughter's in love!'

My mom's beaming, she's so excited. As for my dad? His brows are furrowed and he's eyeing Jason like he's going to have to prove he's good enough for me. I knew my dad would react that way. He's very protective of me. But I'm confident Jason can win him over. He won me over the first night I met him.

'Mom. Dad. I know you might think this is soon,' I say, 'but like you always told me, when you know, you know. And Jason and I know we're right for each other.'

My mom gasps. 'Mia, are you . . .' She waits for me to say it.

Jason beats me to it. 'Mia and I are engaged.'

Chapter 16

Mia

'Oh my goodness.' My mom claps her hands. 'This is wonderful!'

'What are you so excited about?' my dad says. 'We don't even know the kid. For all we know, he's some deadbeat.'

'I can assure you,' Jason says with a smile. 'I'm not a deadbeat. I'm a high school science teacher and baseball coach.'

'See Dad?' I say. 'That's something you and Jason have in common. You love baseball!'

He grumbles something under his breath.

'When's the wedding?' my mom asks, her eyes bouncing between Jason and me. I don't think I've ever seen her this excited. I'm hoping her excitement about the engagement will overtake any disappointment she'll feel when she finds out I'm pregnant.

'We don't know yet,' I say. 'We haven't picked a date.'

'Let me see the ring.' My mom looks at my hand.

'We don't have it yet. It's at the jeweler's being sized.'

'I bet it's beautiful,' my mom gushes.

The waitress comes by with our drinks. 'Hey, Jason.' She smiles at him. 'How was Nick's wedding last night?'

'It was good.' He picks up his menu and looks through it.

'I bet it was pretty at the orchard with all the trees in bloom.'

'What orchard?' my mom asks. 'Is it that one in town? The one everyone talks about?'

'Yeah,' the waitress says. 'Kanfield Orchard. Jason's parents own it. His brother got married there last night.'

'Perhaps you two should get married there too,' my mom says to Jason and me. 'Oh, Walter, we have to go see it today!'

'What do you mean?' the waitress says. 'Jason's not—'

'We should order,' Jason says, interrupting her. 'I'd suggest the pancakes, but the omelets are good too.'

Mom smiles at the waitress and points to Jason and me. 'They just told us that they're engaged! We're beyond the moon happy about it, aren't we Walter?'

He grunts and picks up his coffee.

'What are you talking about?' The waitress laughs. 'Jason's not engaged.'

Jason clears his throat. 'Actually, I am.' He gives me a look like this plan is already turning into a disaster. But it's just the waitress. She's not going to tell anyone.

'You're engaged?' the waitress says to Jason. 'I didn't even know you were dating anyone.'

'Hi.' I turn to the waitress. 'I'm Mia. Jason's fiancé.'

She gives me a confused look. 'I don't get it. I've never seen you before. And just a few weeks ago Jason was going out with—'

'A friend,' Jason says. 'I was out with a friend.' He puts his arm around me. 'You haven't seen Mia because she lives in Madison. I usually go there to see her instead of having her come here.'

'Oh.' The waitress eyes him like she doesn't believe him. 'Well, congratulations!'

'Are we gonna order?' my dad says as he looks at the menu. 'I've gotta eat. Gotta take my pill.'

'Yes, dear, we know you have to eat,' my mom says as she scans the menu. 'I'll go with Jason's suggestion and get the pancakes.'

'I will too,' I say.

'I want eggs and bacon,' my dad says, setting his menu down.

'And for you, Jason?' the waitress asks.

'I'll have the usual.'

She nods and takes off for the kitchen.

My mom grabs my hand and gives it a squeeze. 'I'm so happy for you, honey. I just wish you'd told us about Jason sooner. Where did you two meet?'

I glance at Jason as I try to come up with a story.

'The orchard,' he blurts out. 'Mia was there last fall with her friend.'

'Nora,' I say. 'Mom, you remember Nora. You met her last summer.'

'Yes, the professor with the big hair and big glasses.'

'Yeah, that's her. Anyway, we went to the orchard to pick apples and Jason was there.'

'I was driving the tractor,' he says. 'Taking people to the fields.'

'You can drive a tractor?' my dad asks, sounding slightly impressed. He used to be an engineer, but he grew up on a farm in Vermont. He talks about it all the time. Sometimes I think he would've been happier being a farmer than an engineer.

'I've been driving it since I was a teenager,' Jason says. 'My brothers and I always had to pitch in at the orchard in the fall. We still do.'

'That orchard is quite well known,' my mom says. 'Even our friends back in Boston had heard of it. They saw it mentioned in some of the travel magazines.'

Jason nods. 'Yeah, we get a lot of media coverage, especially in the fall.'

'Your parents are still running it?' my dad asks.

'They help out, but Nick, my older brother, took it over last summer.'

'We'll have to meet your parents while we're here,' my mom says. 'Maybe today!'

Jason gives me that look again, the one that says this is getting out of control.

'They aren't feeling well,' I say to my mom. 'Jason talked to them this morning and it sounds like they might have the flu.'

My mom frowns. 'Oh, that's a shame. Perhaps they'd be up for a phone call.'

'You ever been to Boston?' my dad asks Jason.

'No, I never have.'

'Hope you've saved up some money. Houses there are going through the roof.'

'Walter, don't be so negative,' my mom says. 'I'm sure they'll find something that's more reasonably priced.'

Jason clears his throat, like he's signaling me to tell them we haven't decided we're living in Boston. But why tell them that? It would just upset them, and it's not like any of this is real. When our fake engagement ends, I'll go to Boston and Jason will stay here.

Two women race up to Jason, a younger woman with blonde hair and an older lady with dark hair.

'Is it true?' the blonde woman asks. 'Are you really getting married?'

'Um, yeah.' Jason sits up straighter, giving me that look again.

'When did this happen?' the older woman asks.

'Recently,' I answer. 'We haven't told many people yet.'

The older woman laughs. 'You don't have to. In a town this size, everyone will know by the end of the day. And you're the lucky lady, I assume?'

'I am. Mia Daniels.'

The waitress comes back with our food. 'Can you believe it?' she says to the two women who remain next to Jason. 'Another Kanfield boy, taken.'

'There's none left,' the blonde woman says. 'I heard Sawyer's going to propose to Gina soon. Brody will be after that.'

'Can we eat without all this chatter going on?' my dad says.

'Oh, sorry,' the waitress says with a laugh. She leaves, along with the other two women.

'Who were they?' I ask Jason.

'Sorry, I should've introduced you. They're teachers at the high school.'

'Mia loved teaching,' my mom says to Jason as she pours syrup on her pancakes. 'I think she's going to miss it in her new job.'

'You got a job?' Jason asks me.

'No. She means when I get one. But Mom, I'll still be working with students, just in a different way.'

'This food isn't too bad,' my dad mutters, stuffing a piece of bacon in his mouth.

'It's wonderful,' my mom says. 'These are the best pancakes I've ever had.'

'We eat well in Haydon Falls,' Jason jokes.

'Hey, I didn't know you'd be here,' I hear someone say.

I look back and see Brody and Sawyer walking up to our table. Oh, no. This isn't good. This is bad. Very, very bad.

'Hey,' Jason says to his brothers. 'We're having breakfast. I'll talk to you guys later.'

'Are you two Jason's brothers?' my mom asks. 'Because you sure look like him.'

'I like to think I'm better looking,' Sawyer kids. 'But yeah, that's us. I'm Sawyer and this idiot is Brody.' He points to him.

'Are Gina and Kate with you?' I ask.

'No, they wanted to sleep in,' Brody says. 'We wanted to eat and neither of us has food at our place.'

'We're Mia's parents,' my mom says to them. 'Mia and Jason just told us their news. It was certainly a surprise, but we're beyond thrilled!'

'Our parents are too,' Sawyer says. 'This will be their first grandchild.'

I freeze, my fork held over my plate. My parents weren't supposed to know about the baby yet. I was going to let the engagement news sink in before I told them.

'Grandchild?' my mom says, sounding confused.

I feel Jason staring at me. He's waiting for me to say something, but I can't come up with any words.

'You didn't know?' Sawyer says. 'Shit.'

Brody shoves him. 'Now who's the idiot?'

Sawyer turns to Brody. 'How was I supposed to know what she's talking about? She said they told them the news.'

'I was referring to their engagement,' my mom says. 'Mia, are you having a baby?'

I slowly lift my eyes to hers. 'Yes.'

'Wait—you guys are engaged?' Brody says. 'When did that happen?'

'It doesn't matter,' Jason says. 'Would you guys get out of here?'

My dad points to Jason. 'I knew you were trouble! Getting my daughter pregnant before you've even married her?' He huffs. 'It's a disgrace!'

'Oh, Walter, calm down.' My mom pats his hand. 'You know these things happen. It's not like back in our day.' She gives me a weak smile, which tells me she feels the same way as my dad but is trying to be okay with it. 'It's wonderful news. I assume you'll get married before the baby arrives?'

'Um, I don't know,' I say, glancing at Jason. 'We still have a lot to talk about.'

'Do Mom and Dad know?' Sawyer asks Jason.

'Would you get out of here?' Jason says. 'We're trying to have breakfast.'

Brody laughs. 'If they don't know, they're about to find out.'

Jason turns back and sees his parents talking to the girl at the hostess stand. 'What are they doing here? Did you know they were coming?'

'We weren't sure,' Sawyer says. 'They said they might.'

Martha squeals so loud we can hear it at the table.

'Mom knows,' Brody says, laughing.

'Great,' Jason mutters, sinking back in his chair.

I lean over to him. 'I'm so sorry.'

'Those are your parents?' my mom asks. 'I thought they had the flu.'

'The flu?' Sawyer says. 'Who told you that?'

'Mom!' Brody says, waving her over. 'He's over here.'

'I'm going to kill you,' Jason says under his breath.

Martha and Carl make their way to our table.

'I just heard the news!' Martha says to Jason and me. 'It's wonderful! I'm just so surprised.'

'It does seem a little soon,' Carl says, 'being that you two haven't known each other long.'

'It's been almost a year,' my mom says. 'I think that's plenty of time.' She gets up from her chair. 'Hello, I'm Harriott, Mia's mother. And that's my husband, Walter.'

Martha shakes my mom's hand. 'Welcome to Haydon Falls. I'm Martha, Jason's mom, and that's Carl, his dad.'

'Good to meet you.' Carl shakes my mom's hand, then goes around the table to shake my dad's.

'Sorry I can't get up,' my dad says. 'Had hip surgery awhile back and I'm still taking it slow.'

'I know what you mean,' Carl says. 'I had heart surgery last summer. I'm still running slower than I used to.'

'Heart surgery, huh?' my dad says. 'You have a heart attack?'

Carl nods. 'I did. Got to the hospital and had surgery a few days later.'

'You have that surgery where they saw you open?'

'Dad,' I say, feeling embarrassed. He loves talking about health problems and procedures. He didn't used to. It started when he retired and needed something to talk about. 'Maybe Carl doesn't want to talk about his surgery.'

'He doesn't mind,' Martha says, waving her hand toward him. 'He tells everyone about it.'

'Why don't we see if we could move to a larger table,' my mom says. 'So you all could join us.'

'Yes, let's do that,' Martha says. She catches the hostess going by. 'Ann, do you mind if we take the table in back? We'd all like to sit together.'

Ann smiles at her. 'It's all yours, Mrs. Kanfield. Just go ahead and go back there. I'll get the plates.'

'Thank you.' Martha goes around the table. 'Follow me.'

We all get up.

'Guess we're all having breakfast,' Sawyer says, smiling at Jason.

'Guess so.'

As everyone moves to the larger table, Jason pulls me aside. 'You see why I didn't want to do this?' he whispers. 'Now my family thinks we're engaged.'

'At least they seem happy about it,' I say, trying to stay positive.

'Mia, this is a disaster and it's only going to get worse. Your parents are already pressuring us to get married before the baby arrives.'

'That doesn't mean we're going to. I'll talk to them. I'll explain that we'll be picking the wedding date, not them.'

'What about Boston? They're acting like we should be going there, picking out a house. Soon!'

'I'll talk to them about that too.' I hold onto his arm. 'Jason, relax. They're just excited. Did you see how happy they were when I told them we were engaged?'

'Your mom was. Your dad looked like he wanted to kill me.'

'He just has to get to know you. He takes awhile to warm up to people, especially men I'm dating. We need to get back to the table.'

'Yeah, before they have the whole damn wedding planned,' Jason mutters.

I know he's stressed about this, but it would've been even more stressful if I'd told my parents he's the father of my baby and we aren't even dating. At least now they think we're together. I haven't yet figured out how I'll tell them we broke up, but I'm taking this a day at a time. I'm sure I'll come up with something by the end of August when I move back to Boston.

'We were just talking about your living arrangement,' Martha says as Jason and I sit down at the table. 'Harriott was saying Mia's summer job can be done from anywhere.'

'It doesn't make sense for you to stay in Madison,' my mom says to me. 'You need to move here and be with Jason.'

'Oh, no, I don't think that's a good idea,' I say. 'I already have my apartment in Madison. I don't want to find an apartment here and sign a lease just for the summer.'

'You wouldn't,' my mom says. 'You'd live with Jason.'

'Before I'm married? But Mom, you always said—'

'To not live with a boy before marriage,' she says. 'But given the circumstances, with you two expecting a child, your father and I won't object to you living with him.'

'Speak for yourself,' my dad says. 'I still don't think it's right.'

My mom glances at him, then back at me. 'Have you and Jason discussed this?'

'Yes, and we—'

'Agree it's a good idea,' Jason says.

I stare at him. What is he doing? We didn't agree to this.

'We haven't moved in together yet because we didn't want to upset anyone,' he says, 'but if everyone's okay with it, then we're good with it too.'

I'm still staring at him, but he won't look at me.

'Your apartment is far too small for the two of you,' Martha says. 'You should find something larger.'

'They could live in the Carson house,' Brody says.

'That's an excellent idea,' Carl says. 'It's a house we got with some land we bought,' he explains to my parents. 'Martha's nephew works construction and fixed it up last fall. It'd be perfect for them.'

'It's a beautiful old farmhouse,' Martha says to my mom. 'You'll have to come see it.'

'Perhaps after breakfast,' my mom says.

They make plans to go there, insisting Jason and I go too. To our new home. The house we'll be sharing for the summer.

Why did Jason agree to this? Did he think he had to, to make our story more believable? I don't know why else he'd agreed to it.

This whole thing was a bad idea. The engagement was just supposed to be a little white lie to help my parents accept the pregnancy. But now Jason's family knows and soon the whole town will. Whenever we go out, we'll have to act like a couple. What was going to just be a day or two of pretending to be engaged is now going to last the whole summer.

I really messed this up.

Chapter 17

Jason

'What a beautiful home,' Harriott says as we go into the Carson house. I shouldn't call it that anymore since now it's mine, at least for the summer.

Mia's probably angry at me for saying we'd live together, but I was thinking about it, and if we're really pretending to be engaged, it doesn't make sense that we'd live apart. Her job is the only thing keeping her in Madison, but that excuse went away when her mom said Mia could work remotely. So when Harriott gave us her blessing to live together, I ran with it. I decided it'd be good for us to live together. If we're going to be parents, we need to get to know each other better and living together will force us to do that.

And I want to live with Mia. I want to help her through the pregnancy, go to doctor's appointments with her, get her whatever food she's craving, and just be there for her. This may be the only chance I have to do this. Given my dating history, I may end up single for the rest of my life. This might be the only child I have, so I want to be part of this. I don't want to be left out. I want to be with Mia during the pregnancy, even if she's mad at me for it.

We haven't talked since leaving the restaurant. She drove here in her car and I took my truck. We got here at the same time, but Mia raced inside the house with her mom. I think she's avoiding me, but she can't do it forever. We need to talk about this.

'Oh, honey, isn't it lovely?' Harriott asks Mia as she looks around.

'Yes, it's really nice. I love how it's decorated.'

'Kate did that,' Mom says. 'After Nash finished renovating the house, we added some furniture but nothing decorative. Then Brody started dating Kate and she couldn't wait to add her touch to the place. I think she did a wonderful job.'

'And they didn't want to live here?' Harriott asks. 'Your son and his girlfriend?'

'Brody and Kate already have a house, close to downtown.' Mom heads to the stairs. 'Let's go upstairs. I'll show you the bedrooms.'

Harriott walks to the stairs, then looks behind her. 'Where in the world did Walter go?'

'He's outside with Carl,' Mom says. 'I believe Carl is showing him the land he plans to convert to more pumpkin fields.' She sighs. 'I swear that man just keeps making this place more work.'

Harriott laughs. 'Men. Sometimes I wonder if they're worth all the headaches they cause us.'

'You two go ahead,' Mia tells them as they go upstairs. 'I'll be up later.' She waits until they're gone, then turns to me. 'I guess this is our house now.'

I go up to her, keeping my voice down. 'Mia, I know you're angry, but if you just let me explain.'

'I'm not angry. It was a good idea. People are more likely to believe this is real if we're living together. I just wasn't prepared for this. I'm going to have to get rid of my apartment, move all my stuff.'

'I'll help you with that. Whatever you need. I'm your fiancé. It's my job to help you out.'

'Only if this was real. Jason, I don't want you feeling obligated to do things for me now that we're in this situation. Nothing has to change. Well, other than our living arrangements.'

'Mia, everything's going to change. This is our life now. We have to act the part. Everywhere we go.' I take her hand. 'We have to act like a real couple.'

She looks down at our joined hands. 'Do you think you can do this for the whole summer?'

'Yeah. Can you?'

'I can. I just—'

'Just what?'

She shakes her head. 'Nothing.'

She's having doubts. I am too, but we're stuck in this now. Our only way out of it is telling the truth, and Mia doesn't want to do that. I don't either. I kind of like the idea of having a whole summer with her, even knowing it's going to make it that much harder when she leaves.

'Now that we're going to be living together, I want to be part of this.' I glance at her stomach. 'I want to be part of the pregnancy. I want to go to doctor's appointments with you, shop for baby stuff, and whatever else dads do.'

She turns and walks away from me. 'Jason, I don't think that's a good idea.'

'Why?' I go over to her. 'I'm the father. Why can't I be involved? Why wouldn't you want me to be? Do you really want to do all this alone when I'm right here?'

She looks at me a moment. 'You really want to go to appointments with me? And look at baby stuff?'

'More than anything.'

She smiles slightly. 'Okay.'

I hear my mom talking at the top of the stairs.

'You want to give them a show?' I ask Mia.

'What do you mean?'

'Our moms are coming back. We should kiss. Show them how in love we are.'

She hesitates, then quickly nods as we hear our moms walking down the stairs.

I take Mia in my arms and kiss her. It's an innocent kiss, no tongue, but still manages to stir up feelings in me.

How am I going to do this? How am I going to live with a girl I've completely fallen for, am insanely attracted to, and who's carrying my baby, and act like we're just friends? I can kiss her when we're out in public, and hold her hand, but it won't be real. We'll be putting on an act. What's going to happen when we're here, alone together? Can we really go all summer without something happening?

'Oh, would you look at those two?' Harriott says. 'Aren't they just darling? I remember when Walter and I were like that.'

Mia backs away from me. 'Mom.' She turns to her. 'I thought you were upstairs.'

'I was. Martha showed me the bedrooms. You should go up and see them.'

'I'll go with you,' I say, taking Mia's hand.

As we go up the stairs, I hear Harriett say, 'Maybe we shouldn't be sending them up there if they can't even keep their hands off each other down here in the kitchen.'

Mom laughs. 'I think it's too late to worry about that. She's already expecting.'

'Yes, that's true,' Harriott says, laughing with Mom.

It sounds like they're getting along. I wasn't sure if they would. I thought they'd be too different. My mom's not as strict as Mia's mom. She accepts that her kids do stuff she may not approve of, like Brody and me going out with a different girl every week, which we did for awhile a few years ago. My brothers and I have done plenty of stuff Mom doesn't like, but she still loves and accepts us.

'What do you think?' I say, taking Mia into the master bedroom. It's got a queen-sized bed with a black iron headboard and white down comforter. There's a nightstand on each side of the bed and an antique trunk at the end that's filled with extra blankets.

'I love it,' Mia says, walking around the room. 'Is it mine?'

'Well, yeah. Or . . . ours.'

'Ours?'

I walk over to her. 'We need to talk about this. The separate bedroom thing. If we do that, we risk the chance of one of my family members stopping by unannounced and finding out we're not sleeping together.'

'That would be bad.' She pauses. 'Do you really think they'd stop by unannounced?'

I laugh. 'Have you met my family?'

She laughs too. 'Yeah, I guess I could see that.'

'So what do you want to do?'

She glances at the bed, then back at me. 'I guess this is our room.'

Our room. The one we're sharing. At night. Together in the bed.

This is going to be impossible. How am I going to keep my hands off her? How are we going to go all summer without acting on our attraction to each other? We couldn't even make it through last weekend without having sex. And now Mia agreed to share a bed with me. What does that mean? That she wants to continue this pretend engagement when we're alone? I'm not sure how I feel about that. I want to be intimate with her, but I also know it'll make me more attached to her, which isn't what I want when I know she's leaving.

'Mia,' Harriott yells from downstairs. 'Your father and I are going to go check into the hotel.'

Mia races out of the room and down the stairs. I follow behind and see Walter and Harriott standing by the door.

'You're leaving?' Mia asks, going up to her parents.

'Your father's tired from the trip. We're going to check into the hotel so he can rest.'

'I'll go with you.' She looks back at me. 'I'll text you when I'm heading back to your place. If you're not there, I'll just go wait somewhere.'

'You don't have a key?' Walter scowls at me. 'You should give her a damn key. What's wrong with you? You don't trust my daughter?'

'Dad, of course he does,' Mia says as she goes around him to open the door. 'I just haven't been here enough to need one. Let's go. I'll meet you guys at the hotel.'

'Aren't you going to say goodbye to your fiancé?' Harriott says.

'Bye!' She gives me a wave.

'Mia, that's not how you say goodbye. Go give him a proper goodbye.'

Her eyes pause on mine, then she quickly walks over to me and gives me a hug. When she pulls back, I hold onto her and give her a kiss. 'Bye. I'll see you soon.'

Mia and her parents leave.

'I'm going to head out too,' I say, walking to the door.

'Not so fast,' Dad says in a stern tone.

I turn back and see him giving me the look he gave me when I was a kid, the one he used when I was in trouble.

Shit. They know the engagement is fake. I thought they believed it. They acted like they did back at the restaurant.

'What do you need?' I ask, as if I have no idea what this is about.

Dad points to the couch. 'Have a seat.'

'Dad, I really don't have time—'

'We either do this now or we do it later. What's it going to be?'

I want to say later, but I'd rather just get this over with. I walk over to the couch and sit down. My parents sit across from me on the leather chairs. I feel like I'm on trial. In a way, I am. They know this is all a lie and they're going to make me sit here until I admit it.

'It wasn't supposed to turn into this,' I say with a sigh.

'Jason, what the hell is going on here?' Dad says, raising his voice. He rarely does that, which tells me he's furious. 'Lying to people? Making up crazy stories?'

'I don't understand. If you knew it wasn't real, why'd you act like it was back at the restaurant? Saying I should live with Mia in this house? Taking her parents here? Why would you do that if you didn't believe it was real?'

'Because for a moment there, we thought it was,' Dad says. 'That show you put on was pretty damn convincing. But on the drive over here, your mother and I came to our senses and realized it was all a hoax. Some girl shows up in town and suddenly you're engaged?' He huffs. 'You really think we'd believe that?'

'She's not just some girl. I met her at Noah's wedding. I told you about her.'

'After the wedding, yes, but that was it. You didn't mention her again until she showed up in town.'

'Lying to people is not how you were raised,' Mom says. 'Why would you do something like this?'

'It was Mia's idea. She was afraid her parents would be upset if they found out we weren't together. They're old-fashioned. They think you have to be married to have a baby.'

Mom smiles a little. 'I will say we're very happy about the baby. I can't wait to be a grandma!'

Dad looks at her. 'Martha, we talked about this on the way over. Don't be getting soft on me because of the baby.'

Mom shuts down her smile and looks back at me. 'Your father and I think you should call this off now before things get out of hand.'

'I can't. I told Mia I'd do this, and now it's done. And you saw how happy her parents were. They would've been devastated if they'd found out she was pregnant and alone.'

'So how exactly does this end?' Dad asks, folding his arms over his chest. 'You planning to actually marry her?'

'No. It'll end when she leaves. She'll tell her parents it didn't work out and we called off the engagement. By then her parents will have had time to accept the pregnancy and get excited about it, which will hopefully help them get over the disappointment of us not getting married. And Mia will probably have a job by then, and an apartment, so they won't have to worry about her, or they'll worry less than they would now when things are more uncertain.'

'What do you mean when she leaves?' Mom asks. 'She's really not staying here?'

'You heard what she said at breakfast. She's moving back to Boston at the end of August.'

Dad's brows furrow. 'And you're okay with this? With your child living on the other side of the country?'

'No, but what am I going to do? I'm not leaving Haydon Falls. My life is here.'

Dad glances at Mom, then back at me. 'You and Mia have talked about this? And neither one of you is willing to move?'

'She can't. She needs to take care of her parents. Her mom's in good health, but her dad's health isn't very good. You saw how hard it is for him to get around. Mia wants to be close to them to help them out. And I want to be close to you and Mom. It doesn't work for either of us to move.'

Dad rubs his hand over his jaw and glances at Mom again. 'I still don't think this is right. You're messing with people's lives here, including your own.'

'Yeah, well, this wasn't supposed to happen. We were only going to tell Mia's parents about the engagement. Nobody else was supposed to know.'

'You really thought that was possible in a town this size? After that show you put on at the restaurant, everyone in town probably knows by now. How are you going to explain this to people?'

'I don't know. I haven't figured that out yet.'

'You were going on dates with other girls just a few weeks ago,' Mom says. 'And now you're engaged and having a baby? Just think how that looks.'

'You always told me not to worry about what other people think.'

'Yes, but you're a teacher, Jason. Your students look up to you. What are you going to tell them?'

'I don't know. I haven't thought about it. I haven't thought about any of this because this wasn't supposed to happen.'

Dad shakes his head. 'Maybe next time you'll think of these things before getting yourself into messes like this.'

'Are we done here? I need to get back to the apartment in case Mia shows up.'

The door opens and Brody walks in, with Sawyer right behind him. They both have huge grins on their faces.

'What are you two doing here?' Dad asks.

'We came to congratulate the groom,' Sawyer says, laughing. 'So Jason, when's the big day?'

'Shut up,' I say, because it's not funny. My parents are right. This is a fucking mess.

'Is she really pregnant?' Brody asks, laughing. 'Or did you guys make that up too?'

'Why would we make that up? You saw how upset Mia was when she told me. And we didn't know you guys were standing there. We weren't putting on a show.'

'Boys, this isn't funny,' Dad says. 'Everyone in town is going to be asking us about this, and until we figure out how to handle it, I want you both to keep quiet. Just tell people this is a family matter and leave it at that.'

'Like that's going to work,' Brody says. 'That'll just make people come up with their own story, which is always worse than the truth.'

'How are we going to explain Jason going on dates the whole time his girl's been knocked up?' Sawyer asks.

'You don't,' Dad says. 'You keep your mouth shut. Let them make up stories about us, if that's what they want to do. It's not like it hasn't been done before.'

'Are you really living here?' Brody asks me.

'Just for the summer,' I tell him.

'Unless he comes to his senses and tells the truth,' Dad says.

'I'm not doing that,' I say. 'I told Mia I'd do this and I'm not going back on my word.'

I'm not telling him the other reason I'm doing this, which is to be with Mia. He'd tell me I'm being stupid and setting myself up for heartbreak. I probably am, but I still want to be with her.

'How's this going to work?' Sawyer asks. 'You sleeping in separate rooms?'

They all stare at me, waiting for an answer. I keep quiet.

'Guess that's a no,' Brody says with a laugh. 'So what does that mean? Are you guys dating?'

'We're not dating. We're just—I don't know what we are. Friends who are . . . having a baby.'

'More like friends with benefits,' Sawyer says, smiling at Brody.

'Stop that,' Mom says. 'We shouldn't be talking about this.'

Brody smiles back at Sawyer. 'At least he can't get her pregnant.'

'Not again.' Sawyer looks at me. 'How the hell did that happen? Don't you teach sex ed at school? You should know this shit.'

'I only taught it for one semester, when the health teacher left and they couldn't find a new one.' I glare at Sawyer. 'And yeah, I know how birth control works, but it's not always a hundred percent effective.'

Mom gets up. 'I think we've heard enough. Jason, when will you be moving in? I'd like to wash the bedding before you do. I'm sure it's dusty, having gone unused for months.'

'Mia's graduation is next weekend so we'll probably move in after that. And don't worry about the bedding. I'm sure it's fine.'

'This whole house is dusty,' Mom says, looking around. 'I'm going to have to do a thorough cleaning.'

'Mom, you don't—'

'Just let her be,' Dad says as Mom goes upstairs. 'Nothing you say is going to change her mind, especially with her future grandchild living here.'

'Her grandchild won't even be born until October,' I say.

'October?' Sawyer says. 'That's her due date? Shit, I hope she doesn't have the kid the same weekend as the fall festival. Nick's got you down to drive the tractor again.'

'If she's due that weekend, he's not going to be here,' Dad says. 'He'll be out in Boston with Mia.'

He's right. I hadn't thought about that. I haven't let myself think beyond the summer. But what happens after that? I can't miss my baby's birth. I'll need to be in Boston. What if Mia has the baby early, or late? I can't take weeks off from work, but if I don't, I might miss the birth.

'She's still moving away?' Brody asks.

'At the end of August,' I say, feeling my anger rise as I think about how little I'll see my kid with Mia living in Boston. I've been trying to be okay with it, knowing it's just how it has to be, but it's not right. It's not what I want. I want to see my child every day, not a few times a year. And I don't want him or her growing up in a big city in some tiny apartment.

Mia and I need to talk about this. I've been going along with whatever she wants, but this is my baby too and I'm going to have a say in how our kid is raised.

Chapter 18

Mia

It's been three days since my parents arrived and Jason's still acting distant. He barely talks to me, and when he does, he seems angry. He started acting this way on Sunday after we went to see the house we'll be living in. He was fine when we were there, but later, when I met up with him at his apartment, he was quiet and withdrawn.

'You want breakfast?' I ask, taking a box of cereal from the cupboard.

'No.' Jason walks past me to the fridge. 'I need to get to the school for a meeting. Shit, I forgot to make a lunch.'

'I could make you a sandwich.'

He shuts the fridge door. 'I'll just get something from the vending machine.' He grabs his keys from the counter. 'Have a good day.'

'Jason, wait!' I race up to him, catching him before he gets to the door. 'When are we going to talk about this?'

'About what?'

'About whatever you're angry about. You've been like this since Sunday when we went to see the house.

Did something happen? Did your parents say something after I left that upset you?'

'Yeah,' he huffs. 'They said they're pissed at me for lying and to end this and tell the truth.'

'Wait—your parents know we're not engaged?'

'Of course they know.' He throws his hands up. 'I was dating other girls all last spring. And then one day you show up and we tell them we're engaged? They're not stupid. They knew we made it up.'

'Then why did they go along with it at the restaurant?'

'Because for a minute we had them convinced it was true. It wasn't until they left the restaurant that they realized it didn't make sense.'

'So you're angry because of your parents?'

'I'm angry that I agreed to this. Now, because of this fake engagement, my whole family has to lie. Everyone in town is asking my family about us. For now they're saying it's a family matter and not talking about it, but they can't keep doing that. People are already spreading rumors about us—about me—about how I've been cheating on you, going out with girls here while you're in Madison. They're saying you never came here because I told you not to, because I didn't want you running into girls I'd been out with. My whole damn reputation is being ruined because of this.'

'Jason, I didn't know. Why didn't you tell me this sooner?'

'Why? Telling you isn't going to change anything. This is what you wanted. And I agreed to do it. I just have to deal with the fallout.'

'Why would people say that about you? You grew up here. These people are your friends. And you said everyone here is nice.'

'Most people. Not everyone. Some people think my family has too much influence in town. That's why my dad got off city council. He was sick of hearing that he made all the decisions for the town, which wasn't even close to being true. The council votes on decisions. It wasn't my dad deciding. Anyway, those are the people who start rumors about us. My mom usually shuts them down before they can spread, but this time she can't. She doesn't know what to say, how to explain this.'

'Then we need to find a way to make the rumors stop. Maybe when you get home later we could talk about it and figure out what to tell people. I'm sure we could come up with something.'

'Mia, you're not getting it.'

'Getting what?'

'I don't want to do this. I don't want to keep lying to people. The fake engagement was bad enough. I'm not making up even more lies. It's just going to make things worse.'

'So what do you want to do?'

'Nothing. I just have to deal with it and hope people move on to something else soon. Maybe Sawyer will get engaged. That'll give people something new to talk about.'

'The rumors are why you've been so angry at me? Or is there something else?'

He checks his phone. 'I need to go. I'm going to be late for this meeting.'

There's something else bothering him, but he won't tell me. Maybe this is all too much for him. Finding out about the baby. The fake engagement. Having to give up his apartment and live in that house with me. His whole life is changing and it's happening really fast.

'Jason, I think I'm going to head back to Madison.'

He was halfway out the door but turns back. 'When?'

'Today. Tomorrow's Wednesday and I have a lot to do before my parents get there on Friday.'

'Is that the only reason, or is there something else?'

'I think you need some time alone. Time to think, without me around.'

'When are you coming back?'

'I don't know.'

'What do you mean? You're moving here. We're living together.'

'It doesn't have to be right away. My parents fly home on Sunday. Once they're back home, they won't know where I'm living. I can tell them I'm here but still be in Madison.'

Jason comes back into the apartment and shuts the door. 'What are you saying? That we're not doing this? That we're not living together?'

That's not what I want, but I think Jason does. I think he regrets doing this. Actually, I know he does. It's the reason he's angry, the reason he hasn't been talking to me.

I shrug. 'We wouldn't have to. Your family already knows the truth. There's no reason to pretend we're engaged when they know we're not.'

'The town knows. If they never see you, more rumors will start.'

'You can tell them my morning sickness is really bad so I'm staying home. Like you said, after a few weeks they'll probably get tired of talking about us and talk about something else.'

'Mia.' He sets his hand on my shoulder, which is the most he's touched me since Sunday. 'When I said all that stuff about the rumors, it didn't mean I don't want you here.'

'I know, but maybe it'd be easier if I wasn't.'

He sighs. 'I'm sorry I've shut you out the past couple days. I'm still trying to go through all this in my head. And you're right. I'm angry, about more than just the rumors. I'm angry about this whole situation.'

'You mean the baby?'

'I mean you living in Boston and me living here.' He walks past me, rubbing his jaw. 'I don't want my kid living a thousand miles away. I don't want him living in a big city, or in an apartment where he's stuck inside all the time.' Jason turns back to me. 'I don't have an answer here. I'm just saying, I don't want that for my kid.'

'It's OUR kid,' I say, getting angry. 'And I don't like that you're implying I'm doing something wrong here. You knew I was moving back. And you know why I have to. If you really want to see our child, then move to Boston with me. I know you'll miss your parents, but you can still come back and see them. And if anything happens to them, your brothers can help. My parents don't have that. They only have me.'

He checks his phone. 'Shit, I'm late. I have to get to work.'

'I'll pack up my things and clean up before I go. We can talk this weekend after my parents leave.'

He walks up to me. 'What about graduation?'

'You don't have to go. I'll tell my parents something came up and you had to work.'

'Mia, I'm going to your graduation. It's a big deal. I should be there.'

'If you were my fiancé, then yes. But you're not. Don't worry about my parents. I'll come up with something to explain why you're not there. I need to go clean up. Have a good day.' I race off, straight to the bathroom where I turn on the shower so he won't hear me crying.

Why am I getting worked up about this? My relationship with Jason isn't even real. But I wanted to see if it could be, which is why I wanted to live with him. I had this dream of us falling in love and Jason wanting to go with me to Boston at the end of the summer. We'd find a small house to buy in a suburb that was safe and clean and had good schools. Jason and I would find jobs and raise our child and maybe have a couple more.

That's never going to happen. I knew it never would, but I was excited about spending the summer with him. Now I don't think I will. I don't want to be around Jason when he's angry at me, or have him keep doing this back and forth thing where he's nice to me one day and not talking to me the next.

After I pack my stuff and clean up the apartment, I go to the hotel where my parents are staying. I tell them the professor I'm working for wants to meet tomorrow so I have to go back to Madison. They don't question it, and actually seem relieved I'm not going with them to sightsee today. I think I wore them out yesterday. I forget how tired they get.

* * *

On Wednesday, I meet Nora for lunch at a sandwich shop near campus. I tell her what's happened since we last talked, which was Sunday, before I left to meet my parents for breakfast.

'So let me get this straight,' Nora says. 'You were going to move there and live on his parents' farm, but now you're not because you and Jason got into a fight.'

'No, it's because we don't need to live together. My parents will be in Boston. They won't know where I'm living.'

'Do you still like him?' she asks before taking a bite of her sandwich.

'Jason? Yes. Why does that matter?'

'Do you still think he's hot?' she asks, her gaze going to a guy as he walks past us.

'Yes, but again, why does that matter?'

'That's Professor Wren,' she says, smiling, as she watches him fill his drink at the fountain dispenser. 'What do you think?'

I glance back at him. 'He's old.'

'He's not old. I heard he's 35. That's only five years older than me. That's nothing.'

'Have you talked to him?'

'Not yet, but I'm thinking about it.' She looks back at me. 'So anyway, what was I saying?'

'You asked if I was still attracted to Jason.'

She nods and picks up a potato chip from her plate. 'Are you going to date anyone this summer?'

'No.' I laugh. 'Who would go out with me? I'm pregnant.'

She shrugs. 'Some guys are into that.'

Just then, a guy stops by our table and smiles at me. 'Hey, how's it going?'

'Good.' I don't know this guy. Or do I? My memory hasn't been great since I got pregnant. 'What's your name again?'

'Craig. We're in boot camp at the gym.'

'You must be thinking of someone else. I'm not in boot camp. I'm not even sure what that is.'

Nora laughs and turns to the guy. 'Are you asking her out?'

She's so bold, which I admire, but it also embarrasses me sometimes.

'I was just saying hi.' He looks back at me. 'But what do you think? You want to have dinner this week? I could tell you all about boot camp. Maybe you could come with me sometime.'

'I don't think so.' I look at Nora. 'But maybe you could go with my friend, Nora.'

'I'd rather go with you,' he says in a flirty tone.

'She's pregnant,' Nora says, chomping on her chips.

He backs away, like I have a contagious disease. 'Is she serious?'

'Yes.' I rub my stomach. 'I'm due in October. Twins!'

'Okay, well, I need to get going.' He takes off.

Nora stares at me, her eyes bugged out. 'You're having twins?'

'No, I just said that to get rid of him. I told you guys won't go out with me. Did you see how fast he ran out of here when I said I'm pregnant?'

'I think it was the twin thing. He might've been okay with it if you said you're just having one.' She pops a chip in her mouth.

'I'm pretty sure he wouldn't, which is fine. I'm not looking to date right now.'

'So, to summarize, you like Jason, you think he's hot, and you're not dating anyone else.'

'Yeah? What are you saying?'

'I think you should go live with Jason. Spend the summer with him.'

'I don't think he wants that.'

'You said he's the one who suggested it.'

'Yes, but then later that day, he barely talked to me. I can't take all his back and forth. One minute he's kissing me and the next he's acting like he just wants to be friends.'

'Maybe you should cut him some slack. You did kind of appear out of nowhere and tell him he's having a kid. The guy's probably just confused.'

'I know he is, but I don't want to spend all summer with him going back and forth between wanting to date me and wanting to just be friends.'

'What do *you* want?'

'I don't know,' I say, looking down at my half-eaten sandwich. I haven't had much of an appetite since leaving Jason's apartment yesterday.

'Yeah, you do.' Nora nudges my knee under the table. 'What is it you want, Mia?'

'I can't have what I want. That's the problem.'

'You could have it for the summer.'

'And get close to him and then have to leave? Why would I do that?'

'You never know.' She wipes her hands on her napkin. 'Maybe spending three months with him would change things.'

'He's not going to move to Boston. And I can't stay here.' I slump back in my chair. 'I never should've done the fake engagement thing. It messed everything up.'

'If you're really that upset about it, it's not too late to get out of it.'

'Meaning I should tell my parents the truth?'

'Maybe. From what you said, they seem okay with you having a baby. Maybe they'll be okay with you not being engaged.'

'They will be eventually, but not yet. Monday, when I was sightseeing with them, my mom kept telling me how lucky I am to have found a great guy like Jason who didn't run off when he found out I was pregnant. Then she went on to tell me how hard it would've been to raise the baby on my own, to the point that I started to think I couldn't do it.'

'Of course you can,' Nora says, reassuringly. 'Your mom's from a different era when women didn't make the kind of money they do now.'

'Even if I get a good job, Boston's expensive. And so are babies. What I make may not be enough.'

'Isn't Jason going to help?'

'We haven't talked about it.'

'You need to. Even if you two decide not to live together this summer, you still need to talk to him. Why don't you call him tonight?'

My phone rings. Jason's name lights up the screen. 'I think he heard us talking about him.' I show her my phone, then answer the call. 'Hey, Jason.'

'Hey. I was wondering about this weekend.'

'What about it?'

'I need to know what time to be there.'

'For the graduation? I thought you weren't coming.'

'Of course I'm coming. It's Saturday, right? I was thinking I could come Friday after work. We could take your parents to dinner.'

'Um, yeah, that'd be nice.'

'Great! I'll be there around five. Just text me your address.'

'Okay. But wait, don't you have a game on Friday?'

'It's tonight. And tomorrow I'm having an end-of-season party for the team. Nothing fancy. Just pizza and ice cream. Mia, I hate to run, but I have to grade quizzes before class.'

'Okay, bye.' I end the call and text him my address.

'What'd he want?' Nora asks.

'He's coming to graduation.' I set my phone down. 'And he wants to take my parents out Friday night.'

'See? He's not angry at you. You've been worrying for nothing.'

'He's only doing this for my parents. To keep the fake engagement story going.'

'Or he has feelings for you and wants to see you.' She spots the professor guy by the trash can. 'I'll be right back.' She bursts up from her chair, taking her tray with her. She stands beside the guy, waiting for him to clear his tray. 'Are you new here?'

'I am.' He turns to her and shakes her hand. 'Steve Wren.'

'Nora West. Where are you from?'

'Arizona. I worked at a small college there. I assume you work at the university?'

'I'm a professor in the physics department.'

'Physics.' His brows rise. 'Impressive. I work in the English department.'

'Have they given you the campus tour?'

'Briefly, but I still find myself getting lost.'

'I'd be happy to show you around.'

'I'd like that.' He smiles at her like he's interested in more than a tour. 'Do you have time now? I'm supposed to pick up my staff ID and I have no idea where the administration building is from here.'

'I can show you.'

'Great! Let me get this for you.' He takes her tray.

As he's dumping it, Nora texts me, *He's even hotter up close! And he smells amazing!*

'Ready to go?' the guy asks.

'Just a minute.' She runs over to me. 'Sorry to rush off but—'

'It's fine. We were almost done anyway.'

'I'll call you tonight!' she says as she hurries back to the guy.

Seeing her with that guy makes me wonder how long it'll be before I date again, or if I ever will. I wonder how long it'll be before Jason finds someone. I'm surprised he hasn't by now. He's smart, funny, athletic, hot. I wish I'd stayed in touch with him after the wedding. Maybe things would've turned out differently. If we'd dated before finding out about the baby, would I have been able to convince Jason to move to Boston with me?

There I go again, fantasizing about what will never be. Jason and I aren't a couple. We can't be. I just need to be okay with that.

Chapter 19

Jason

'Hey,' Nick says, sitting beside me at the bar. 'Care if I join you?'

We're at Sawyer's brewery. I came here hoping it would get my mind off Mia, but so far, it's not working.

'What are you doing here? I thought you were still on your honeymoon.'

After the wedding, Nick and Lyndsay drove down to Chicago and stayed at a resort hotel with a spa.

'We got home this afternoon. And don't call it a honeymoon, especially around Lyndsay. I promised her I'd take her on a real honeymoon later this year.'

'Where does she want to go?'

'Somewhere in the Caribbean. I would've taken her now, but she didn't want to leave the orchard when we've got so much work to do. So how was your game? It was the last one, right?'

'Yeah, we lost.'

'Hey,' Sawyer says to Nick. 'What are you drinking?'

'The stout.'

'How was Chicago?' Sawyer asks as he gets the beer.

'Good. Nash, Jake, and Uncle Mitch met us for dinner last night.'

Sawyer brings Nick the beer. 'Did you tell them the good news?'

'About Jason getting married and having a kid?' Nick glances at me. 'Nah, I figured he should tell them himself.'

'Would you stop it with the marriage stuff?' I say, keeping my voice down so the people around us don't hear. As far as the town knows, I'm still engaged. People have been asking me about it all week, wanting to know who Mia is and where she's from and why they never saw her before now. I told them Mia and I have been on-and-off dating since last year and that just recently it got serious, but people are still spreading rumors about us that aren't true.

'You never know.' Nick drinks his beer. 'Maybe the marriage will actually happen.'

'Yeah, I don't think so. Who told you about it?'

'I did,' Sawyer says.

'I could barely understand him when he called,' Nick says. 'He couldn't stop laughing.'

'You think this is funny?' I say to Sawyer.

'Dude, if you saw your face at breakfast that day when Mom and Dad showed up, you'd be laughing too.' He glances behind me. 'I have to go check on a table.' He takes off.

'Sawyer said Mia went back to Madison,' Nick says.

'Yeah, yesterday morning. She said she had things to do before her parents got there.'

'Was that really the reason, or was it something else?'

'I don't want to talk about it.' I gulp down my beer.

'So something else. Let me guess. You got scared and pushed her away?'

'I'm not scared. What the hell would I be scared of?'

'Getting closer to her. Falling for her even more than you already have.'

I take another drink of my beer, annoyed that he knows me so well.

'What are you going to do about it?' Nick asks.

'I don't know. I'm going there Friday night. We're taking her parents to dinner and then Saturday is her graduation.'

'And she's not planning to come back with you after that?'

'She hasn't decided.' I sigh. 'I fucked up. I got angry at her before she left. And this was after barely talking to her for the two days before that. I'm not surprised she left.'

'And you haven't talked to her since?'

'Only about the graduation. I don't know what to do. Part of me wants her to live with me, but the other part is telling me to stay away from her. Being with her is just going to make it that much harder when she leaves.'

'What do you want more? To be with her this summer or to protect yourself from feeling like shit when she leaves?'

I pause a moment. 'To be with her. I miss her. I can't stop thinking about her. But that's what worries me. If I miss her this much now, think how bad it's going to be when she leaves in a few months.'

'You can't worry about that. If you do, you're going to get scared again and push her away. If you decide you want to live with her this summer, you need to stop this back and forth shit. And you both need to decide what this is—if you're just going to live together as friends or if it's something else.'

'We've tried being friends, but it keeps turning into something else.'

'Then you have to be okay with that. And so does she. You're basically dating for the summer.'

'Which is stupid. Why would I do that?'

'Because you're not ready to lose her.' He takes a drink of his beer. 'There's nothing wrong with dating her as long as you both know what you're getting into.'

'What would you do?'

'I can't tell you that. Besides, it doesn't matter. You and I aren't the same.'

'You'd move with her. You'd move to Boston.'

'It's different for me. I lived in New York all those years, so yeah, leaving Haydon Falls wouldn't be as big a deal for me as it is for you.' He turns to me. 'I'm not saying you should go. I'm saying do what feels right today. Don't worry about three months from now. You've been crazy about this girl since the night you met her. What if she's it? What if you were meant to meet her that night? Do you want to go the rest of your life wondering what might've happened if you'd spent the summer with her?'

I look at him. 'So how do I get her back?'

'You go there this weekend and tell her you fucked up and want another chance.'

'Chance for what? I don't even know what I'm asking for.'

'You've got two days to figure it out.' He finishes his beer, then gets up.

'You're leaving?'

'Yeah, I need to get up early tomorrow.'

'Did you just come here to get me to do something about Mia?'

He cracks a smile. 'I'm taking over for Dad. He said talking to you is like talking to a brick wall. He needed a break.'

'So he sent you?' I shake my head. 'I love how all of you talk about me when I'm not around.'

'Like you don't do the same thing?' Sawyer says, appearing behind the bar as Nick leaves. 'So what'd he tell you?'

'To stop worrying about what happens when she leaves.'

Sawyer nods. 'It's tough, man. I get why you're worried. But Nick's right. You'll never have a chance with her if you keep thinking about her leaving.'

'Her leaving is the reason why I *don't* have a chance with her.' I rub my jaw. 'Shit, I did it again. I'm thinking about her leaving.'

'You'll work it out. You want another beer?'

'No, I need to get home. Hey, if I move in the Carson house, you want my apartment for the summer? It's a lot bigger than your place.'

'Maybe. I'll think about it.'

I leave and go back to my apartment. It feels empty without Mia there. She was only here a few days, but it was long enough for me to miss having her around. I always tell people I don't mind living alone, but I'd rather be with someone. I'd rather be with Mia.

* * *

On Friday, I get to Mia's apartment a few minutes early, wanting to talk to her before her parents get there. I've done some more thinking and have no doubt that I want her to stay with me this summer. I'm just not sure she'll agree to it.

'Jason,' Mia says, greeting me at the door. 'Come on in.'

'Hey, before your parents get—' I stop when I see they're already there, sitting on the couch in Mia's tiny apartment. It's much smaller than I was expecting.

'Mom and Dad got here early,' Mia says.

'I see that.' I smile at them. 'How was the trip?'

'Wonderful,' Harriott says. 'It's so easy to drive around here. There's almost no traffic.'

'It's a big change from Boston,' Mia says to me. 'They're not used to it.'

Harriott gets up and gives me a hug. 'It's good to see you again, Jason.'

'You too, Mrs. Daniels.'

'Call me Harriott,' she says, going back to the couch. 'You're going to be my son-in-law soon.'

I look at Mia, but she looks away.

'When's dinner?' Walter asks. 'I'm starving and I've gotta take my pill.'

'We could go right now,' Mia says. 'There's no reason to wait now that Jason's here.'

'You haven't even kissed him hello yet,' Harriott says, winking at Mia.

'Oh. You're right.' She walks up to me and gives me a quick peck on the lips.

I guess I have my answer. She's not going to live with me. She doesn't even want to kiss me. I screwed up too many times.

'Walter!' Harriott yells.

Mia and I look back and see Walter on his knees, holding onto the chair by the couch.

Mia races over to him. 'Dad, are you okay?'

'I'm fine. You just got too much damn furniture in too small of a place.'

'Let me help you up,' I say, reaching under his arm. He looks annoyed, like he doesn't want my help, but he lets me lift him up to standing.

'It's that damn hip of mine,' he grumbles. 'I think that damn surgery made it worse.'

'Walter, watch your language.'

'It can take awhile to heal after joint surgery,' I say, keeping hold of him as he slowly makes his way to the door. 'I tore my shoulder the summer before college. It took the whole next year to heal. Lost my baseball scholarship.'

'You were good enough to get a scholarship?' Walter asks, sounding impressed.

'I was.' I smile at him. 'But then I hurt my shoulder and it ended my chances of playing again.'

'You play in a rec league,' Mia says, walking ahead of us with her mom.

'Well, yeah. I meant college ball.'

'That's a shame,' Walter says, holding onto my arm as he walks. Mia said he hates using his cane so tries to go without it, but after falling just now, I think he wants some extra support.

Mia keeps looking back at me and smiling as I help her dad. I know she's had it with me, but I hope she at least knows I'm a nice guy. I only treated her the way I did because I was stupid, and afraid. Nick's right. I was afraid of getting close to her so I pushed her away.

We go to dinner and I feel like Mia and I are a couple again. But it's all for show. We're back to our fake engagement routine, except this time Mia isn't being as affectionate. She's not holding my hand or touching my arm or sitting as close to me as she did last weekend.

As we're finishing our meals, a guy stops at our table.

'Mia,' he says, smiling at her. 'How have you been?'

'Kurt. Hey.' She clears her throat. 'I've been good. How about you?'

'Same. Just busy with work. Hey, I was thinking of you the other day. They're having a concert in the park next weekend. I was wondering if you'd want to go with me.'

What the hell? Does this guy not notice me sitting here? Does he think I'm her brother?

'Mia won't be here next weekend,' Harriott says before Mia can answer. 'And she's engaged, so perhaps you could find some other girl to go with.'

'Engaged?' He laughs. 'Is this a joke?'

'Kurt, these are my parents,' Mia says. 'And we were just about to leave so—'

'You're not really engaged, are you?' he says. 'You couldn't be. We were going to go out like a month ago. Hey, sorry I couldn't make it that night. I—'

'A month ago?' Harriott looks at Mia. 'You were going out with this boy a month ago?'

'No. Mom, it's not what you think. We're just friends.'

'You leave my daughter alone,' Walter says to the guy. 'She's engaged to Jason and they're having a child soon.'

The guy rears back. 'Wait—what?' He looks at Mia. 'You're pregnant?'

'She is.' I put my arm around Mia. 'And we're trying to have some family time here so if you could just . . .'

'Yeah, whatever.' He turns and walks away.

Mia looks at her parents and forces out a smile. 'Well, should we go?'

'What about dessert?' Walter asks.

'I have ice cream at home,' Mia says, hurrying to get up. She wants to get out of here after that awkward encounter with Kurt. Who is that guy and how did she meet him? Was she really going to date him? How many guys has she dated since that night we spent together?

I feel on edge, my pulse going faster, as I think about Mia with other guys. I know she's not mine. I know I have no right to be jealous, but I am. I don't even like thinking about her with someone else. When Kurt came over here and flirted with her, I wanted to punch him. I almost did, but I knew Mia's parents wouldn't be too pleased with that.

On the drive back to Mia's apartment, Walter nods off and starts snoring.

'I know it's early,' Harriott says to Mia as we get out of the car. 'But I need to get him to bed. It's been a long day and he's tired. And I'm sure you'd like some time alone with Jason.' She winks at me.

'Will you come by in the morning?' Mia asks. 'For breakfast?'

'Yes, we'll be here.' Harriott leans into the car and shakes Walter. 'Walter, wake up.'

He rouses and mutters something.

'Walter, wake up,' Harriott says. 'We're going to the hotel.'

His eyes open and he looks at all of us, finally realizing he was asleep. He holds onto the car as he gets out.

'Goodnight, Dad,' Mia says, kissing his cheek.

He narrows his eyes at me. 'You better take good care of my girl.'

'Yes, Sir. I will.' I put my arm around Mia.

'Goodnight, honey,' Harriott says, smiling at us as she helps Walter to their rental car.

We remain on the sidewalk, my arm still around Mia, as we watch them drive off.

'I worry about them,' Mia says.

'I know you do.' I lean down and kiss her head, not even thinking about it.

She looks up at me. 'Thanks for helping my dad. After he fell in my apartment, I didn't think he'd be able to make it to dinner.'

'He was fine. He just needed a little help.'

She softly smiles. 'Want to go inside?'

'I should probably get going. I need to go find a hotel. Any recommendations?'

'You're not staying with me?'

'I didn't think you'd want me to.'

'Of course you can stay. C'mon.' She takes my hand and heads to the building.

We go into her apartment and she sits down on the couch and closes her eyes.

'You okay?' I ask, sitting beside her.

'I'm just tired.' She opens her eyes. 'I've been like this for months. I've heard I won't be as tired later on in the pregnancy, but right now, I have to take naps or I won't make it through the day.'

'You want to go to bed?'

'No, I just needed to sit down.' She turns to me. 'Hey, do you think you could help my parents get to the ceremony tomorrow? I have to be there early. My mom knows where to go, but I'd feel better if you were with them, to help my dad if he needs it.'

'Of course. I'd be happy to.'

'Thanks. I'm sure they'd be fine on their own, but I'd feel better if you were there.' She gets up. 'You want something to drink?'

'No, I'm good.' I watch as she goes to the kitchen and fills a glass with water. 'Mia, I need to talk to you about something.'

'Go ahead.'

'Could you come over here?'

She sets the glass down and comes back to the couch. 'What is it?'

'I need to apologize for how I acted when you were in Haydon Falls. And I don't just mean last weekend. I mean every time you've been there.'

I pause to let her say something, but she doesn't. She just looks at me, waiting for me to continue.

'I keep doing this hot-and-cold thing with you. I know it's wrong. And I know it's why you left.' I turn to her and take her hand. 'But I swear, I'm going to do better. I want you to come back, Mia. I want you to move into the house with me like we planned.'

She shakes her head, looking down at her hand in mine.

'What does that mean?' I ask.

Her eyes rise to mine. 'I can't do this, Jason. It's wrong. I never should've suggested it. I'm going to tell my parents the truth. Tomorrow, after the graduation ceremony.'

'What?' I stare at her in disbelief. 'Mia, why would you do that? After everything we went through to convince them we're engaged, why would you tell them the truth?'

'Because I don't like lying to them. And I hate that I caused you and your family so much trouble. I never wanted that to happen.'

'I know you didn't. But Mia, it's done. The story's already out there. Why not just keep it going?'

'It's not fair to you, Jason. You need to live your life. You should be with someone you really want to be with.'

'I want to be with you. This whole time we've been together, I haven't been pretending. I felt like we were a real couple. But then I'd remind myself that you were leaving and I'd shut down. I'd pull away. That's why I treated you like a girlfriend one minute and like a friend the next. But I figured that out and now I know what I want.'

'Jason, I'm still leaving.'

'I know you are, but I still want the summer with you. I want to date you, for real, and for more than a night. I want to spend the next three months with you or however long I have until you move away.'

'Why? If you know it's going to end, why would you do this?'

'Because three months is better than nothing. Mia, that night we shared is one I'll never forget. The moment I saw you I felt something—something I'd never felt before. I can't explain it, but whatever it was, I haven't stopped feeling it.' I look into her eyes, pleading her to do this. 'I need more time with you, Mia. And if I only get three months, I'll take it. So will you do it?'

'I don't know.' She pulls her hand from mine and moves back. 'I think doing this would just make things harder. And what if you pull away again?'

'I won't. I'm committed to this. I want to do this, Mia.'

She gets up. 'I need to go lay down. I'm really tired.'

'Okay,' I say, getting the hint she needs time to think about what I said.

She goes down to her room and returns with a pillow and blanket. 'Is this enough or do you need more blankets?'

'This is good.' I get up and take the pillow and blanket from her and toss it on the couch.

'Okay, well, goodnight.' She gives me an uncomfortable smile.

I don't know what happened. We've never felt uncomfortable around each other, even when we first met, but something changed. From the time she left my apartment until now, something changed in her and now she's acting like she wants nothing to do with me.

I guess I deserve that. I screwed up. I thought of myself when I should've been thinking about her. I protected myself, when I should've protected her.

'Mia.' I step up to her and give her a hug. I keep her in my arms for as long as she'll let me, which isn't long. I feel her pulling away and let her go, then watch as she goes down to her room.

She's not going back with me. And I don't know how to change her mind. I had a plan. I had a speech. I had a ring. But none of that matters now. She's made her decision.

Chapter 20

Mia

'The ceremony was lovely,' my mom says as we head back to the car. We're going slow for my dad, who's holding onto Jason. It warms my heart seeing Jason help my dad. It just confirms what I already knew—that Jason's kind and caring and will be a great father to our child.

'They could've spoken up more,' my dad says. 'You could barely hear what they were saying.'

The speakers in the auditorium were plenty loud enough. My dad's just losing his hearing. This past week I've noticed how much my dad's health is declining. It scares me, and reminds me how little time I have left with him.

It's the reason I can't stay here, and the reason I can't be with Jason. Last night, when he asked me to live with him this summer, I almost said yes. He told me all the things I've been wanting to hear. But I couldn't do it. I couldn't tell him yes. I've already messed up his life enough. I'm not going to keep doing it for another three months. I need to end this fake engagement so Jason can go back to living his life.

I haven't told him this yet, but I've decided not to wait to go back to Boston. I've already sublet my apartment for the time remaining on the lease. I don't need to stay in Madison. I only planned to because I wanted to be close to Jason to see if we might have a future together. But we don't, so I might as well leave. I can do my summer job from Boston and be close to my parents.

'What a beautiful garden,' my mom says, stopping to look at an area on campus filled with flowers and surrounded by trees. There's a stone path that winds through it and some benches.

'Why don't we go check it out?' Jason says, giving me a look to go along with it. He glances at my dad and I notice he's slumped over, like he needs a break from all the walking.

'Let's go sit on the bench,' I say, walking over to one.

'Mia, remember these?' my mom says, pointing to a patch of pink flowers. 'We planted some just like these when you were a little girl. I let you pick them out.'

'I picked them because the color matched my doll's dress,' I say to Jason. 'It was the same pink.'

'She loved her dolls,' my mom tells Jason. 'She talked to them, tucked them in at night, read them stories.'

'I was practicing being a mom,' I say, laughing. 'I wanted to have ten kids someday. Five boys and five girls. Then I got older and started babysitting and realized how much work it would be to have ten kids.'

'You good?' Jason says to my dad as he helps him sit on the bench.

'I'd be better if this damn hip of mine would work like it's supposed to.'

'You did well today,' my mom says, sitting beside him. 'We've done a lot of walking, more than we do back home.'

'I only made it that far because I was hanging onto him.' He motions to Jason.

'Me?' Jason says, sounding confused. 'I was hanging onto you. That hill by the auditorium was steep.'

My dad cracks a smile. 'Glad I could help.'

It's moments like this that I love Jason and wish I could be with him. But since I can't, I need to end this. I'm tired of lying. Tired of pretending.

'Mom. Dad.' I stand in front of them as they're seated on the bench. 'I need to tell you something.'

'What is it, dear?' my mom says, with concern in her voice. She can sense something's wrong because I'm no longer smiling, and I'm sure my eyes are red because I feel like I'm about to cry.

'Jason and I . . .' I look at him beside me and notice he looks surprised, like he wasn't expecting me to do this now. I look back at my parents. 'What we told you when you got here, about us getting married.' My heart's racing and my throat is dry. I'm finding it hard to get the words out.

'What is it, Mia?' my mom asks. 'Just tell us.'

I take a breath. 'It's about the engagement. It wasn't real. It was—'

'What she means,' Jason says, interrupting me, 'is that it didn't feel real because I didn't have the ring.'

Jason turns to me. He reaches in the pocket of his suit pants and pulls something out. My jaw drops when I see it's a ring.

'Jason, what are you—' I stop when he drops to one knee and takes my hand.

'Mia, will you marry me?'

I hear my mom gasp and my dad mumble something, but my eyes remain on Jason. What is he doing? Why is he proposing? This was supposed to be the end of our engagement, not the beginning.

'Mia, say something,' my mom whispers.

'Um, I don't know.'

'What'd she say?' my dad says really loud to my mom.

'Nothing, dear. Just give us a minute. Mia, can I talk to you?'

I look over at her. 'Mom, there's nothing to talk about. I just need to finish what I was saying.'

She gets up and takes my arm. 'This won't take long.'

We walk down the stone path to an area with a small fountain and another bench.

'Mom, I just have to say this.'

'Honey, I already know.'

'You do?'

'Of course. I'm not senile. I know what's going on here. You think your father and I will be upset that the only reason you got engaged was because of the baby.'

'Mom, that's not—'

'But you couldn't be more wrong. Your father and I are proud of your decision. I know it's not easy to commit to someone for the sake of your child, but the best things in life aren't easy. They take work. They take time. And I know with some time and effort, you and Jason will grow to love each other.' She smiles. 'I think part of you already loves him. And I can he tell loves you.'

'Mom, no. Jason doesn't—'

'He does.' She takes both my hands in hers. 'In his own way, he does. You just have to open your heart to see it.'

What is she talking about? Jason doesn't love me. He likes me. And he's attracted to me. But he doesn't love me.

'I know you have doubts,' my mom says. 'But just give it some time. And remember, you're doing this for the baby.' She hugs me. 'Your father and I couldn't be more proud of you, honey.'

This isn't how this was supposed to go. But after that speech she gave me, I feel like I have to stay engaged to Jason. And it's not just because of the baby, but because of what she said about the best things in life not being easy. Am I giving up on Jason too soon? Should I commit to a summer with him and see if we could make this work?

We head back to the bench where my dad is sitting.

'Wait,' I whisper, stopping my mom before we get there.

Jason's on the bench next to my dad. He's leaned over, his forearms resting on his knees, the ring still in his hand.

My dad's talking to him. 'Hang in there, kid. She'll come around. Women are always changing their mind.

And just when you think you know what they want, they change their damn mind again. It's frustrating as hell, but what are you going to do? You can't change them.'

'I wouldn't want to change Mia,' Jason says. 'I like everything about her, but you're right, I don't always know what she wants.'

'But you love her, right?'

Jason glances at my dad. 'I do.'

My heart nearly stops. Jason loves me? Is he just saying that to please my dad or does he really mean it? He can't mean it. We've barely spent any time together.

'I knew I loved her mother the moment I laid eyes on her,' my dad says.

'Really?' Jason says.

'When you know, you know. You don't need years to figure it out. In fact, the night I met her, I walked right up to her and told her I'm going to marry her someday.'

Jason laughs. 'And what did she say?'

'She told me I'm crazy and to go away. But I didn't listen. I knew she was the one. I just needed some time to convince her of that.'

'You never told me that story,' I whisper to my mom. 'Is that really what happened?'

'I couldn't stand him when I met him,' she whispers. 'But over time, I grew to love him.' She smiles as she gazes at my dad.

Jason stands up. 'Maybe I should get out of here.'

'Didn't you hear a damn thing I said?'

Jason looks at my dad. 'What do you mean?'

'For crying out loud.' He pushes himself up to standing. 'If you want to marry Mia, then what the hell you running off for?'

'I'm not running off. I'm just giving her some time to think.'

'About what?' he huffs. 'You kids these days think too much. Back in my day, we took action. We didn't stand around thinking all day. Thinking just leads to coming up with problems that didn't exist before you did all that thinking. If you want Mia, go get her. Stop thinking so damn much.'

I come out from the bushes we were hiding behind and walk up to Jason and my dad.

'Jason, I—'

'I want you to come back with me tomorrow,' he says in a forceful way. 'Back to the house where we'll be living this summer.'

Glancing at my dad, I see his lips turning up.

I look back at Jason. 'Okay.'

'Wait—what? You'll really do it?'

'Yes. Didn't we already decide this?'

'Yeah, but then you said—'

'Hey, kid,' my dad says, nudging Jason. 'What did I say about women?'

Jason looks over at him and smiles. 'You're right.'

'Damn straight. Now put that ring on her finger.'

Jason takes my hand, looks in my eyes, and slides the ring on my finger. I don't know if he's pretending or if it's real, but it feels real. I feel like something's changed between us, like there's a commitment that wasn't there before.

'It's lovely,' my mom says, looking at the ring. It's just a gold band, and probably not even real gold. But it doesn't matter. I like how it feels on my finger, and how Jason looked at me when he put it on.

'What are you waiting for?' my dad says. 'Kiss her.'

As Jason leans down to kiss me, I hear my dad talking to my mom. 'You gotta teach these damn kids everything these days.'

'Walter, your language.'

Jason pulls back from the kiss and smiles at me. 'Your dad's a smart man.'

'She knows I am,' my dad says. 'Now let's get out of here. I need to eat and take my pill.'

We leave the flower garden and head back through campus to the car, but this time Jason and I walk in front, holding hands, while my parents walk behind us, also holding hands.

I'm still not sure what's happening here, if it's real or pretend, but I'm committed to this summer. I'm committed to living with Jason, being with him, and letting myself feel whatever I want to feel.

* * *

That night, Jason doesn't sleep on the couch. He sleeps in my bed. And we make love, like a real engaged couple. I didn't ask Jason to explain what happened earlier or what it meant. I didn't want to know, not yet.

Or maybe I'll never ask. It might be better to not know and just continue as if this were real.

In the morning, we take my parents to the airport. If Jason and I had broken up yesterday, I would've told my parents I'd see them next week and would be moving into my old room until I found an apartment. But instead, I'm moving to Haydon Falls. Jason called Brody, who agreed to come here today and help move everything out of my apartment. It shouldn't take long. It's a really small apartment and I don't have much stuff.

This is all happening really fast, which is good. Having more time would just make me think about it and I might change my mind. Like my dad told Jason, thinking just leads to coming up with reasons for not doing things. It's better to just take action.

'We're here,' I say to Nora as I answer her call. We're meeting her for a quick breakfast before going back to my place to pack. 'Where are you?'

'Outside on the patio. I'm the really hot girl with the black tank top and denim shorts, sipping a mimosa.'

I smile. I'm going to miss her unique sense of humor. I spot Nora as Jason and I go out to the patio.

'Over here.' I keep hold of Jason's hand as I lead him to the table where Nora's sitting.

She jumps up when she sees me and gives me a hug. 'Tell me you're not leaving today.'

'I know it's soon. I'm sorry. I'm really going to miss you.'

'I'll miss you too, but it's only an hour away. And now I'll have somewhere to go on the weekends.' She looks at Jason, smiling as her gaze moves down his body. 'You're Jason, huh? You are not what I expected.'

'I'm not sure what that means,' he says with a laugh.

'It means she thinks you're hot,' I tell him. 'I told her you were, but I don't think she believed me.'

We sit down at the table.

'We have different definitions of that word,' Nora explains as she picks up her mimosa and takes a sip. 'Like when Mia set me up with this guy. She said he was cover model hot and well . . . let's just say he was not my type.'

'He looked better at the bar,' I tell Jason. 'But the lighting was dark and I'd had a few drinks.'

'I never let her set me up again,' Nora says.

'Mia said you're a professor,' Jason says.

She nods. 'I teach physics to pimply teenagers who complain constantly and don't want to be there.'

'So you like your job,' Jason kids.

'Love it.' She sips her drink.

'Speaking of professors,' I say, 'did you ever call up the one from the sandwich shop?'

'Yeah, we already went out. We met during lunch at the frozen yogurt place, which I know is really lame for a date, but we didn't have much time.'

'How was he? Do you like him?'

'I'm not sure.' She crinkles her nose. 'He ate his yogurt with one of those tiny spoons. You know the kind they give you for the samples?'

'Maybe he was trying to make the yogurt last longer.'

'I don't know, but it was weird. That might be our last date.'

'Because he used a tiny spoon? I think you're being too hard on him.' I look at Jason. 'What do you think?'

'It's weird. Why would a grown man use a spoon that small? And he uses it on a date? That's weird.'

'See?' Nora says to me. 'Even your boyfriend agrees.'

'Fiancé.' I show her the ring. 'He made it official.'

She laughs. 'I know you told me that on the phone, but it's not real, right? You were just playing along. You're not actually engaged.'

Jason and I don't answer.

Nora's eyes bounce back and forth between Jason and me. 'What's going on? Why aren't you saying anything? The engagement is fake.' She pauses. 'Right?'

Jason looks at me. 'I meant what I said yesterday. To me, this engagement is real.'

I'm too shocked to say anything. I wanted his proposal to be real, but I didn't think it actually was.

'I'm going to go use the restroom,' Nora says, getting up. 'Let you two talk.'

Jason waits for her to leave, then turns to me. 'I know we're not ready to get married, and I know it may never happen, but I'm committed to this, Mia. I'm committed to trying to see if this could work.'

'But what does that mean? You said you wouldn't move.'

'We'll talk about that when it's time. For now, I want to focus on us. We need to figure out if we actually *want* to be together, but we can't do that if we're just pretending, or telling ourselves that's all it is. We need to give this a real chance, with a real engagement. We need to stop playing games and take this seriously.' He pauses. 'Mia, say something. Anything.'

'I agree. With everything you just said. I just can't believe you said it. I didn't think you wanted this. The way you kept going back and forth—'

'Forget all that. I was just scared. I still am. But fuck, I'm going to be a dad soon. I need to grow the hell up and stop running from things that may not work out. We have one chance here, Mia, and I'm not letting it slip away.'

'So we're really engaged,' I say, gazing down at my ring.

'The engagement is real, but the ring's not. I don't have the money right now to get you a real ring.'

Nora returns, sitting across from us. 'So? What'd you decide? Should I be ordering champagne?'

'If I wasn't pregnant, then yes,' I say.

'Are you serious? This is real?'

'It's real,' Jason says, holding my hand.

'Congratulations!' Nora pops up from her chair and comes around the table to give me a hug.

We have breakfast, and as we're waiting for the check, Jason leaves to answer a call from Brody.

'You're really getting married?' Nora says in a hushed tone, even though Jason's nowhere near us. 'You barely know him.'

'I feel like I know him better than guys I've dated for months. There's something about Jason that feels so familiar, like I've known him forever.'

'Yeah, but still. Are you really going to marry him?'

'We don't know if we're getting married, but the engagement is real. We're going to live together this summer and see if this is really what we want to do.'

'All this from a one-night stand?' She sighs. 'I don't even get a text the next day and you get a proposal.'

'But I'm also pregnant. I don't think you'd want that part.'

'Not yet. Kids are few years off.' She reaches across the table and puts her hand on mine. 'As crazy as this is, you look really happy.'

'I am. I'm also scared it won't work out.'

'If it doesn't, you'll be okay. You know that, right? You're strong, smart, and more than capable of doing this on your own.'

I smile. 'Remind me of that if it doesn't work out.'

'I really hope it does. He seems like a good guy. And damn, he's hot. I was not expecting that. Hey, didn't you say he had brothers?'

'Yes, three, and they're all taken.'

'Of course they are,' she says, rolling her eyes.

'You'll find someone.'

'Yeah, guys who eat frozen yogurt with tiny spoons.' She holds up her phone. 'He texted me just now. He wants to meet for coffee.'

'Are you going?'

'Maybe, but if he drinks it out of a miniature cup, we are definitely done.'

Jason returns. 'Brody will be at your place in a few minutes. We should head over there.'

'Yeah, okay.'

We say goodbye to Nora, then go to my apartment and pack up my things. A few hours later, everything's loaded in Jason's truck, Brody's truck, and my car. I say goodbye to Madison, my home for the last two years, and head to my new home in Haydon Falls.

There's no turning back now. I'm doing this. No more fake fiancé. No more fake engagement. This is real. From here on out, it's all real.

Chapter 21

Jason

'What do you think of Zeus?' Mia asks, trying to hold back her smile.

'No.'

'Apollo?'

'No.'

'Oh! I got it. This one is perfect!' She pauses for dramatic effect. 'Atlas.'

'Nope.'

'Jason, you love maps!' She turns toward me on the couch. 'How could you not like Atlas?'

'An atlas is a book of maps. It's not a name.'

'According to this list, it's definitely a name.'

I take the tablet from her and read the screen. 'Names inspired by Greek Gods. Sorry, but no.'

She laughs. 'Okay, I'll keep looking.'

Mia and I are having a baby boy and I couldn't be more excited. I actually teared up when they told us during the ultrasound. My mind filled with images of me taking my son to baseball games, teaching him how to catch and throw a ball, coaching his Little League team.

Mia's excited about having a boy too, but she was surprised when we found out. She thought for sure we were having a girl.

Now we're trying to pick a name. Mia thinks it's hilarious to suggest names she knows I'd never go for, like the ones she just told me. It's become a game to her. She finds lists of names that are completely ridiculous just to see how I'll react.

We've been living together for a month and so far, it's been great. Every morning we get up together, have breakfast, then she gets on the computer for work while I go to the school to teach summer classes. Haydon Falls High has a summer program for teens in and around the area who are falling behind in school and need to catch up. I teach the math and science classes, which only takes up two hours of my day and then I spend another two hours tutoring. It's an easy job and I like helping kids who might've dropped out of school if it weren't for this program. It's over at the end of June and then I'll start my summer baseball camp. I also do private coaching. This year, I've cut back the number of kids I'm coaching so I'll have more time with Mia. She's done working at three so I try to be done then too. That way we have the rest of the afternoon and evening to go out and do stuff or just hang out at home. Like right now, it's just after four on a Monday and we're relaxing on the couch.

'How about Hermes?' Mia asks, looking at her tablet.

'How about you take a break from the names?' I take the tablet from her and set it down on the table.

'But I was having so much fun.'

'I can think of some other ways to have fun.' I kiss her.

She smiles. 'Let's go upstairs.'

Since moving in together, Mia and I have sex all the time. All I have to do is kiss her and we end up in bed, or the shower, or other places in the house. We've done it in every room, even the kitchen. I think it's the pregnancy hormones making her this way, or maybe she just really likes sex. Either way, I'm loving every second of it.

'I might need a nap after that,' Mia says as she lies in my arms.

'Go ahead and sleep.' I kiss her forehead. 'You did all the work that time. You need a nap. I'll take one too.'

She turns on her side and kisses me. 'I already want you again.'

I laugh. 'Are you serious? Because I'm totally up for it. I just need a few minutes.'

'I can't help it.' She runs her hand up and down my chest. 'You really turn me on.'

'All I have to do is look at you and I'm turned on.' I kiss her.

'I love that we're so good together.'

'I love it too.' I look at her. 'I love everything about us. These past few weeks have been great.'

She rests her head on my shoulder. 'I think so too.'

'I love you, Mia.'

She lifts up to look at me. 'You what?'

'I love you.' I smile. 'Why do you look surprised? I thought you knew this.'

'I wasn't sure. I still find myself trying to figure out what's real and what's not.'

'It's all real. We talked about this when we moved in together. No more fake relationship. This is real.'

She slowly smiles. 'So you really love me?'

'I really do.'

'I really love you too.'

I wrap my hand around her face and press my lips to hers, feeling even closer to her after telling her that and hearing her say it back. We make love again, then fall asleep. When we wake up, I make dinner while she reads off more crazy baby names.

This is the life I've always wanted. Living with the girl I love, planning for the baby we're about to have, sleeping next to her every night. On weekends, we hang out with my family, having breakfast with them on Saturday morning and dinner with them on Sunday. Sometimes during the week, Mia and I will go hang out with Brody and Kate or we'll meet up with Sawyer and Gina for dinner. Nick and Lyndsay are always at the orchard, which is less than a mile away, so we see them all the time, along with Mom and Dad.

I have everything I ever wanted. My family. The girl I love. And a baby on the way. But it's all going to change soon and I'm still not ready. I don't want to leave all this and move away.

* * *

Friday night, Mia and I are lying on the couch watching a movie when she says the words I've been dreading to hear.

'I applied for a job. I know I said I'd wait, but the deadline to apply was today.'

I don't say anything. I'm not sure how to react. Do I pretend to be happy even though I'm not? I love her, so I should support her, but if I'm being honest, I don't want her to get the job. I know it's wrong of me to think that, but I don't want her getting a job and leaving. We've only had a few weeks together. We need more time. We agreed to live here for the summer and the summer just started.

'Jason, say something.'

'What do you want me to say?'

She sits up. 'You could at least ask me about it.'

'What kind of job?'

'Director of a youth center.'

'You said you wanted to work at a school.'

'I do, and I'll apply at some schools, but this job pays more and I'd be able to help more kids. Kids from bad homes who really need help.'

'If that's what you want to do.' I pick up the TV remote and flip through the channels.

'Jason, don't get mad at me for this. You knew I was going to apply for jobs.'

'And we decided not to talk about it until after the summer.'

'I can't wait that long. If I get a job at a school it would start at the end of summer. I'd have to be out there in August.'

I turn off the TV. 'So now it's August? That's when you're leaving?' I get up and walk to the kitchen. 'So staying here for the summer was really just June and July.'

'Jason, you know how it works. You're a teacher.'

I open the fridge. 'Do you want something to eat? We didn't have much for dinner.'

She comes over to me. 'Why are you doing this? Why won't you talk to me about this?'

'Because it wasn't supposed to happen yet.' I shut the fridge door and turn to face her. 'The summer wasn't supposed to end in a few weeks.'

'It won't. We have the rest of June, all of July, and part of August.'

'Unless this place hires you and wants you out there now.'

'And what if that happens? What are you going to do?'

'I don't know. I need more time.'

She throws her hands up. 'How much time do you need? If you love me and want us to be a family, then why won't you go with me to Boston?'

'Because that's not where I want to live. It's not where I want to raise a family. Mia, we could have a good life here.'

'Jason, we've been over this a million times. I need to take care of my parents. I want to. I may only have a few years left with them.'

'I'm going to the store.' I grab my keys and walk to the door.

'That's it? You're just leaving?'

'There's nothing more to say. And staying here is just going to lead to us fighting.'

'You said you wouldn't pull away from me again. But here we are, a month into this, and you're leaving.'

She's right. Why do I keep doing this?

I know why. It's because I love her so damn much that I can't handle the thought of her leaving. I don't want to talk about it or think about it. I just want to run away and pretend it isn't happening.

The way to fix this is to go with her to Boston, but I can't make myself do it. I'm not there yet. I love Mia, but I also love my family and the life I have here.

Coming back inside, I walk up to her and take her in my arms. 'I'm sorry. We'll keep working on this, okay?'

We don't talk about the job or moving away for the rest of the night. But it was a reminder that this is happening. I can't keep pretending it's not. I have to make a decision and I have to do it soon.

* * *

'I'm done.' Darren hands me his quiz. 'Can I go now?'

I look over the quiz. 'You only answered half the questions.'

'That's all I could do.'

'Go back to your seat. We'll talk after class.'

'But I'm done. Why can't I—'

'Darren, go back to your seat.'

He rolls his eyes and lets out an exaggerated sigh. Most of the kids in this program don't want to be here. They have problems at home so school is the last thing they care about. I try to give them hope for a better life and tell them how finishing high school could help with that, but it's hard to get them to believe that when they go home to a house with no food or have an abusive parent who tells them they're worthless.

It's Monday morning and as much as I love teaching, I didn't feel like coming here today. Last weekend wasn't good. Mia was really quiet. She barely talked to me. She turned away from me in bed at night. We didn't have sex. We've been living like strangers the past couple days.

I know the reason why, and I know I need to address it. I didn't last weekend because I'm still angry and didn't want to express that anger to Mia. I'm not angry at her. I'm angry about the situation. I want things to be different, but they can't be, so then I get angry at myself for not accepting that and dealing with it.

After class, I wait for everyone to leave, then call Darren up to my desk.

'Did you study for the quiz?' I ask.

He shrugs. 'Not really.'

'You know this quiz is ten percent of your grade. You didn't even finish it.'

'What's the point? I'm not going to college.'

'What are you doing after graduation?'

'Working for my dad.'

His dad has a farm outside of town.

'Is that what you want to do?'

'No. I hate it here. I want to leave and go somewhere else.'

'And do what? What would you do for a job?'

'I want to work on cars. But my dad says I'm too stupid and no one would hire me.'

The door opens and Mia walks in. 'Oh, sorry. I thought class was over.'

'It is. We're almost done here. Is everything okay?' I ask, worried something's wrong with her or the baby. Mia never stops by like this.

'I'm fine.' She gives me a reassuring smile. 'I just wanted to talk to you. I'll wait outside.' She leaves, shutting the door behind her.

'Is that your girlfriend?' Darren asks, smiling.

'Yes. So going back to—'

'You knocked her up?' Darren laughs. 'Way to go, Mr. Kanfield.'

I clear my throat. 'About your quiz. If you promise to study, I'll let you take it again.'

His phone dings with a text. He checks it. 'My ride's here. I gotta go.' He takes off.

'Darren, what about the quiz?'

He's already gone, probably halfway down the hall by now. It's frustrating that I can't get through to him. I can't get through to most of these kids. I'm only able to address their problems at school, not all of their other problems, so nothing ever changes. I get maybe one or two kids every summer to take school seriously, but that's not much when I'm working with 30–40 kids.

I walk to the door and go out to the hall. 'Mia?' I look around but don't see her.

Did she leave? I check my phone. She didn't text me that she was leaving. I send her a text, asking if she's still here. She texts back that she's in the bathroom. I hope she's not getting sick. She hasn't had morning sickness since we moved in together.

Going back to my desk, I start grading the quizzes. A lot of the kids didn't finish. It was an easy quiz and we've gone over this material more than once. I know a lot of them didn't study, but I feel like I failed as a teacher when they do this poorly.

'Jason?' I hear Mia's voice and look up and see her standing at the door. 'Can I come in?'

'Yeah, are you okay?' I get up as she comes over to me.

'I'm fine. I was in the bathroom and found a girl crying so I stayed there and talked to her.'

'Who was it?'

'She said her name's Janelle. Do you know her? Short pink hair. Lightning tattoo on her neck.'

'I've seen her, but I don't know her. She's not from Haydon Falls. She's from one of the other towns around here. Why was she crying?'

'She thinks she might be pregnant. She's scared and doesn't know what to do. She saw that I'm pregnant and was asking me how I knew.' Mia smiles a little. 'I didn't tell her I went four months without figuring it out. Anyway, I told her I'd help her any way I could.'

'And what did she say?'

'She's going to take a test when she gets home. She was afraid to, but I told her it's better to know if she's really pregnant than to worry if she might be. Putting it off isn't going to make it any easier.'

I feel like she's talking about me. I keep putting off what I know I need to do, hoping the situation will just go away. I'm like that girl, wanting my life to stay the same but knowing it's going to change.

'I gave her my number,' Mia says, 'in case she wants to talk.'

'That was nice of you.'

'It's what I want to do, what I went to school for. I want to help kids who have no one to talk to. She said she can't talk to her parents. Her dad isn't around and she said her mom will kick her out if she's pregnant.'

'I hope you're able to help her. Maybe you could help Darren too.' I tell her about him, and about how he's lost all interest in school.

'I'd be happy to talk to him, if he's willing.'

'I'll ask him. So what are you doing here? Not that I'm not happy to see you. You're just usually working right now.'

'The research software is getting an update so I couldn't do anything. Since we didn't leave the house last weekend, I thought I'd get out and go into town.'

'I'm glad you came by.' I put my arms around her. 'I've been thinking about you all morning, and about last weekend.'

'That's why I'm here.' She pauses. 'Jason, I don't want to fight with you. I love you, and I want us to be able to get through disagreements without us turning against each other.'

'I agree.' I kiss her.

'Oh, shit, sorry,' someone says.

I look behind Mia and see Tyler walking out the door.

'Tyler,' I say, stopping him.

He turns back. 'I just had a question about the homework, but I can come back later.'

'No, come on in.' I look at Mia. 'Let's talk more tonight.'

'I'll see you later.' Mia smiles at me as she leaves.

Tyler watches her walk out.

'What's your question?' I ask.

He looks back at me. 'That's your girlfriend? She's hot.'

'She's my fiancé.'

'When are you getting married?'

'We don't know yet.'

Mia and I haven't even talked about it. When we decided to make the fake engagement real, it was so that we'd stop feeling like we're pretending to be a couple and feel like we're in an actual relationship. It wasn't a promise to get married. I don't think we're ready to get married. There's too many things we still have to work out.

'Aren't you supposed to get married first and then have a kid?' Tyler says, jokingly.

'Yeah, well, it doesn't always happen that way. So what was your question?'

We go over his homework, but my mind keeps wandering to Mia. Time's running out. I can't keep stalling. This is happening whether I like it or not.

When Tyler leaves, I get out my phone and search for jobs.

Chapter 22

Jason

It's the end of July and not much has changed. Mia still doesn't have a job for the fall. We're still engaged. Still living together. And there's still unresolved tension between us. But we don't let that tension come to the surface. We ignore it for the sake of getting along.

I know our relationship would be better if we could talk about the future, but until Mia gets a job, we're not in a hurry to discuss it. I've applied for five teaching jobs in and around Boston, but haven't heard back from any of them. I haven't told Mia about the jobs because I don't want her getting her hopes up. I'd rather wait until I have an offer.

'Hey, neighbor,' Nick jokes when I come into the kitchen at my parents' house. My summer classes are done, leaving my mornings free, so sometimes I come over here so I'm not bothering Mia when she's trying to work.

'Shouldn't you be out in the fields?' I grab a mug and fill it with coffee.

'I'm taking a break. It's hot out there. I've been going out at six every morning to avoid the heat later in the day.'

'Yeah, the heat's bad this week. The humidity bothers Mia. She's been staying inside.'

'How are you guys doing?'

'Good.' I sit across from him at the kitchen table. 'How about you and Lyndsay?'

'Lyndsay's upset that she's not pregnant by now. I keep reminding her we've only been trying a few months, but it doesn't seem to help. And it doesn't help that you got Mia pregnant on the first time, which Lyndsay keeps bringing up when I tell her we need to be patient.'

'It's not like I tried to get Mia pregnant. Maybe that's what you two should do. Try not to get pregnant and then you will.'

'Yeah, maybe. It'll happen eventually. We just need to keep trying.' He sips his coffee. 'How's the baseball camp going?'

'Great! I've already got a sign-up list for next summer.'

'Why do you have sign-ups for next summer? You won't be here.'

I get up and go to the counter where Mom left out a plate of her apple pastries.

'Jason, you're not staying here,' Nick says.

I take a pastry and go back to the table.

'Jason,' Nick says in his advice-giving, big-brother tone. 'You love her. And you're having a kid together. You have to go with her.'

'Nothing's been decided. She doesn't have a job there, and maybe she won't by next year.'

'She will. You know she will. Even if she doesn't have a job, she wants to be with her parents.'

'And I want to be with mine. Dad almost died last year. What if something like that happens again and I'm not here?'

'I'll be here. So will Brody. Sawyer. Mom. Dad has people here to care for him. Mia's parents don't.'

'I get that, but I still want to be here if something happens to Mom or Dad.'

'Then you'll get on a plane and fly here. You think I didn't feel the same way when I lived in New York? I always worried something would happen.'

'But you wanted to leave. You wanted to be in a big city and have that life. I don't. I never did.' I sigh. 'I know I need to move with her. I just wish I felt better about it.'

'Nick!' Mom yells from upstairs. 'Are you down there?'

'Yeah, Mom, what do you need?' he yells back. He gets up, concern on his face because she sounded panicked and we can hear her running down the stairs.

We meet up with her in the hall. 'Your father's having chest pains. We need to get him to the hospital.'

'Can he walk?' Nick asks.

'I'm not sure,' Mom says, her voice shaking. 'He's in a lot of pain.'

'Get the truck going,' he tells her. 'Jason and I will get him down the stairs.'

My heart's pounding, memories from last summer coming back. Images of my dad in the hospital. The doctor telling us he could've died. Waiting for him to make it out of open heart surgery.

This is why I don't want to leave. This is what's holding me back.

'We got you, Dad,' Nick says, as we help him get up from the bed.

'I just need my medicine,' Dad says, clutching his chest. 'I don't need a doctor.'

'We're going to take you there anyway,' Nick says. 'Just to have them check you out.'

I admire Nick for being so calm. He's always been that way. I think it's an older brother thing. He takes charge when things like this happen. I panic and can't think straight. Sawyer and Brody are like that too.

Nick and I help Dad down the stairs and outside to the truck. Mom gets out to let Nick drive.

'Call Brody and Sawyer,' Nick says to me as he gets in the truck.

'Don't be doing that!' Dad orders. 'I'm fine.'

'Call them,' Nick says, ignoring Dad. 'Then meet us at the hospital.'

They drive off, and instead of calling my brothers, I call Mia without even thinking. She's the first person who comes to mind now when things like this happen.

'Hey, are you coming home?' Mia answers.

'No.' I tell her what happened and that I'm going to the hospital.

'Can I come with?' she asks. 'He's my dad too.'

She's right. He treats her like a father does, and if we get married, it'll be official. She's part of my family, so why am I treating her like she's not? Am I pushing her away without even realizing it?

'I'll be there in a minute.' I drive down to the house and pick her up, then call my brothers as we head to the hospital.

Mom and Nick come up to us when we get there.

'They think it's angina,' Mom says. 'But they're going to keep him here overnight to run some tests.'

'It sounds like he'll be fine,' Nick says to me, knowing I'm panicking.

'Do you need anything?' Mia asks Mom. 'Coffee? Tea? I could run to the cafeteria.'

'Thank you, but no. I'm fine.' She smiles, glancing at Mia's belly, which has grown a lot the past couple months. 'Let's go sit down. Get you off your feet.'

Mom takes her over to the chairs in the waiting area while Nick and I stay behind.

'We talked to the doctor before you got here,' Nick says. 'He said it's angina and that they probably just need to adjust the meds he's taking.'

'Angina means he's not getting blood to the heart. That's serious.'

'The doctor said we shouldn't worry. They'll run some tests, but the doctor thinks it's most likely a narrowing of the arteries, not a blockage. Taking the meds and watching his diet should help. He doesn't think Dad needs surgery.'

'You see why I don't want to move away? What if this happened when I was in Boston?'

'You'd get on the next flight and be here. It's no different than if something happened to Mia's parents while you guys were here.' He checks his phone. 'Lyndsay just got here. I'm going to go meet her outside.'

I walk over to where Mom and Mia are sitting.

'Nick went outside to meet up with Lyndsay,' I say, sitting beside Mia.

'Mrs. Kanfield?' A nurse walks up to her. 'I need you to answer some questions for the insurance.'

'Of course.' Mom gets up and follows the nurse to a room near the waiting area.

'Nick said Dad's probably okay,' I tell Mia. 'They'll just need to adjust his meds.'

Mia reaches over and holds my hand. Just that small gesture makes me feel better. It's good she came. I like having her here. The more time I spend with her, and the more things we go through together, the more I realize how much I need her in my life. How much we need each other.

Mia's phone rings. 'It's my mom. I'll go outside. I don't think I'm supposed to use my phone in here.' She answers the call as she hurries to the door. 'Hey, Mom.' She stops. 'He what? Wait, slow down.' She continues out the door.

She sounded worried. Something must've happened. I get up and follow her outside.

'Mom, are you sure?' Mia's hand is resting on her stomach and I notice she has tears in her eyes.

I come up beside her and put my arm around her. ‘What’s wrong?’

She holds her hand up, signaling me to be quiet so she can hear. ‘Mom, don’t worry about me. I’m not too pregnant to fly. I could be out there tomorrow.’ She nods. ‘Okay, I’ll let you know.’ She ends the call.

‘What happened?’ I ask, moving in front of her.

‘Dad fell down the stairs. He’s in the hospital. He broke his arm and maybe a rib. They’re not sure yet. They’re still running tests.’

‘Is he going to be okay?’

‘My mom said he probably will, but at his age, it’ll take him a long time to recover.’ Mia looks up at me. ‘I’m going to go out there and stay with them. For as long as they need me. I know I promised you the summer, but I need to do this, Jason. I’m sorry.’

‘Mia, you don’t have to apologize. You’re going.’ I hold her hands. ‘We’re both going.’

‘But you can’t. You have baseball camp and your dad and—’

‘And you. We’re a couple. I go where you go. And while we’re there, we’ll look at some apartments.’

‘Does that mean . . .’ She waits for me to tell her.

‘Do you really think I’d let you move out there alone?’

‘Jason, this whole time you’ve resisted the idea of moving. You wouldn’t even talk about it.’

‘Because I was thinking of myself and what I wanted. But it’s not just me anymore. I have to think of all of us. You. Me. Our baby. Your parents. We’re all a family now.’

‘But what about your family here? And your job?’

I get out my phone and show her the texts confirming all the applications I submitted. 'I haven't heard back from any of them yet, but I'm hoping I will soon.'

'Why didn't you tell me you'd applied for jobs?'

'I was waiting until I had an interview. I didn't want to get your hopes up for something that may not happen. Mia, I'm sorry I've been putting off talking about this. I was being stupid, thinking something would change and we wouldn't have to move. But it's time we stop waiting and just do this. Your parents need us and it'll be easier for us to find jobs if we're already out there.'

Mia's face lights up with that beautiful smile that drew me to her the moment I met her. 'You're really doing this?'

'WE'RE doing this.' I kiss her, then take her hand and we go back inside.

Mom walks up to us. 'You two can go. There's no reason to stay. He's resting and will probably be asleep soon.'

'Can I go see him?' I ask.

'Yes. Go ahead.'

'I need you to come too. I need to talk to both of you.'

She looks at me with concern. 'What's this about?'

'I'll tell you when we're with Dad.' I turn to Mia. 'I'll be right back.'

She nods.

Mom and I go into Dad's room. He hears us coming in and his eyes flutter open.

'Martha, what are the boys doing here?' he says, sounding annoyed. 'I told you I'm fine. Even the doctor said so.'

'Jason has something he wants to tell us,' Mom says.

I walk up to Dad. 'I'm going to be moving to Boston with Mia.'

'Yeah. So what do you want to tell us?'

'What I just said. That I'm moving.'

'Honey, we already knew that,' Mom says.

'How? I told you I hadn't decided.'

Dad shakes his head. 'You decided the moment that girl showed up in town. We all saw it. Your brothers. Your mom and me.'

'Saw what? What are you talking about?'

Mom sits on the bed next to Dad. 'You've been fighting against being with Mia for months now. Telling yourself and us and anyone who would listen that she wasn't the girl for you. You didn't want it to be true because admitting it meant having to leave us. Leave your home. Leave Haydon Falls.'

'We could've saved you some time and heartache and just told you to go,' Dad says. 'But we thought it'd be better if you came to that decision yourself.

'Wait—so you're okay with this?'

'We'll miss you,' Mom says, 'but you need to do what's best for you and Mia, and right now, that's moving to Boston.'

'I never expected you boys to stick around,' Dad says. 'I wasn't surprised when Nick left. I thought Sawyer would leave too. You and Brody were the only two I thought might stay, but I knew the right girl could convince you to leave. And now you've found her.'

Mom smiles. 'And we're very happy for you.' She looks at Dad. 'We'll be making a lot of trips to Boston to see our grandson.'

'And your son,' I remind her.

She laughs. 'Well, yes, of course.'

'We're going to go out there tomorrow,' I say, 'or as soon as we can get a flight.'

'You're moving this week?' Mom says, sounding alarmed.

'No, we're going out there to see her parents. Her dad fell down the stairs and is in the hospital. We'll go see him and check on her mom and look for an apartment. I've already started applying for jobs. Next week, I'll tell the school that I'm leaving.'

'I know you'll miss it here,' Mom says, 'but I think this is the right decision.'

There's a knock on the door. 'Am I interrupting?'

It's Matt, Nick's best friend. We all went to high school together. Matt's a real estate agent in town. He sold Brody the house he fixed up and the one he's living in now.

'We just finished up,' Mom says. 'Come on in.'

Matt walks up to Dad. 'How are you feeling, Mr. Kanfield?'

He huffs. 'I'd be better if people stopped treating me like I'm dying every time I have a pain.'

'He's a little grumpy today,' Mom says to Matt.

'Me too,' Matt says. 'Just had a house sale fall through. The people who were going to buy it decided it was too small and backed out.'

'That's too bad,' Mom says.

'It happens.' Matt looks over at me. 'How are you doing? Getting ready to be a dad?'

'I don't think I'll ever be ready.'

Matt laughs. 'I felt that way too with the first one. With the second one, I wasn't worried at all.'

'Jason just told us he and Mia will be moving to Boston soon,' Mom says to Matt.

'Yeah, Nick said that might happen. That's gonna be a big change.'

'I'm going to miss being here,' I say, 'but Mia needs to be close to her parents. Her dad's almost 80 and has some health issues and her mom can't care for him on her own.'

'Why don't they move here?'

Mom, Dad, and I all look at Matt, not saying anything.

He shrugs. 'It was just an idea. You know how I am, always trying to get people to move here.'

'How did I not think of that?' I say, mainly to myself because I can't believe the thought never occurred to me. It hadn't occurred to any of us. We just assumed Mia's parents had to stay in Boston. But why would they have to stay there? They don't have jobs keeping them there, or family. They just have a house. But they could sell their house and move here, to Haydon Falls.

'Do you think they'd consider it?' Mom asks me.

'I don't know why they wouldn't. Why would they have to stay there?'

'They have a house, don't they?' Dad asks.

'Yes, but they could sell it. They'll have to, now that her dad fell down the stairs. They'll need a house that's all one level.'

Matt smiles. 'I got the perfect one. That sale that didn't go through? It's a one-level house. It'd be great for her parents. And the previous owners fixed it up so it's move-in ready. It has a yard, but they could hire Brody to take care of it for them.'

'He wouldn't charge them,' Mom says. 'They're family.'

'What do you think?' Matt asks, directing the question to me. 'I can send you the link to the listing.'

'Yeah, do it. I'll talk to Mia.'

'Talk to her right now,' Dad says. 'What are you waiting for?'

I leave his room and return to the waiting area where I find Mia talking to Lyndsay.

'Mia, we need to go,' I say. 'Hey, Lyndsay.'

'Hey.' She smiles at me. 'What are you so happy about?'

My excitement must show on my face.

'I'll tell you later.' I take Mia's hand. 'C'mon. We need to go home and talk.'

'Um, okay,' she says. 'Bye, Lyndsay.'

'Bye!'

When we get outside, Mia asks why I'm in such a hurry. I don't tell her. I want to wait until we're home where we can discuss this without being interrupted.

'Would you please tell me what's going on?' Mia says the moment we get in the house.

'Do you like it here?'

'Where? This house?'

'This town. Haydon Falls.'

'Yes. I love it. It's beautiful.'

'So if we could stay here, you would?'

'Definitely. But we can't, so why are we talking about this?'

'I think we should move your parents here.'

She doesn't say anything as she slowly walks to the couch and sits down.

'I'm not saying we have to. I was just thinking there isn't really a reason they need to stay in Boston, is there?'

Mia's staring straight ahead, looking lost in thought. 'I can't believe I never even considered that.'

'I know, right?' I go to the couch and sit next to her. 'This whole time it's been an option and nobody thought of it.'

'I just assumed because their house is there and because they're from there that they couldn't leave. But they're going to have to sell the house. My dad can't live in a house with stairs.'

'What do you think of this one?' I get out my phone and show her the house Matt told me about.

Mia gasps. 'It's perfect.' Her eyes light up as I flip through the photos. 'My dad would love the brick on the outside. And Mom would love the built-ins in the dining room. And that kitchen looks like the one in the house Mom grew up in. When was this built?'

I read the description. 'It says 1950, but Matt said the owners have done a lot to fix it up.'

Mia takes my phone and scrolls through the listing. 'Did you see the price? That can't be right. It's too cheap.'

'Houses are cheaper here. A lot cheaper than Boston. What do you think? Could we convince them to move?'

'I don't think we'll have to convince them. They loved this area when they came to visit. I could totally see them living here.'

We just need them to agree to it. I don't know why they wouldn't. Living here is cheaper, safer, it's easier to get around, and they'll have not just Mia and me, but my whole family to help them out if they need it.

I was prepared to move to Boston, but staying here and having Mia's parents with us is a better option for all of us. I can't believe I didn't think of it sooner.

Chapter 23

Mia

'We should be going,' my mom says, getting up from her chair.

We've been with my dad in his hospital room for the last half hour. He has a broken arm and some bruises and a cut on his lip, but other than that, he's okay. He was lucky. The doctor said his injuries could've been a lot worse.

'Mom, before we go,' I say. 'Jason and I want to talk to you both.'

'Let's do it later. You dad needs his rest.'

'I don't need rest,' he says. 'I'm wide awake.' He looks at Jason and me. 'What is it? You having twins?'

I smile. 'No. It's not about the baby. It's about you and Mom.'

'What about us?'

Jason takes my hand. I told him he could tell them, knowing my dad would like it if he did. It's the whole man-taking-charge nonsense that's sexist and outdated but how things were done when my dad grew up.

'We want you to move to Haydon Falls,' Jason says.

We wait for my parents to respond. We could list out all the reasons why they should move, but we decided to let them think about it before we try to sell them on the idea.

'You two aren't moving here?' my mom asks.

'We could,' I say, 'but we'd rather stay where we're at. We both like Haydon Falls and you guys liked it when you were there. I know it'd be a big change but—' I stop when I feel Jason squeeze my hand. We said we'd be quiet and let them decide.

'We'll be right back,' Jason says, pulling on me to leave with him.

We go out to the hall.

'They were really quiet,' I say.

'Is that a bad sign?'

'It might be. I'm worried they're going to say no.'

'Then we'll go over all the reasons why this is a good idea. Mia, the more I think about this, the more I'm convinced this is the right thing to do. We're having a baby soon. Taking care of a baby and your parents is a lot. We'll need help, which we'll have in Haydon Falls.'

'Mia?' My mom comes out to the hall.

'We're here, Mom.' I walk up to her.

'Your father wants to talk to you.'

Jason and I follow her back into the room.

I walk up to my dad. 'Mom said you wanted to talk to me?'

'I want to talk to him first.' He points at Jason.

Jason comes up beside me.

My dad moves so he's sitting up more. 'Those tractors your father's got.'

'What about them?' Jason says.

'You think he'd let me drive them?'

Jason smiles. 'Of course. Whenever you want.'

'What about that workshop of his, the one in the old barn. You think he'd let me use it, just to tinker around, maybe do some woodworking?'

'He'd do it with you if you didn't mind hearing his stories. He's got a lot of them.'

Dad smiles. 'I do too. I could use someone new to tell them to.' He glances at my mom, then back at me. 'I guess we could move. But you'll have to find us a house.'

'We already did.' Jason pulls up the listing.

'Mom, look.' I motion her to come over to see Jason's phone. 'You're going to love it!'

She's in love the moment she sees it. She loves it even more than her current house.

That night we go home and my mom and I start going through what she wants to keep and what she wants to get rid of. It's going to take time to go through everything so I'm going to stay here and Jason will fly back tomorrow.

I'm thrilled we're all going to be together in Haydon Falls. I love it there, and I know my parents will too.

* * *

Two weeks later, I'm getting off the plane in Madison and run into Nora at the airport.

'What are you doing here?' I ask, giving her a hug.

'Picking you up.'

'Jason's picking me up.'

'He just said that so he wouldn't ruin the surprise.'

'What surprise?'

She smiles. 'Your baby shower. Surprise!'

'We're doing this now?'

'Yes. We've been planning it for a month.' She looks down at my belly and her eyes widen.

'Yeah, I know, I'm huge.' I laugh. 'And no, I'm not having twins.' We walk to the baggage claim area. 'Where's the shower?'

'In Haydon Falls, at some store downtown.'

'Kate's store?'

'Is she related to Jason?'

'She's dating his brother, but I'm sure they'll get married.'

'Then yeah, that's her. She closed the store and has it all decorated in blue and white. She sent me pictures. It's adorable, like something you'd see in a magazine.'

'She's a decorator. She's really good at it. She decorated the house Jason and I are living in.'

'I've got it,' Nora says, racing ahead of me to grab my suitcase. 'This is heavy. What do you have in here?'

'Some of my mom's stuff. I had room so I threw some of her things in.'

We head to the parking lot.

'I can't believe your parents are moving here,' Nora says.

'I can't believe I didn't even consider it until a couple weeks ago.'

She stops and sets my suitcase down. 'Seriously, Mia, what is in here? Did you pack bricks from their fireplace?'

'Need some help?' a guy says.

Nora turns to the guy. 'Steve.'

It's the guy from the sandwich shop. The professor Nora was hitting on the day we had lunch.

The guy smiles at her. 'It's been awhile.'

'Yeah. What are you doing here?'

'Just back from a conference in London.'

'London. Great. Well, I need to get going.'

'Can I help you with the bag?'

'Sure!' I say, knowing Nora won't ask for help.

She glares at me. She says she doesn't like the guy, but every time I talk to her, she brings him up. She never went on that coffee date with him. She couldn't get over the tiny spoon thing on their yogurt date.

Steve picks up the suitcase and walks beside Nora as we head to the car. 'Are you going to introduce me to your friend?'

'Oh. Yeah. Steve meet Mia. Mia meet Steve.'

'You teach at the college?' he asks me.

'No, but I'm working for a professor there, just compiling data. It's not too exciting.'

'She just finished grad school,' Nora says. 'She's going to be a school counselor.'

Actually, I don't know what I'm going to do. I've decided to hold off on applying for jobs until after the baby arrives, but when I'm ready for a job, I don't know if I'll find one in Haydon Falls. The schools don't have any openings. I don't know where else I could work.

We get to Nora's car and Steve puts my suitcase in the trunk.

'You open to going for that coffee we never had?' Steve asks Nora.

'Oh, I don't think so. I'm really busy.'

'C'mon. Just one coffee?'

She gives him a slight smile. 'Sure. Maybe tomorrow. I'll send you a text.'

'Sounds good.' He waves at me. 'Nice meeting you.'

'You too.'

When we're in the car, she takes off, going faster than she should. 'Did you really have to do that?'

'Let him take my suitcase? Yes. As slow as you were going, it would've taken an hour to get to the car.'

'I told you I'm not going out with him again, and now I somehow got talked into having coffee with him.'

'You need to let go of the tiny spoon thing. He's smart. He seems nice. And he's handsome.'

'And weird. I want a normal guy. Is that too much to ask for?'

'Hey, there he is.' I point to him waiting at the stoplight. 'Nice car.'

It's a black luxury sedan.

'Would you stop trying to sell me on him? I agreed to get coffee with him.' She glances at me. 'Let's talk about you. Did you and Jason pick a wedding date?'

'Not yet. I told him I just want a simple wedding, maybe at the orchard. I'd like to get married before the baby arrives, but I don't think Jason is ready.'

'I don't know about that.'

'What do you mean?'

She darts into the other lane. 'Why is everyone driving so slow today? Hey, did you need to get something to eat before we leave town?'

'No, I brought snacks.'

Nora seems more distracted than usual. It's probably because of Steve. Seeing him again got her all flustered.

A little over an hour later, we're in downtown Haydon Falls. There's a light blue banner outside Kate's store saying it's closed today for a special event. It's so nice of her to do this.

We go into the store and find everyone waiting for us—Martha, Kate, Gina, Lyndsay, some of my friends from Madison, and Lacey, my friend from college. She's the one who got married the night I met Jason.

'Lacey!' I race up to her. 'I haven't seen you since the wedding!'

She hugs me. 'I couldn't miss your shower, especially since my wedding was kind of the reason for it.' She laughs.

I hope nobody heard her. Only Nora and Jason's family know that Jason and I met at the wedding. Everyone else thinks we met last fall at the orchard, the fake story we told as part of our fake engagement.

'I can't believe you guys did this,' I say as I look at everyone. 'And that you kept it a surprise.'

'It helped that you were gone the past couple weeks,' Kate says.

Looking around, I notice a table topped with desserts on white pedestals and jars filled with blue candies.

In the middle of the room is a long rustic wood table lined with blue and white floral arrangements. White wood folding chairs are along each side of it and at the end is a plush white chair with a blue pillow on it that has 'mom' embroidered on it. I guess that's where I'll be sitting.

'The store looks beautiful,' I tell Kate.

'Thanks! I had so much fun I'm thinking of hosting more showers here. It could be a side business.'

Lyndsay walks up to us. 'Mia, someone wants to say hi to you.' She brings me over to the long table where a laptop is set up.

I see my mom's face on the screen. 'Mom!'

She waves at the screen. 'I didn't want to miss your shower.'

'Mom, you've got to see how Kate decorated the store.' I pick up the laptop and walk around to show her.

'Oh, it's lovely. I wish I could be there.'

'You will be soon.'

The day after my dad got out of the hospital, my parents put an offer in on the house Jason and I showed them and the sellers accepted the offer that night. Their house in Boston is going up for sale next week. We're hoping it'll sell quickly, but even if it doesn't, they plan to move here within the month. This is going to be a huge change for them, but they're excited about it.

The baby shower goes all afternoon. Around four, my friends from Madison get up to leave, saying they need to start driving back.

'Before you go,' Kate says. 'We have one more surprise for Mia.'

Everyone looks behind me.

I turn and see Jason coming out from the back room, wearing a gray suit, white shirt, and light blue tie. He looks hot. Seeing him in the suit reminds me of when we met and the night we spent together. The night that led to a baby that led to us getting engaged. Sometimes I still can't believe that going to a wedding ended up changing my entire life.

I smile as Jason comes over to me. 'What are you doing here?'

'I needed to give you your gift.'

'You're the dad. You don't have to give me a baby gift.'

'This one isn't for the baby. It's for you.' He takes my hand. 'I need you to get up for this.'

I stand up and face him. 'What's this about?'

He looks into my eyes. 'I screwed this up, so many times. I went back and forth. Pushed you away. Confused you. Made you wonder if we had a future. And what's really messed up is that this is what I always wanted. A wife. Kids. A home. But when I got the chance to have it, I ran from it. Because it didn't happen the way I wanted, the way I imagined. I was selfish, and I'm sorry.'

'Jason, you don't have to—'

'Mia, I need you to know that my feelings for you were always real. No matter what we said this was, it was always real to me. And just to make that perfectly clear, I'm going to do this one last time.' He takes something from his pocket and gets down on one knee. 'Mia, will you marry me?'

He holds out a ring. Not a gold band, but a diamond ring.

I hear people whispering, but my gaze remains on Jason.

'Yes.' I smile. 'For the last time, yes, I'll marry you.'

He slides the gold band off my finger and slides the diamond ring on, then gets up and takes me in his arms. He leans down and talks in my ear. 'The ring is real this time. No more faking it. It's all real, from here on out.'

'You guys, come check out the ring!' Kate says. 'It's gorgeous!'

They all run up to me as Jason steps aside.

'How did you guys meet?' Haley asks as she looks at the ring. She's a friend from school. She was in all my classes. 'I never heard the story.'

'They met at my wedding,' Lacey says, a proud grin on her face. 'At the reception. They were seated next to each other at the singles' table.'

'Wedding?' I hear my mom say from the laptop.

'I thought you met at the orchard,' Candace, another friend from school, says.

I look at Jason.

He comes up beside me and quietly says, 'It's up to you.'

I'm not ashamed of how Jason and I met. I don't care if people know. I just didn't want my parents finding out.

'Orchard?' Lacey laughs. 'No. They met at my wedding back in January. They were so adorable, dancing and looking into each other's eyes. And now they're engaged!' She smiles at Jason and me. 'I'd like to take at least a little credit for that.'

She says it jokingly, but no one's laughing. Gina, Kate, and Lyndsay are giving me sympathetic looks like they want to help me out but don't know what to say. The other girls look confused.

'Mia, what is she talking about?' my mom asks. 'You said you met Jason last year when you went to the orchard.'

My fear of disappointing my parents rises up again, just like it did when I found out I was pregnant. Trying to please them led to a fake engagement and then the town finding out and all the craziness that followed. It turned out okay in the end, but I should've just told my parents the truth. They might've been disappointed, but I know they love me no matter what.

'We didn't meet last fall,' I say as Jason reaches over to hold my hand. 'Lacey's right. We met the night of her wedding.'

'You met in January?' my mom says. 'But that would mean—' She stops, her brows drawing together, which she does when she's thinking. 'Oh. I see.'

'Mom, I didn't mean for that to happen. But it did, and I can't change it.'

'I wouldn't want you to,' Jason says, his arm going around me. 'If it didn't happen, you wouldn't be here with me now.'

I smile at him, then look back at my mom. 'I should've told you the truth. I just didn't want to disappoint you and Dad. So I told you we met last fall and then told everyone else that.'

'Sorry,' Lacey says to me. 'I didn't know.'

'It's okay,' I tell her. 'The truth needed to come out. I don't know if Jason and I could've kept that story going forever.' I look at him. 'Although we might tell our kids the orchard story.'

Jason laughs a little. 'That's probably a good idea.'

'Maybe we'll keep telling your father that story too,' my mom says. 'You know how he is. He's stuck in how things used to be. He doesn't keep up with the times.'

'Yes, I know,' I say, not pointing out that she's the same way. But she's starting to come around. She doesn't even seem upset by the news of how Jason and I met.

'What's important is that you're happy and have a whole new wonderful family there,' she says, 'and a beautiful baby boy on the way.'

'And soon I'll have you and Dad here.'

'Oh! The real estate agent has someone interested in our house. It's not even on the market yet. We might be out there sooner than expected.'

'That's great, Mom! I'll call you later and we can talk about it.'

She logs off and I thank everyone for coming. As they leave, I start to clean up.

'That's not your job,' Jason says, taking the stack of plates I was holding and setting it back on the table.

'He's right,' Kate says. 'You're the guest of honor. You don't clean up. Besides, you have plans. You have to go get ready.'

'Ready for what?'

'I'm taking you to dinner,' Jason says, taking my hand and leading me out of the store. 'We're going to the place we went when you first came to town.'

'That's a nice place. Can I go home and change?'

'Yes, the reservation isn't until seven. You have time to shower, take a nap, change clothes, whatever you want.'

I smile at him as we walk to the truck. 'I might skip the nap for something else.' My gaze drops to his body. 'You look really hot in that suit.'

'I'm all for skipping the nap.' He walks faster. 'I would've suggested that myself, but I was trying to be a considerate husband.'

'Husband?' I say as he helps me into the truck. 'We're not even married yet.'

He shuts the door and gets in the other side. 'What do you think of September?'

'For what?'

'Getting married. The leaves will be changing. The weather will be cooler. Your parents will be here by then.'

'Wait—you mean this September? Like next month?'

'Yeah. Why? Is that too soon?'

'No. It's perfect.' I'm thrilled he wants to get married that soon. I thought he'd want to wait.

'We could get married at the orchard,' he says as he drives out of the parking lot. 'The place where we met.' He chuckles.

'Yeah, that story didn't last,' I say with a sigh. 'I don't know why I ever thought we'd be able to keep it going. I should've known the truth would come out eventually. Do you think my mom was mad when she found out?'

'I think she was surprised, but she wasn't mad. Mia, your parents love you. Despite what you think, you could never disappoint them.'

'Maybe, but I'm sure my mom's not happy about me hooking up with a guy at a wedding and getting pregnant.'

'Hey, I'm not just any guy. I'm a Kanfield, of the famous Kanfield Orchard.'

I smile. 'That's right. I keep forgetting I'm marrying a celebrity. But I'm not sure that makes what we did that night any more acceptable to my mom.'

'How would you feel if it was our kid who did that? Would you be disappointed in him?'

'Not if he felt something for the girl and wasn't just using her for sex.'

'Is that what you think I was doing that night? Using you for sex?'

'No, not at all. That's one of the reasons I liked you so much. You didn't pressure me. In fact, I felt like I was the one trying to convince *you* to do it.'

'You didn't have to try too hard.'

'It was such a great night.'

'It was.' He reaches over and holds my hand. 'And we've got a lot of great ones ahead of us.'

Tonight is one of them. We go home, make love, then go to the restaurant where we had our first date. I guess that wasn't a date, but it felt like one, and it confirmed that Jason wasn't just a one-night stand but a guy I could actually see myself with in the future. And now, here we are, living that future.

Chapter 24

Three Months Later

Jason

'Can you help me with my dress?' Mia asks, turning her back to me. 'I'm not sure it'll fit, but I'm going to try.'

I come up behind her and kiss the side of her neck as I zip up the dress. 'You look beautiful.'

She looks in the mirror. 'I feel fat. But at least the dress fits.'

I turn her away from the mirror. 'You're not fat. Stop saying that. You're beautiful.' I kiss her, slowly, my tongue slipping past her lips. I want her so damn bad, but the doctor wants us to wait another week. I'm counting the days.

The baby fusses and Mia pulls away from me.

'He's fine,' I tell her, knowing how worried she gets every time the baby cries or fusses. She's always calling her mom or mine to make sure he's okay and she's doing everything right.

She walks over to the bassinet where Milo is sleeping. We finally agreed on a name. We didn't decide until we saw him and then it's like we just knew. Mia looked at me, said the name Milo, and I told her yes. We didn't even have to think about it.

I walk over to the bassinet and pick up Milo. 'What are you fussing about?' I gently rock him. 'Are you telling us to hurry up and go?' I kiss his cheek. 'You love these family dinners, don't you? You get nonstop attention.'

'And everyone fighting over who gets to hold you,' Mia says to him.

It's Sunday, which is when we have family dinner at my parents' house. It's one of my favorite traditions, especially now that my brothers are busy with their own lives and I don't see them as much as I'd like. Mia's parents come over too, and after dinner, my dad and Walter go out to the barn and do whatever old guys do. I think Walter's making a wooden toy tractor for Milo, but he won't confirm it. He just tells Mia and me to stay out of the barn.

Mia's parents moved here the first week of September. Kate and Mia helped them decorate the house and Nick and I did whatever small repairs needed to be done. It's a cute little house and perfect for the two of them. And the best part? Walter hasn't fallen once since living there.

Mia and I got married at the orchard on a beautiful fall day—September 15th, four months after Nick's wedding. I went to that wedding thinking I'd never get married, that I'd always be a bachelor. I never in a million years thought I'd be getting married four months later. But I didn't see a need to wait. I knew Mia was the one. I knew it the night we met. Nobody would believe me if I told them that, so I don't. I keep it to myself. But I really did feel that way, like Mia was meant for me. I think sometimes you just know. It's like what Walter told me on campus that day—when you know you know. I just kept denying I felt that way because I never thought I could be with her.

'You think your mom would watch him tomorrow?' Mia asks. 'That meeting with Sheryl got moved to tomorrow at nine. She just texted me.'

I chuckle. 'You really think my mom would tell you no? She begs us to let her watch him.'

'Yes, but she's been really busy with the orchard. She has all that baking to do. She may not have time.'

'Trust me, she is not going to say no. So the meeting tomorrow is about the grant?'

'Yes, we're going to finalize it and then submit it. I'm getting really excited. I think this might actually happen.'

Mia and Sheryl, the woman who runs the summer school program, are trying to get a teen counseling center approved. It'd be based in Haydon Falls but would serve teens in all the surrounding towns. For now, it'd just be a room in the high school and Mia would be the only counselor, but if there was enough of a need, it could grow.

'It's going to happen,' I tell her. 'And you're going to be great. The kids will love you. Look how good you were with Darren and Janelle.'

Janelle, the girl Mia found crying in the bathroom, took a pregnancy test later that day and found out she wasn't pregnant. She called Mia and told her, then wanted to talk about other stuff. Mia's easy to talk to so I can see why teens open up to her. As for Darren, Mia talked to his father and got him to agree to let Darren take an auto repair course through the community college as long as he kept working for his dad on the farm. I helped him enroll for the class as part of a dual enrollment program for high school students. Darren's loving it and getting good grades. Even his grades in his high school classes got better. He just needed something to motivate him and he found it, thanks to Mia.

When we get to my parents' house, I stop before going in. I look down at Milo in my arms. 'You ready for this?'

Mia laughs. 'He'll be fine. He's getting used to it.'

'Okay, here we go.' I open the door.

'The baby!' Mom squeals as we come into the house. She races up to me and takes Milo.

'Nice to see you too, Mom.'

She laughs. 'Sorry, honey. He's just so adorable, he takes my attention away from everything else.' She smiles at Mia. 'Your parents are here. Your mom's in the kitchen and your dad's outside with Carl.'

Mia laughs. 'Dad's favorite place. It's either that or the barn.'

Walter's always outside with my dad or Nick, asking about the orchard. He wants to know all about how the trees are grown and the different varieties of apples.

My dad and Nick could talk about that stuff all day so it works out well.

'Milo's here!' Lyndsay races up to Mom and the baby.

'I think we're invisible,' I say to Mia.

'Oh. Hi!' Lyndsay gives us a quick wave before looking back at Milo. 'Aww, look at his tiny little hands.'

The door opens and Brody walks in with Kate.

'Milo's here!' Kate squeals, running up to him.

It's like this every time we're here. Mom, Kate, and Lyndsay can't stop gushing over the baby. Gina likes seeing him too, but she's not as baby-crazy as the other girls, maybe because she grew up playing sports instead of playing with dolls.

'I'm going to the kitchen,' Brody tells Kate. She doesn't hear him. She's too busy looking at Milo and listening to Mia tell her whatever cute thing Milo did this morning.

'I'll go with you,' I tell Brody.

We pass Harriott on our way to the kitchen.

'He's in the living room,' I tell her, knowing she was about to ask where Milo was.

'It's like I don't exist anymore,' I say to Brody as he goes to the fridge.

'And you're surprised by this?' He laughs. 'You saw how Mom was with Nash's kid. Now she's got her own grandkid, and it's her first.' He closes the fridge and takes a brownie from the plate of them that Mom left out. 'At least with the baby distracting her she's not in here yelling at me not to eat before dinner.'

'Even if she was in here, she wouldn't notice what you were doing if Milo was around.'

'I still can't believe you're married with a kid. A few months ago, you didn't think it would ever happen.'

'Yeah, I know. Sometimes I can't believe it either.'

'You going to stay in the Carson house or find something else?'

'We'd like to stay there for now, if Mom and Dad are okay with it.'

'Why wouldn't they be? No one else wants it.' He takes another brownie. 'Does it ever bother you being that close to Mom and Dad?'

'No. It's been great. Mia likes having Mom close by in case she has questions about Milo. And of course Mom loves helping her out.'

Sawyer walks in with Gina.

'You guys want to try my new stout?' Sawyer sets the bottles on the counter.

'I'll try one,' Brody says.

'Sawyer thinks he's going to win the hard cider competition next weekend,' Gina says with a laugh. 'In his dreams.'

'Say whatever you want,' Sawyer says. 'But I've had a year to work on it and I guarantee I'm going to win.'

'Don't you two ever get tired of competing?' I ask.

They look at each other. 'No,' they say at the same time.

Brody turns to Gina. 'Why aren't you in there with Milo? I lost Kate the moment she saw him.'

'He's too tiny. I feel like I'm going to break him. I'll be more comfortable around him when he's older.'

'She doesn't like holding him,' Sawyer says. 'She always thinks she's going to drop him.'

As he says it, Nick walks in. 'I dropped Sawyer all the time when he was a baby and he turned out okay.'

'I don't know about that,' Gina says, smiling at Sawyer. 'Okay, I'll go see the baby, but I'm keeping my distance.'

When she's gone, I say to Sawyer, 'What's she going to do when you guys have kids?'

'Probably wrap them in bubble wrap. Or make me hold them until they can walk.'

'I can see it now.' Brody laughs. 'Sawyer holding the baby with one hand and serving beer with the other.'

'Did you guys pick a wedding date yet?' Nick asks Sawyer. He proposed to Gina back in August.

'We can't decide. Maybe next spring. She really wants her dad there. She keeps asking him when he could be here but he won't give her a date. Even if he did, I doubt he'd show up.'

'Tell her Dad will walk her down the aisle,' I say.

'Yeah, I might. He already told me he'd do it.'

'When are you going to propose to Kate?' I ask Brody.

'Maybe at Christmas. She loves the holidays.'

'The family's getting so big we're going to have to get another table for these dinners,' Nick says.

'Any news with you and Lyndsay?' I ask, referring to their babymaking efforts.

He cracks a smile but doesn't answer.

'She's pregnant,' Brody says. 'Look at his face.'

'Is she?' Sawyer asks.

A full-on smile takes over Nick's face. 'Yes. We're going to announce it at dinner so act surprised.'

We all congratulate him. We must be too loud because Dad comes in and scolds us.

'What's all the ruckus in here? I could hear you boys from down the hall.'

'Nothing, Dad,' Nick says, giving us a look not to tell him. 'We were just talking.'

Walter comes in behind Dad. He walks slow and uses a cane, but he seems to be moving better now than last summer. He gets more exercise here and goes out more than he did back in Boston. Mia said when he lived there, he spent all day in a chair, watching TV. Here he's made some friends and actually does stuff with them. And he loves coming here and hanging out at the orchard and the barn.

'What are you boys doing drinking?' Dad asks. 'It's not even noon.'

'Sawyer wanted us to try his new stout.' Brody offers Dad one. 'Try it. It's not bad.'

'I'll have one later.'

'I'll take one,' Walter says. 'I don't have any rules about drinking before noon.'

Sawyer laughs and hands him a bottle. 'Drink up. Let me know if you like it.'

We remain in the kitchen, talking, drinking, and joking around. If Mia and I had moved to Boston, we would've had a completely different life, in a place I didn't want to be. But I've realized it's not about the place. It's about the people you're with, and as long as I was with Mia and our baby, I'd be happy.

I really didn't think we'd end up here, but I'm thrilled that we did. And so is Mia. She loves it here, and loves that her parents are with us. Little Milo will love it too when he's older and can run around the orchard.

I'll tell him how I met his mom here one beautiful fall day and how I asked her out and we started dating. He doesn't need to know the real story. Walter doesn't either.

It doesn't really matter how I met Mia. What matters is where we are now. Happy and together, surrounded by the people we love.

About the Author

Allie Everhart writes swoony, heartfelt, spicy romances that whisk readers away on an unforgettable emotional journey. With over 40 books published, including small-town romances, sports romances, and romantic comedies, Allie's stories are always full of passion, heart, and a dash of humor.

When she's not writing, Allie enjoys long walks, cozy cafés, and baking up delicious treats. Her love for food, holidays, and nature often makes its way into her books.

If you're ready for a romance that will make you laugh, cry, and swoon, you can explore all of Allie's books at www.allieeverhart.com.

About Embla Books

Embla Books is a digital-first publisher of standout commercial adult fiction. Passionate about storytelling, the team at Embla believe our lives are built on stories – and publish books that will make you 'laugh, love, look over your shoulder and lose sleep'. Launched by Bonnier Books UK in 2021, the imprint is named after the first woman from the creation myth in Norse mythology. Embla was carved by the gods from a tree trunk found on the seashore; an image of the kind of creative work and crafting that writers do, and a symbol of how stories shape our lives.

Find out about some of our other books and stay in touch:

X, Facebook, Instagram: @emblabooks
Newsletter: https://bit.ly/emblanewsletter